COURAGE TO CHANGE

Sylvie Nickels

Published in 2013 by Oriole Press (through FeedARead.com
Publishing – Arts Council funded

First Edition

A CIP catalogue record for this title is available from the British
Library.

By the same author
The Young Traveller in Finland Phoenix House, 1962
The Young Traveller in Yugoslavia Phoenix House, 1967
Travellers' Guide to Yugoslavia Cape, 1969
Travellers' Guide to Finland Cape, revised 1977
Welcome to Yugoslavia Collins, 1984
Welcome to Scandinavia Collins, revised 1987
The Big Muddy – *a canoe journey*
     down the Mississippi Oriole Press, reprinted 2006

Fiction
Another Kind of Loving Antony Rowe, 2005
Beyond the Broken Gate Oriole Press, 2007
Long Shadows, Oriole Press, 2010
Village 21, *an anthology of short stories,* 2011
The Other Side of Silence, Oriole Press, 2012

Educational aids
Assassination at Sarajevo Jackdaw Publications 1966
Caxton and the Early Printers Jackdaw Publications 1968
Scott and the Antarctic Jackdaw Publications 1971
The Vikings Jackdaw Publications 1976

For Ann, Helen, Alison and, above all, Bill W.

Prologue

This is a story about growing up. In particular, it's about what happens when things go completely the opposite way to all your plans.

A lot of it is hazy, for reasons which will become clear, but I did keep a sort of diary and, though it's now eons later, the sequence of events and how I felt are things I hope I never forget.

I'm now what is termed a Young Adult, but the story began long ago, a few weeks after I started at Greenley High and just before my twelfth birthday. I may have changed some of the conversations, but it's how I remember it all in my head.

October 2002

1

"Sorry, Nicole," Mother said. "That's a really bad idea. And do stop chewing your hair."

It was always Nicole rather than Nikki when she thought I'd got things wrong. I allowed myself a moment of defiance before removing the end of my ponytail from my mouth and glowered at her. "I just don't see why," I protested, my voice coming out squeakier than intended. "I... we'd planned it all so it wouldn't be extra work for you. I think you're really *mean*, Mother." Her elevation from Mum to Mother seemed relevant to my own recent elevation to the High. I went on: "Laura's bringing sandwiches, Madge's mother is making a gigantic cake, Jane's aunt has this magic recipe for éclairs, and Rachel's Mum does these dreamy iced things."

"And you, Nicole ... what are you doing?"

"I'm providing the venue. And of course the birthday." I tried to look my most appealing. "Mum ... Mother, this is a really special day. It'll be my first birthday at the High when I can invite my new friends. And I'll be *twelve* for heaven's sake."

"And what about your father?"

"Oh, Dad." He hadn't been elevated to Father status yet. I felt something tight, like a clenched fist in my midriff. We'd stopped pretending that Dad's behaviour was anything but an embarrassment. Mother explained that it wasn't his fault, he just couldn't tell when he'd had enough to drink, so he just went on until he became very silly or ill or noisy. And embarrassing. I didn't understand why it wasn't his fault. If I did anything stupid, I was expected to make up for it: do extra jobs or something. Then I had a brilliant idea. "Can't you take him out somewhere? Have a meal out that evening, or something?"

"Who's taking me out somewhere?" Dad asked cheerily, coming in from the conservatory. Mother and I exchanged glances. From his mood and demeanour, we could tell that he'd had a drink or two, but not enough yet to make him stupid.

"Did you remember to get the bread, James?" Mother asked.

He clapped a hand to his head. "Oh sorry! Sorry, darling, I bumped into a couple of chaps from the cricket club and we decided to have a quickie at The Lion. And you haven't told me who is taking me out somewhere or why."

"It was my idea." I said quickly. "You know it's my twelfth on the 12th, and it's the first party when I can invite my new friends from the High. I thought if you and Mother went out …."

Dad gave a roar of laughter, "… so we wouldn't see what mischief you were getting up to. Great idea. It's ages since I took your mother out." That was true enough.

"I'll get the bread," I said. I was ashamed of my part in the conspiracy and couldn't meet his eye.

It was only a ten-minute walk to the Co-op, along the side of the park, past a garage and a hotel. Pete was coming out of the shop as I went in. He was in his running kit and grinned "So how are you getting on at the High?"

The fact that Pete would be at the High had been one of the few pluses about going there. Most of my friends were moving to independent schools, but apparently we couldn't afford it. Of course Rachel, one of my best friends at Primary, was going to the High, too. But though I like her *enorm*ously, she's, like, mega brainy and always has her nose in a book. So quite soon I palled up with Madge, Laura and Jane who all came from another Primary and had some wicked ideas. In fact Jane, because of her birthday being when it is, is already in Year Two. She is Laura's special pal.

"Yes, OK," I said in answer to Pete. "It's just a bit awesome."

He nodded. "Yep, I felt like that first. You'll get used to it. Isn't it your twelfth soon?"

How did he know that? Oh, probably his younger sister.

"Mmm. Everyone's been marvellous helping me plan a party." I hesitated, then added, "Sorry you're not invited, but it's girls only."

He grinned. "Don't think I could cope with all those girls."

"Anyway, Mum's helping me to organise it, though she and Dad will be going out for a meal that evening."

Pete looked away. "Ah," he said. He knew, of course, about Dad. Everyone knew about Dad. There had been too many embarrassing occasions for everyone not to know. Pete added "I'm glad for you." Which was particularly nice of him as he wasn't invited.

I'd always got on well with Pete, even though he was more than two years older than me. I knew he felt much the same as I did about sport. The other boys were always jeering at him because he

7

was no good at team games. Then someone had found out he was good at cross-country running, so he would go off on sports afternoons on his own, training for county, then regional competitions which he quite often won. I wished I could find something I was good at, but I was rubbish at all sports. Our PE teacher said I lacked team spirit.

"Will I see you at Liz's bash?" Pete asked as he turned to jog away.

"I doubt it. Not really my scene."

"Nor mine." He paused. "Perhaps we could go over to the marsh sometime. I hear there are some egrets in."

"Yeah, that'd be good."

He jogged away and I went into the shop for the bread. Mrs Kumar was on the check-out.

"Hello, dear. And how is your father? I was sorry when I saw him have that fall."

As I said, everyone knew about Dad. "He's OK, nothing serious." I didn't add that it might have been better if it had been serious, because it would have kept him at home out of trouble.

On the way home, I turned into the park and found a seat by the pond. The mallards got very excited as they always do and I wondered what Mother would say if I gave them the bread, but not seriously. "Quack," I told them.

"Quack, quack," they said back.

The ducks waddled about hopefully while I sat and thought about the party and the new friends I had made. Jane was the one I particularly liked. In a way she was rather like Rachel, like brainy, but less buttoned up. She's a special pal of Laura, which is surprising as Laura – although she's a year younger – is much more 'in your face'. Really sure of herself like I've never been. Of course she probably doesn't have an embarrassing Dad. In fact I find Laura a bit scary and I hope my party goes so-o-o well she'll be impressed and want to be friends. When I told Mother how sure of themselves some of the girls were, she laughed and said, "They probably think the same about you." I hadn't thought of that so I practised various expressions and poses in front of the mirror, until I felt stupid enough to stop.

So I went back to thinking about Dad. He travelled around the north-east of the country selling computer stuff – in fact he was the chief regional rep for the area. This took him away from home quite a lot, and sometimes this seemed a good idea. On the other hand I once thought of him as my best pal. He understood things like nobody else.

You know how adults are always telling you how you'll understand things better when you're older. Well, I've always *known* that I could understand anything if only someone took the trouble to explain. When I told Dad that he really understood.

"I know Tuppence," he said, using the name he calls me when we're talking about serious things. "It must be very frustrating. I'll try and help." And that year for Christmas he gave me a huge dictionary. I love words and spent ages looking through it. There were some amazing words, like, you could never imagine using - words like epitomise, or fallibility, or inappropriate. It was one of the reasons I kept on liking the Beatles, even though everyone else said they were *so* yesterday. Instead of just shouting, their songs had words that meant things. Like the one called *The Nobody Man* that no one ever noticed because he never had opinions or did anything.

"Clever Tuppence," Dad said when I pointed it out to him. But he had just arrived back from work and sounded a bit funny as he often did when he arrived home. Mother said he stopped off at the pub on the way home and that can make you a bit funny. It began to happen more and more. In the end I gave up trying to have a proper talk with him when he was like that. Once or twice he fell down in the street and it was so embarrassing because everyone could see.

I really did not understand about this drinking business. Some of the girls said they had a glass of wine at home and got giggly but I didn't believe them. It was the same when they got giggly if there was a group of boys hanging about. Well, that had begun happening since I started at the High. We'd had the sex classes in Primary and it didn't sound a lot to get excited about. Mother had explained a bit more and made it sound more interesting, but I hated the idea of all that fumbling and messing about. That was one of the reasons I liked Peter. You couldn't think of him like that. He had far more interesting things to talk about.

The first time I met him – I mean properly met him to talk to – was one afternoon last year when I was upset with Dad because he'd made a fool of himself in front of neighbours who had come in for a drink. At his invitation. Mother never asks anyone in for a drink.

Anyway I rushed out of the house while they were still there. There's a public footpath running past our back garden, which goes down a slope to a marshy bit of land. People take their dogs for walks along it, and I sometimes go down there when I want to be alone. There's a stump of a tree which I sit on and look across the marsh or up at the sky. You wouldn't believe how the sky changes from angry to happy or just boring. That day it was just boring – milky grey all over, so I looked across the marsh and saw a figure coming towards me.

"Hi Nikki," Peter said as he got nearer. "Would you like to see something interesting?"

Anything would be better than sitting there thinking about my embarrassing Dad, so I followed him down the track. It was spring and there were a lot of birds flying about.

"Go quietly," Peter whispered and began walking very slowly,

Then I saw it: a black and white bird called a peewit, limping along the track ahead of us, its left wing trailing. "It's hurt!" I cried out. "We must help it."

But Peter only shushed me and pointed in another direction to where several small balls of feathery fluff were huddled together, squeaking and restless. "It's all right," he whispered. "She's not really hurt. It's the mother lapwing luring us away from her babies."

So not only did I learn that peewits are also called lapwing, but they are really clever at tricking us humans. After that I went more often down to the marsh, sometimes meeting Peter down there by chance, or we'd arrange to meet if he'd found something particularly interesting. So I gradually learned about the resident birds and those that came here for the summer or winter. I really got into this migration stuff. Then I had my first triumph. I rang him to say I'd found a new bird, very small and nondescript, but definitely new to me, so he came rushing over and said it was the first willow warbler of the summer and he'd never seen one that early before. I thought he was going to hug me for a moment, and the idea didn't seem so bad.

The ducks had got fed up with waiting for me to produce something to eat and had waddled back to the lake where a little girl was flinging small fistfuls of crumbs at them. Beyond them, on the water, were two pairs of widgeon, and then several of something smaller. I hadn't got my identification book with me so I stared at them hard, memorising their details: a flash of green near their tail feathers, and a lovely green streak over the head.

Then I thought I'd better get back with the bread, which was just as well as Dad was about to come looking for me.

Over the next few days, my party became *the* topic of conversation with Mother. Then she said, "Why don't you bring the girls back for tea so that I can meet them." So I did, choosing an afternoon when I knew Dad was going to be late at the office. Rachel couldn't come because there was a documentary on television she didn't want to miss (I *ask* you!), but Madge, Laura and Jane arrived about an hour after I got home from school. I saw they had changed and brushed their hair, and it felt like a really special occasion. Laura looked particularly pretty and quite grown up; she has reddish brown hair and I think is beautiful.

It was one of those early October days when everything is golden and warm. Mother had set the tea out in our small conservatory, and with the doors open on to the garden, it felt even more special. Jane, who is tall, asked Mother all sorts of questions about the garden, so we went out to have a look at it. I watched Laura wandering off on her own, then bending down to look at some plant and calling out a comment. Jane clearly made quite an impression on Mother who said afterwards that she would make a good role model. Usually Mother is saying what a bad role model some celebs are, and I have to say I felt a bit jealous.

It was next morning she raised the question "Are you sure you don't want any boys at your party. I thought you liked that Peter who knows about birds. And Madge happened to say she would like to bring someone called Roy." As for Peter, I knew he'd hate it. And Madge's Roy is a terrible show-off.

The truth was that I'd worried over it a long time, changing my mind and then changing it back again. I knew Jane had a boy friend, so if Madge brought hers, Jane would want to bring … Clive. I think that was his name. At the High I couldn't help noticing that most of my new friends were becoming different in all sorts of ways: always changing their hairstyles, spending Saturday afternoons window shopping and checking out the latest fashions instead of cycling out to the local woods as we all used to. And talking about boy friends. They never kept the same one for long. Anyway I stuck out against inviting boys, but I did invite several more girls so it would be more fun.

Of course people kept asking me what my Dad was giving me for my birthday. Well, I wasn't going to say 'Nothing, as far as I know', so I said 'Dunno yet. It's like a surprise.'

Mother asked "So what are you planning to do at this party?"

"Well, I've got some CDs from the library," I said. "And I'm getting some dressing up stuff as most of them are mad about clothes at the moment. Then there's charades. I've asked each of them to

11

bring a special object in a box without saying what it is, then they'll have to do a charade for the rest of us to guess. And if we can't, they get a prize." I stopped. "Oh, prizes!"

"Yes," mother agreed, "you'll need some prizes with those sorts of games." She went off and came back a few minutes later with a marvellous bag of different bits of make up – nail varnish, eyebrow pencil, lipstick samples, hair combs. She had once worked in the cosmetics department of a store, and according to Dad one of the salesmen took a fancy to her and kept giving her samples. He pretended to be jealous, but I don't think he was serious. Mother said now that she was glad to find a use for them.

I hugged her. "You're a star, Mother."

She hugged me back, "You're not so bad yourself."

In due course Mother also found me scraps of material, some old hats and scarves to contribute to the dressing up events. And although I had told her everyone was bringing lots of goodies, she made two smashing cakes oozing with cream and a small mountain of profiteroles.

2

Everything was going so well until Madge rang up to say she couldn't come. Unexpected visitors were her excuse, but I knew it was because I had said no to boy friends. Mother said "Never mind", and spent the whole morning on the day of the party helping me to make everything look nice. She is very good with making decorations and arranging flowers and by the time she had finished, the living room looked something out of one of those telly advertisements. Mother had helped me choose an outfit which apparently fitted into the category of 'smart casual'. She knew I hated wearing dresses, so she helped me choose a denim trouser suit which I really liked. Even Jane described it as cool when she arrived.

She was the first guest and I could see Dad was impressed. Soon after that, he and Mother left for their evening out, so I had no time to feel nervous. Jane was full of admiration for the way we had decorated the living room and wrote things down in a little notebook which she put in the blue sparkly bag she had brought which went with her blue sparkly dress. Then Laura turned up in one of those peasanty skirts, with rusty tinges that matched her hair. She turned out to be the real life and soul of the party. She could change herself from funny to serious just by putting on a hat or pulling back her hair or making herself old and stoopy. We had shrieks of laughter over the dressing up games, and later some of them did great charades to describe the objects they had brought. We couldn't guess three of them, and the prizes were greeted with whoops of delight.

After that we were all ready for a breather. I'd just put on my favourite old Beatles album and was in the kitchen fetching some more cartons of juice from the fridge when I heard the front door being shut, then a chorus of surprised greetings. Yeah, I know the Beatles are really retro, but I'd been brought up with Mother humming all their stuff and kind of inherited them into my genes. Anyway, I assumed the disturbance in the hall was some gatecrasher, but soon after there was a squeal that might have been pleased or protesting followed by a yell that definitely meant everything was not well.

When I reached the hall there was quite a scrum going on with several of my friends pulling and screeching. Towering above them all was the unmistakeable figure of Dad. I was horrified and looked frantically round for Mother.

"Dad?" It came out as an unenthusiastic squeak.

"Stop it! Please, stop it, Mr Wood! " shrieked Jane's voice. And for once she was not looking at all self assured. Then I saw Dad had lifted her up, and was swaying about as though he was dancing with her. The other girls stood back, aghast, not sure what to do. As soon as Jane saw me, she gasped "Nikki, stop him. Why is he doing this?"

But Dad just went on grinning and burbling about wanting to be part of my party.

"Stop it, Dad. Stop it!" I threw myself into the fray, scrabbling at his fingers. "I hate you! Hate you!"

It seemed to go on for ages, with Jane struggling and me fighting Dad, and everyone babbling incoherently. Except Rachel, who stood by the door staring at her feet. I didn't hear the scrape of a key in the lock, but the front door opened again. And there was Mother. The other girls melted away into living room, leaving me still helplessly scrabbling at Dad.

"James!" thundered Mother. "Put Jane down. At once! And go upstairs." To me she added more quietly, "I'd slipped off to the loo and he'd gone when I came back. I got here as soon as I could."

Dad looked at her, round Jane's bobbing head. "It's all right, dear. I just wanted to see how my baby's party was getting on."

"Upstairs, at once!" Mother repeated, and Dad put Jane gently down and went up the stairs.

Jane was sobbing and I was crying too in humiliation and anger.

Mother shepherded us into the living room to a babble of 'did you see?', and 'can you imagine?' and 'poor Nikki with that awful father'. Rachel was sitting hunched in a small armchair, still staring at her feet. Even Laura looked subdued. The babble died down as we went in, and Mother spoke quietly to us all. I don't remember all she said, except that that it was something about Dad not being quite himself and perhaps it would be better if we ended the party now. So everyone got out or borrowed each other's mobiles and rang parents to collect them unless they were near enough to walk. All except Jane. Mother wanted her to stay a bit longer and said she would ring Jane's mother herself.

I'd thought of Jane as my most grown-up friend and she soon calmed down. I was too embarrassed to speak to her, but Mother was marvellous, explaining how sometimes grown-ups acted strangely when they had things on their minds, and how splendidly she, Jane, had coped. She gave her something to drink and telephoned her mother.

All I could think of was that never ever could I go to school and face my friends again. Their words echoed through my head – 'Poor Nikki and that awful father' – because though he was awful I loved him terribly and wanted him to be his normal self again. The one big relief was that the half-term break started in a few days and by the time that was over, everyone might have forgotten what happened. Though I didn't really think anyone could forget anything so awful.

October 2002 – April 2003

1

Jane's mother came to pick her up, and after that I helped Mother clear up. She was very quiet.

"What will you say to Dad?" I ventured at last.

"He'll be fast asleep, and by tomorrow he'll probably have forgotten all about it." She sounded sort of hopeless and I couldn't think of anything helpful to say. Anyway I wasn't feeling too bright. Perhaps it was something I'd eaten? It felt as thought I'd been kicked in the stomach.

And when I did get to bed I just couldn't sleep. I kept seeing my friends' faces and their expressions, disgusted or pitying. My mind went over and over the evening like one of those old gramophone records stuck in a groove. The pain in my tummy got worse, like having awful toothache in your guts. Eventually I couldn't stand it any longer so I got up and went to the loo, hoping I might get rid of whatever it was. But nothing came, except I noticed there was a funny stain on my pyjama bottoms.

I thought I knew what it probably was, but because I was so tired and upset, I started being frightened as well. The light was on downstairs, so I went down and found Mother having a hot drink and watching a news programme on TV, though I don't think she was taking it in. As soon as I told her, she said, "Oh, sweetheart, that'll be your first period," and started bustling about making me a hot drink and finding a pad for me to wear. It was almost as though she had been sitting there waiting for it to happen.

"Does it always hurt like this?" I asked, clutching my tummy.

"It'll wear off. I'll give you a Paracetamol, and the hot drink will help."

We sat there quite a while, and she was right, the hot drink did help.

"You're falling asleep, darling. Why don't you go back to bed?"

I went to the door. "Don't tell Dad, will you?"

Once he'd been the first person I'd tell anything, but this felt private and anyway I didn't like him much just then.

"I won't tell your father," Mother said.

In seconds I was fast asleep and when I awoke, sunlight was streaming through a crack in the curtains and I saw on my wise owl clock that it was half past ten.

I rushed downstairs. "Mother, you didn't wake me. I'm missing school….."

She stopped me in mid-flow. "It's all right, love. I've rung the school and told them you're not well." She smiled, but her eyes were puffy and she looked anxious. "And how are you feeling?"

I thought about it. "A bit niggly and sickish." Then the memories of the previous evening came flooding back and the miraculous realisation that I didn't have to go and face them all at school. Not today anyway.

"Where's Dad?"

"Out. He went out as soon as he'd had breakfast. Not that he had much of that."

"Did he say anything about last night?"

Mother looked away. "He was far more worried about how he felt. I tried to tell him about it, and he said he was sorry if he spoilt the party, but all he wanted was to join in and he was sure I was exaggerating."

She looked so miserable. I put my arms round her, gave her a hug and said, "Don't worry, Mother. It'll all work out. I'll talk to him."

To my surprise my Mother started shaking and I realised it was not with sobs but suppressed amusement. "Oh, darling. I'm not laughing at you. It's just that you sounded suddenly so grown-up, and I thought that's just what I would have said to you."

After a moment, I saw what she meant. "Well, I am twelve." Then I told her what was really worrying me. "It's the thought of going back to school – I can't bear it."

This time Mother gave me a hug. "I know, love. And I've been thinking about it. I wouldn't normally let you get away with time off even for a first period, but there's half-term in three days. And by the time you all go back, everyone will have forgotten. You'll see."

Even though I wasn't convinced, it was an enormous relief that I wouldn't have to face them all immediately, so when Dad came in an hour later I said, more in sorrow than in anger, "That wasn't very clever was it?"

Dad is quite a big guy but that morning he looked crumpled and shrunk. He said, "Sweetheart, I'll never be able to tell you how

16

terrible I feel. I don't remember exactly what happened – only that I so much wanted to be part of this big day of yours. Then your mother told me that I behaved in a totally … totally inappropriate manner."

"Yes, I guess inappropriate is just the word," I said, and burst into tears.

The next thing he was giving me one of the big bear hugs he hadn't given me in a long time, and I started loving him so much again. so when he said "I promise I'll never, never let you see me like that again," I wanted so much to believe him that I did.

2

We had a wonderful day. Mother told him she'd agreed that I need not go back to school before the half-term holiday though not why, so Dad said we would all go out and have a meal and a country walk, then come home and have a game of scrabble, which was my favourite just then. We had a lovely walk through some woods and along a small lake with lots of ducks that I decided to tell Peter about later. Mother and I looked at each other when Dad took us to a country pub for lunch, but he ordered a glass of wine for Mother, a Coke for me and fruit juice for himself. I kept looking at him through the meal, especially when he went back to the bar for more drinks. His hands looked a bit sort of clenched, but he came back with the same drinks as before. And then I began really to think things were going to be all right.

Half way through the half-term holiday, Jane rang. She had been ringing almost every day since the party, but I wouldn't take her call. Mother said I should because she thought I shouldn't let the rift continue. So when she rang again, I was feeling so good about our great day out together that I decided to talk to her. I started off by saying how sorry I was about what happened at the party, and she brushed it off, saying "Well that's in the past now. And it wasn't *your* fault."

Perhaps I should have left if there and just made plans to meet up with her, but somehow I wanted to defend Dad who was making such a big effort to change. So I said, "I know it wasn't my fault, and Dad was awful, but everything is OK now. He's changed completely. For some reason he had been drinking too much, but now he isn't going to any more."

There was a long silence. Then Jane said in a small voice, "Well, that's good. Though he didn't look very sober when we saw him last night…."

Last night? What had she seen? Or what had she thought she'd seen?. Suddenly I was so angry I couldn't speak. Jane was being mean because Dad had embarrassed her. She was trying to make me doubt him.

So I said, "Well, thanks for ringing. See you after half-term," and put the phone down.

"That was a quick call," Mother called from the kitchen, but I wasn't going to tell her the reason for that.

Soon after I was in town when a voice called "Hi, Nikki. Wait a mo." It was Rachel, the one who usually had her nose in a book.

"Feel like a Smoothie?" she asked.

In fact, I didn't, but it seemed mean to walk away, so we went into the nearest café and ordered a Smoothie each. When we had sat down at a couple of stools by the bar near the window, she said, "That was a great party, Nikki. Sorry about Jane, but she did make rather a fuss."

I was astonished. "Well, Dad was pretty embarrassing"

"Yes, but he obviously didn't mean any harm."

I looked at her with interest. "I wish everyone else looked at it like that."

Rachel shrugged. "Well, you know how they can gang up sometimes."

She was right, I realised and felt cheered. We chatted about GCSE options though they were eons away. She'd already decided she was going to be a librarian, which was hardly a surprise. I still hadn't a clue, though I wanted to do something with words. Not in a library, though. When I said as much to Rachel she exclaimed as though it was obvious, "Well, if you like words, why don't you become a writer?"

It was an amazing thought, and I went on turning it over and over in my mind liking it more and more. At first it seemed scary because when I thought of some of the authors whose books I liked, it didn't seem possible that I could ever be like them. But then they were grown-ups, like, as old as Mother, and if I imagined it being her it didn't seem quite so scary.

Just before the half-term holiday ended, I mentioned it to Dad. He seemed just a bit funny when he got back from work, but I was so full of this idea that I didn't take much notice. When I'd told him, he lifted me up and tried to swing me round, then dropped me saying I was getting much too heavy, but it was an absolutely brilliant idea. Then we told Mother who thought it was a great too, but warned that I would have to work hard at both English Language and English Literature.

Mother was right. By the time we were back at school, everyone seemed to have forgotten about my party. Madge and Laura had both been to France and could talk of nothing else. The others had all been visiting aunts and cousins, one had gone up in a glider (imagine that!) and no one could think of anything but the fun time they had been having. As for Jane, she's in a different year, so I only glimpsed her in the distance. Before long, everyone was talking about Christmas anyway.

Mother decided that she and I were going to stay with the Grampies, that's *her* mother and father, who are some of my very favourite people. Gramp, that's my grandmother, has the most special Christmas tree you've ever seen, decorated with coloured balls and tinsel, but with *real* candles. On Christmas Day we light the candles and every year Grump, granddad, complains that she will set fire to the house, and no one takes any notice. Grump has so many stories to tell because when he was younger he did exciting things in the Arctic and Antarctic, and got frostbite in his toes so that even now he can't feel anything. As for Dad, he had decided to go to a place called Estonia with some friends. I thought it was mean of him to go away at Christmas, but he had started behaving strangely again, so in a way it was a relief.

At school there was a special party, and we all sent each other Christmas cards, posted in a big pillar box which the teachers emptied, then read out the names so we could collect ours. I was a bit worried that I might not get very many, but I did all right. There was one from Pete. We quite often went down to the marshes in December and January because there were some fab birds, even a very rare visitor blown across from North America to the local sewage farm. It was called a lesser yellow legs and wasn't very special to look at, though its legs were very yellow indeed. Pete quite often came over to have a chat in the canteen. Jane didn't though, and she didn't send me a card either.

19

"Did you send her one?" Mother asked when I mentioned it. I shrugged a 'No' and she gave me one of those looks that said 'What do you expect, then?'

The Grampies live in a cottage some distance from Burford. It was cold and crisp and we did a lot of walking and eating, and then there was the Christmas tree which was as beautiful as ever. We all take a guess at which will be the last candle to go out, and Grump is always the one who gets it right. Mother seemed very happy and I did wonder a bit whether it was easier when Dad wasn't there to worry about. When he did get back, he was quite ill. Mother said it was a stomach upset, and the doctor decided he should spend a few days in hospital where he soon got better. I visited him a couple of times with Mother.

That second term I really began to enjoy being at the High. I found I was quite good with computers and the IT department was ace. So was the library. I had started reading books in a different way, trying to imagine how they might end if I had written them. I never seemed to get it right so I soon realised how important it was to be able to surprise the reader.

One evening Dad complained, "I don't see much of you these days, Tuppence," and I realised he was right.

"You are out a lot," I pointed out.

"Yes, well, we're very busy at work at the moment." He was certainly getting home late, and then he usually fell asleep in front of the television. Sometimes Mother would prod him if he started snoring too loudly and he would grunt and say "Wha?" then fall asleep again. Watching him one day as I looked up from my book it struck me how I didn't miss him as much as I used to. It made me feel a bit sad, but also older, as though I now had my own life. It was then I made the great mistake of deciding to have another party.

The following Sunday morning while Pete and I were down on the marshes, I asked him what he thought. "It'll be just a small party, but I thought I'd invite boys as well this time. Would you come?" Then I got myself into a terrible tangle trying to explain that it wasn't because I regarded him as my boy friend, but because I didn't want to be the only one without one. By the end, I must have been scarlet in the face as well as tongue tied. Pete put me out of my misery by roaring with laughter. "How can I resist such an elegant invitation? Of course I'll come. As long as you don't expect me to dress up."

I decided to make it on an evening when I knew Dad was out, just before we broke up for the Easter holidays, and Mother helped me plan it, with a sort of buffet. Madge and Laura had boy friends; Rachel didn't but said she wasn't bothered as long as long as we didn't do dressing up. There was an episode of some talent show on television that I guessed most of them, except Rachel, would want to watch and otherwise I was planning bingo and Scrabble.

"You're not inviting Jane?" Mother asked.

"No," I said and did not feel it necessary to explain that though Jane may have forgotten that last awful party, I hadn't.

3

The evening of the party was blustery and damp, but no one had far to come. Pete arrived on his bike. Madge and Laura came together with their boy friends, driven by Madge's older brother. He was called Adrian and I was surprised how serious and studious he was. Of course we had to invite him to stay. Rachel's father dropped her off. After everyone had arrived, and all the food was set out, Mother said she would pop down the road to see a friend and discuss some community event they were planning. I put some music on and we settled round the television, getting to know the boys who seemed all right, until our programme started. That was on for an hour, then we all wrangled about the results. I said I thought the winners were awful, because they shouted rather than sang, and everyone said I was so old *fash*ioned, except for Rachel and Adrian who both agreed with me.

After the programme, I went into the kitchen to put some quiches and pizzas in the oven to warm, leaving the others to change the CD. Peter came out to give me a hand. I wasn't surprised to hear the familiar thump-thump of what mother calls jungle music – that would be Laura's choice. Peter said he would go and tell them to turn it down a bit and I was about to follow him when I heard a noise from upstairs. At first I assumed Mother had come home, but then thought she wouldn't have done that without popping her head round the door. I opened the kitchen door quietly and listened. Silence. Then a sort of explosion like a really loud burp. And, finally, unmistakeably, a snore.

From the living room, the thump-thump settled into a slightly gentler stride. I crept up the stairs. Mother's and Dad's bedroom was empty, but from the spare room next door came the recognisable rumblings of Dad's snoring. Through the half open door, I glimpsed my father's prone figure covered by a sheet as I slipped past into my room and sat on the edge of my bed, head in hands. The sound of the music from downstairs was still pretty loud.

Eventually I crept downstairs, slipped into the living room and said, "Better turn it down, or we'll have the neighbours complaining." It sounded feeble but had its effect. When the CD ended, Adrian put on another one: piano music, rippling and peaceful. I looked at him gratefully. From then on, it was like being on the edge of a precipice, listening out for unexpected sounds, tummy clenched against the awful happening.

When it did I wasn't ready for it. On our third game of Scrabble, I had become really absorbed in trying to beat Adrian who had come out with words that were not only impressive but high scoring and occasionally so bizarre as to be questionable. I think that Rachel had the same idea. In fact, I was racking my brains to think of a word that had a 'q' but no 'u' in it, when we all stopped dead at the sound of a crash on the stairs. I flew out of the living room to find Dad levering himself up from a fall on the stairs, clinging to the banister and then making his way very slowly and carefully, one step at a time. And he had nothing on but his pants.

"No! No!" I shrieked, which was stupid because it brought everyone out to see what was going on.

Pete was the first and, bounding up the stairs, put his hands under Dad's elbows and managed to turn him round. "You'd probably be better lying down, Mr. Wood," he said gently.

Dad staggered, clung to one of his shoulders and took an unsteady step back up the stairs. "Probably right, Peter, probably right. Good fellow," he slurred. Slow he made his way upstairs, pausing to say "Lubbly party, Nikki sweetheart. Lubbly, lubbly party."

I stood helplessly half way up the stairs looking at my friends clustered at the foot, the tears streaming down my face. "I think you'd better all go home," I gulped.

They began to shuffle about, getting jackets. Adrian said, "We'll give Rachel a lift."

"No," Rachel said. "I'm staying."

The others trickled out through the front door. "It was a good party, Nikki," Adrian said. "I really enjoyed meeting these guys." When I remembered that later I was very grateful, because he was years older and he made it sound as though he really meant it.

By the time they had all gone, Peter had eased Dad up the stairs and into the bathroom where I could hear him being sick. I thought if there was a God, He would let me die now so that I would never ever have to face any of my friends again. Rachel put a hand on my shoulder. "Your Dad can't help it, Nikki. I read somewhere that it's like an illness." I suppose she saw it in one of the documentaries she is always watching, and I wanted to lash out at her and Pete because they were there seeing my shame.

Pete came out of the spare room where he settled Dad back on the bed. "I'll go and fetch your Mum, Nikki," he said.

I couldn't say anything and left it to Rachel to respond with "Thanks Peter. That's a great idea."

Mother was back in a few minutes. By then Rachel had made us each a mug of hot chocolate and I'd sloshed cold water on my face. Mother gave me a hug and went straight up to Dad, returning soon to say he was quite unconscious. I said, "I am never, ever going to speak to him again," and Mother gave me another hug and said, "Oh, darling. We'll sort something out in the morning." Then she said to Rachel, "Thank you so much staying with Nikki."

"Of course I stayed. I just feel very sorry for Mr. Wood. It's an illness, you know."

"Yes, I know," Mother said surprisingly, though how anyone could think that getting drunk was an illness was really beyond my understanding.

4

I couldn't sleep for ages, and I was wide awake at six o'clock as I heard Dad stumbling about in the next room. I heard him go into the room he normally shared with Mother and then a mumble of conversation. It went on for a long time and I must have drifted off for I next heard the shower running, and then a tap on my door before it opened and Mother's head looked round.

"I don't want to see him," I said, and buried my head under the duvet. After a while there was another tap on the door and Dad's voice saying "Tuppence?" He tapped several more times before I heard Mother say, "I think you had better leave her alone."

As I listened to the murmur of voices and sounds from downstairs, misery filled my head. Yes, and fear. It was as though all the certainties I had taken for granted were shrouded in a fog behind me and ahead lay a path through an unpredictable darkness. All I could think of was Dad's swaying figure, bare on top like a monstrous white slug, and his legs sticking out from under his black and white boxer shorts. Even burying my head deep into the duvet couldn't get rid of the picture, or the sight of my friends' astonished faces, except for Rachel who stood in the background staring at her feet. And Pete trying to coax Dad upstairs. What on earth must Pete have thought?

Eventually I heard the back door shut and then the car door slam before the engine started up and the car drove away. Soon after my bedroom door opened and I felt Mother sit on the end of my bed. "You can't stay there all day, Nikki love."

"It's Sunday."

She patted the duvet where my bottom was. "Problems won't go away because you bury your head."

"I don't see how this problem will go away." I started to cry. "And the trouble is I still love him."

Mother's voice said in a wobbly way, "I know, sweetheart. So do I." And I think it was then for the first time I realised how difficult it must be for her. I pulled the duvet down. Mother was sitting there, looking down at her lap, one hand on the hump of the duvet that was my bottom.

"So where is Dad?"

"He's gone to see the doctor

"Doctor?"

"Mm. He thinks there's something wrong. He wants advice."

A flickering gleam in the dark steadied into a glow.

"What will the doctor do?"

Mother shook her head. "Your Dad can't be the only one with such a problem."

I thought for a moment longer then said, "I'll get up."

Mother didn't move straight away. "He'll need all the help we can give him, love."

"I don't see what I can do." I wasn't yet ready to let him off the hook that easily.

"Try not to talk too much about last night."

Dad had ruined my whole life, and Mother didn't want me to talk about it! Then I noticed her sad expression and knew that I must try.

I got up and had some breakfast, then told Mother I'd go down to the marshes for a bit. It was partly because of something she had said: problems wouldn't go away just because you buried your head.

24

I wanted to know what Pete's reaction was, though I dreaded seeing him. I found him down by one of the pools, and he shushed me as I approached. "House martins flying low," he whispered. Wow, that was early. Then I saw them, two of them, dipping and gliding. "What are they doing?"

"Feeding," Pete said in a more normal voice. "May be collecting mud for nests, though it's a bit early for that."

Then I remembered. "Pete. I'm so sorry."

"What for?"

"For Dad. For him being so awful. For ruining the party."

Pete turned and put his hands on my shoulders. "Nikki. What your Dad does is not, repeat is *not* your responsibility. He has an illness. My Granddad was a bit the same. You have to get on with the rest of your life."

I looked back at him, and may be that's the moment I fell a bit in love with him. "He's gone to the doctor," I said.

"That's great. Now you have to play your part."

"How?"

"Mainly by not reminding him too often how awful he was last night."

"That's what Mother said."

"She's right." He took his hands off my shoulders. "And if you look round now, you'll see a marsh harrier heading towards us."

When I got home half an hour later, Mother said Dad was in the living room and wanted to see me. He was sitting in his usual armchair with his head in his hands, but looked up when I came in and gave a wobbly smile. He held out a hand and I took it.

"Tuppence," he said. "I don't expect you to forgive me, but I want you to believe I am sorry more than I can find the words to say for spoiling your party. The doctor thinks there is a problem and is doing some tests. I will do everything he says and I hope I will soon be completely better."

I put my arms round his neck. If the doctor thought there was a problem and was doing some tests, then everything must be all right in the end. When you were ill, doctors made you better. "You can't help being ill, Dad," I said, squeezing him. "And don't worry about last night. I've just been talking to Pete, and he's fine about it."

Dad squeezed me back. "That's a very nice boy," he said. "And now I'm going to have a shower and then help your mother in the garden."

I watched him go slowly up the stairs and thought I had never loved him more.

Things were going to be alright, but even so, for the next few days, I felt as though I was holding my breath the whole time. It had been agreed that I wouldn't go back to school before the Easter holidays. I knew Madge and Laura were moving away from the area so I wouldn't see them next term, which was a relief in one way. Dad's results came through and apparently he had lots of things like vitamins and calcium missing in his body so he had to take a lot of pills. He soon started looking a lot better and was so much like his old self that the party began to seem like a fading nightmare. Rachel came round several times. There was apparently something wrong with her father, so they didn't like visitors coming to the house. Perhaps that was why she read so much.

About a week after that awful party, Dad came home from work looking very pleased. We'd had the shepherds' pie and were on to the apple tart and custard when he said, "I was wondering how you might feel about a trip in the old camper van to France during the holidays?"

"France?" I squeaked.

"It sounds lovely," Mother said more soberly. "But isn't it a bit late to make a booking?"

"Done. It's already done." Dad was beaming ear to ear. "We leave on April 17th, return ten days later."

I was breathless with excitement. Foreign holidays are what everyone else did. I couldn't believe it was actually going to happen.

"I bought the Michelin maps today – they mark all the most attractive routes, and the camp sites. Just where the fancy takes us. I thought Tuppence might like to have a go at canoeing." It didn't seem possible to feel happier.

There really wasn't much time to get ready, and the next few days were a haze of rushing around, buying provisions, making sure we had the right gear, with Mother barking out instructions while Dad and I jumped to it. I'd never felt so happy. I managed to find time to go down to the marshes and find Peter and tell him about it. He was watching a fleet of baby mallards trailing after their mother on the largest pool. Further out a young grebe was riding piggy-back on its parent.

"Lucky you," he said. "I wish I could come." And I found myself wishing he could too.

I found myself babbling, "The doctor says he's got lots wrong with him, but he's already so much better.

Peter said "That's good news. But remember it may take a bit of time." As we made our way across to one of the further pools, he said, "Don't forget to keep a list of birds you see; or if you're not sure, write down a description." He paused to leaf through the identification book. "Look, you might see these – bee eaters, hoopoes. And probably black kites." The bee eaters were spectacular colours, and the hoopoes had big crests on their heads. It was all so exciting, and then he mentioned casually that Jane had been down on the marshes recently.

I said, "Oh? I didn't know Jane was into bird watching."

"She wasn't," Peter said. "But I think she might get to be."

And I didn't like the sound of that at all.

April - October 2003

1

Then we were off and so many new impressions were coming at me that I hadn't head space to think of anything else. The first triumph was that although the sea was what Dad called 'quite choppy', I didn't feel ill at all, and leaning on the rail with the wind in my hair was one of the best feelings I'd ever had. Then we landed and everyone was speaking French of course, and I found I could actually understand some of it, so Miss Beattie's lessons had not been in vain.

It felt very weird driving on the wrong side of the road, but Dad was so cool about it that it didn't feel weird for long. That first night we camped early in a very big camp site. We ate at the on-site restaurant, and it was full of people chattering in different languages. And Dad drank water.

Over the next few days we gradually travelled south. Dad wanted to take us to an area he called the Dordogne, because that is where they have organised canoeing trips. When she saw the river and the way it disappeared into a ravine, then came out rushing over rocks Mother was not very keen on my going, but Dad talked her into it. I must say I was a bit scared when I was sitting there in the canoe – well, it was a big rubbery boat – with my life jacket on, and suddenly we were off and there were Mother and Dad waving on the bank and getting smaller. Then we went round a bend in the river and I couldn't see them any more.

It was absolutely wicked, the speed and the way we rushed at rocks but always missed them, and the steep wooded forests on either side. I thought how Pete would have enjoyed it. Lots of people in the boat squealed with excitement, but I just held my breath until I couldn't hold it any more and let it out in a great whoosh, and started again. It all went too quickly so when we arrived at the end of the trip and there were Mother and Dad waiting for me, my first greeting was "Can I do it again?"

"Not now, Tuppence," Dad laughed. "Perhaps we'll find a different trip for you tomorrow."

In fact, I had two more during the holiday, one of them in a huge proper canoe, and it never lost its magic. Then Dad said, "When we get home we'll find you a local canoeing club and you can have some lessons."

I didn't think it was possible to feel happier.

Because it was the middle of the holiday season, the camp sites were all crowded. Our camper van is a bit small for three people, so Mother and I slept in it, and Dad slept under the awning. Once or twice when I was settling into bed, I noticed Dad had gone off somewhere and that worried me a bit, but he was always there bright and cheerful in the morning, and Mother was quite cool about it. In fact one night they both woke me up, as Mother had decided to go with him. In one camp site I got friendly with a girl of about my age and we giggled a lot, me trying to talk French and she in English.

In between the driving and the canoe trips we went for long walks and wandered round small towns and villages. I thought they had a lot more small shops than we have at home, and every morning you could see people going out to buy fresh bread and come back with long crusty loaves. The bakers smelled gorgeous. There were a lot of greengrocers and butchers too, and we often went in to buy what I learned was called *charcuterie*, a range of marvellous cold meats which we ate for lunch with that crusty bread. We also went into a lot of old churches because Mother likes that sort of thing. They were often rather dark, but the light came through beautiful stained glass windows, making coloured blobs on the floor. I did try to do some bird watching, but somehow it wasn't the same on my own and I wasn't very successful at identifying anything that wasn't very familiar. I didn't see any bee eaters or hoopoes, but there were lots of little birds. I kept a list for Peter and wrote a lot of notes about the ones I couldn't be sure about.

After a while I stopped watching Dad because everything seemed wonderfully back to normal. On the last night before we headed home, we had a meal in the camp site restaurant and Dad said, "Well, let's celebrate a great holiday. How about a small carafe of wine?"

"No, thanks," Mother said.

"OK, I'll just have a glass then."

I'd forgotten all my worries about Dad's drinking, and now they all came flooding back. I watched him anxiously through the meal, but he sipped it from time to time and he didn't have another one.

It was next evening, our last night in France that I heard Dad going off after our supper, and then a short while after Mother said, "Must find your father. We have an early start tomorrow."

It was eleven o'clock when I heard them coming back, Mother's voice in a hoarse whisper but I could tell she was near to tears. "You *promised* James. You promised."

"Goddammit," I heard Dad say. "Haven't I been a pillar of rectitude. What else do I have to do to prove that I'm all right now?" His voice was a bit slurred, but not as bad as it has sometimes been. Not like that ghastly evening of my party.

All the same, I suddenly knew what it was like to have your heart sink.

2

Their voices mumbled on for ages. Try as I did I couldn't make out what they were saying and in the end I must have fallen asleep. The next thing I knew, Mother was shaking me and demanding that Sleepy Head should get cracking. And then we were having breakfast under the awning, with Dad his usual self. Sometimes I give up on trying to understand grown-ups. Presumably I'm going to be like that one day.

"Is everything all right?" I asked Mother as we went over to the camp kitchen to wash up.

"Fine, sweetheart. Why do you ask?"

"I thought I heard you and Dad arguing when you came back last night."

There was only a moment's pause. "Oh that. I was telling him off because, as usual, he hadn't packed up his gear as he said he would."

It wasn't very convincing, but surely I didn't have to start being suspicious of Mother, too?

We had a great drive to Calais and this blip soon went out of my head. Dad was what he termed 'a pillar of rectitude' all the way home, and then did all the unloading of the campervan while Mother got a meal ready.

Things continued to be so normal that I stopped having flashbacks about my last party and began to take normal for granted. But the memories started to return as term time approached and I began to dread going back to school. Of course, it helped that Madge and Laura had moved away, and I had nothing to do with Jane these days. Then the thought of Jane brought the memory crashing back of

Pete's comments that she had started taking an interest in bird watching. When I tried to call him, his mother told me had gone on holiday to Cornwall with a friend and his family. Dad went on seeming fine. Once or twice I thought he looked a bit pink in the face, so I supposed he was still drinking but had it under control.

Then just before term began, I came home to find a big box sitting in the middle of the living room.

"What is this thing?" I grumbled after I'd tripped over it a couple of times.

"Why don't you open it and find out," Mother said, and then I saw it was addressed to me.

And then I also saw the name on the box of one of the best known computer companies and I felt myself going scarlet with excitement, from my face and neck and spreading over me so that I must have looked like a boiled prawn. Dad folded his newspaper and said "I'll give you a hand." He knelt beside me, pulled a little knife from his pocket and began cutting through all the tape that sealed the box.

"This is what you should have had for your birthday," he said as he opened the box and drew out the most beautiful laptop I'd ever seen. He also spilled a lot of those polystyrene things which rolled all over the carpet, but Mother didn't say a word, just watched us both with such a happy face.

I scrabbled about in the box pulling out more things, adding to the mess. There were two speakers, a load of CDs and DVDs from which I saw I had all the latest updates, some photo-editing software, and other stuff I hadn't a clue about.

Dad helped me set it up in my bedroom. We registered for one of those free email programmes, and I sent a message straight away to my cousin in Australia. She's a couple of years older than me and a real computer nerd, and she answered straight away with a page of smiley faces. After that we emailed each other every day, and she told me about good websites to check out.

Since we'd started at the High, Rachel and I had become even more friendly. She still had her nose in a book most of the time, but sometimes she'd surface for long enough for us to do a film together. She's also a great letter writer and kept in touch with Madge and Laura, so I had their news. Soon after term started, Rachel and I were having lunch in the canteen when Pete came over to join us. He wanted to know all about France and told us all about Cornwall. Nothing was said about Jane, and I didn't like to ask.

Rachel was still set on being a librarian. I still wasn't at all sure. The rest of your life seems a long time to be doing anything. Rachel suggested choosing something that offered different possibilities. She's sensible like that. When I asked 'Like what?', she said I was a good communicator so there should be a big choice: like newspapers or magazine, or television, or of course the internet. Well, it was worth thinking about.

3

Things were OK for so long that I should have known it was too good to be true. I came home one evening to what seemed at first an empty house. Mother wasn't downstairs or in the garden, but then I heard movements upstairs. I was amazed to find her in my room, sitting on my bed with piles of my clothes all round her.

"What on earth…?" I began, and then I saw she had been crying.

"I want you to go and stay with the Grampies for a while," she said.

"Dad?" She nodded. "What's happened?"

She shook her head. "It's quite serious. I'd rather tell you when I've had a chance to sort things."

"What can I do?" I wrapped my arms round her.

"The best way you can help is by me knowing you are with the Grampies."

Some of it gradually came out while we were packing my bags and having a cup of tea. Dad had been caught up in a fight the night before and put in a police cell. My Dad in a police cell! He hadn't any identification on him and no one could understand what he was saying. During the night he had collapsed and they had to take him to hospital. By then he had sobered up enough to give his address and the police contacted Mother. She'd rushed off to see him, and he was quite seriously ill. Something to do with his liver.

My feelings were so mixed up. I was afraid for Dad, and I hated him for messing my life up yet again. And I was angry for Mother for letting it happen. Then, as we were driving to the Grampies, I saw how clenched tight Mother's expression was, and her eyes were all red and puffed up. The realisation of how she must be feeling made me feel mean to have had such bad thoughts. I told myself that getting to understand difficult situations like this was part of growing up. And I didn't want to grow up one little bit.

When we reached the Grampies, they were clearly in the picture. They gave me a hug without making too much fuss and said my usual room was ready. I love the room: small, cosy and with a fab view over rolling pastures with what look like toy sheep dotted about. We had supper, then Mother went home and I asked if I could go upstairs to write some emails. With all that was going on, Mother had still remembered to pack my laptop. And it was really weird. Once I was on line, Dad no longer seemed to be my problem.

A few days later, the Grampies said they had arranged for me to go to a nearby girls' independent school, which I guess meant they were paying for it. Though it was mainly a boarding school, I would cycle home each evening as it was not far. It wasn't much fun starting after everyone else, but the girls were nice; friendly but without asking too many questions, so it was quite easy to keep myself to myself. The best thing was when Mother forwarded a letter from Pete. He said how sorry he was that I had gone, and would I let him know if I saw any interesting new birds. That was the best thing that happened since Dad's escapade. Anyway, the school was in beautiful grounds, and in the lunch break I started to go for walks and do some bird watching, then send a note to Pete at the week-end if I saw anything new.

The school had ace IT facilities and I got really good at learning what my laptop could do. The Grampies went to bed quite early, so I had hours to myself. They'd leave me watching the television, but as soon as they'd gone, I switched the box off and my laptop on. By then I'd joined several chat groups, but came off most because they were so boring - everyone trying to score points over everyone else. But there was one I really liked called Junior Connect. It had all kinds of sub-groups, so I joined one on birding. I guess I hoped Pete might be on it until I remembered he hated computers. But I met a lot of other people from all over the world, swapping bird stories. Some of the birds had the craziest names, like the yellow-bellied sapsucker, and thick-billed flowerpecker.

Bit by bit things went on changing. Dad was moved into a Rehab Centre and Mother said he was likely to be there a long time, like maybe months. Then one week-end she came with a serious face and said she had decided we must make some changes. She had been working part-time at one of the main local health centres in Greenley for a while, but now they had asked her to be full time.

33

"So," she said. "It would make sense to sell the house"

I was about to yell a protest, then I saw she was trying hard not to cry, so I shut up as she went on, "I can take a small flat - but of course there'll always be room for you." She paused for a bit, then said "Of course the Grampies wanted to help, but they've already done plenty, and Grump is getting very frail and forgetful." Yes, I had noticed.

At last I managed, "But what about Dad?"

Mother took my hand. "He'll be in Rehab a long time yet, and when he comes out it will be a while before he can take a full-time job." She left unsaid what was in my mind: 'even if he manages to stay sober.' In view of her full time job, she also said it would be better if I spent the summer holidays with the Grampies. Finally she said, "And when you've finished your exams, we'll find a really nice flat in Greenley while you decide what you want to do with your life." But that was yonks away and I couldn't believe she was thinking so far ahead.

When she had gone, I went up to my room and cried and cried until I was nearly sick. It felt as though my life had been completely turned upside down. Then I got on to the computer and went to Junior Connect where someone had recorded some amazing bird sightings the other side of Oxford. For an hour or more I forgot all about Dad and selling the house and Mother looking so tired and sad. I was amazed when Gramp knocked on my door with a mug of hot chocolate. How could I forget what a miserable time Dad was having?

But then he had brought it on himself.

The only cheering thing that happened was a phone call from Rachel who said she missed me dreadfully at the High. When I told Gramp, she said why not invite Rachel over one week-end, so I did. She hadn't any grandparents and loved the Grampies so I said I would be glad to share them from time to time. The odd thing was that because Rachel did not ask a lot of nosy questions, I was glad to share with her a bit about the awful mess my life was in. As she had been at my party, she guessed what some of it was about.

"I think you are a bit hard on your Dad," she said.

"That's all very well, but he brought it on himself."

She looked at me quite crossly. "Do you really think he wants to be like that, upsetting you and your mother and being ill?"

I hadn't thought of it quite like that so when Mother suggested I went with her to see Dad in Rehab, I didn't hesitate. I'd never imagined a hospital like it: it was more like one of those stately homes you can pay to visit - until you got inside, then it smelled like a hospital and you saw the patients wandering around looking as though they'd lost something.

Dad was in a chair out on the lawn. Though Mother had forewarned me, I was shocked at how thin he was. When he saw me he tried to stand up, but was too weak and sank back into the chair. "Tuppence, Tuppence," he kept saying with a big smile. But the smile didn't get to his eyes, which looked blank and sad.

I chattered on and on to fill the silence, all about my new school, and my computer. Especially the computer.

"You want to be careful about those chat groups," Mother said. "You hear all sorts of stories." So I explained how boring most of them were except the birding one I had joined. When I told them about the yellow-bellied sapsucker, Dad actually giggled, and it felt as though I'd been given a present.

On the way home, Mother realised I was upset and explained that it was the drugs that made Dad like that. She said it would take a good many weeks yet. Perhaps months. The good thing was that the police had decided not to charge him. That was a bit of a shock. I hadn't realised it was *that* serious.

When I got back to the Grampies I felt really lonely. There was no one I could talk to about Dad, and all my mixed up feelings. That was when I decided that the next sunny week-end I would cycle back to Greenley to see if I might meet Pete on the marsh.

3

As luck would have it, the following Friday evening was lovely and the forecast was for a great week-end. We rang Mother who seemed really pleased I would be coming over, though she fussed a bit about the bike ride. But I told her precisely the route I would be taking away from main roads, then Gramp made me some sandwiches to take with me and put them in the fridge.

When I set off next morning, I really wished I had someone to go with, but after a while I was glad I was on my own and kept stopping to admire the countryside or identify a bird I had spotted. It was early October and everywhere glowed with autumn tinges. I had chosen a route that went through Burford, and well before I reached it, I found a gateway with a stunning view. I propped my bike against the hedge and clambered on to the gate to eat my sandwiches. I hadn't been there long when a couple of other cyclists stopped. They were quite old but friendly. The man said, "You've found yourself a good place. Can we join you?"

So I said, "Well, like, it's a free country isn't it?"

The woman wanted a pee, so disappeared towards some nearby trees. The man told me they were touring the Cotswolds, staying in campsites. He said they were planning to get married in the New Year, and saving up. When the woman came back, they cycled off. I thought how that was the first time I could remember having a conversation like that with totally unknown grown-ups. I also thought how nice it must be to go for a cycling tour with someone you really liked.

I stopped again in Burford and went into the church where someone was practising the organ. It was a lovely sound and I sat in one of the pews for a while just letting it wash over my mind. I'm not sure about God, but just in case I shut my eyes and asked him to make things all right for Dad.

Mother had been home about an hour when I reached the flat, which overlooked the market place. The flat was small, but I liked the way it was in the middle of things, and you could see everything going on right outside the windows. Mother had made my favourite, spagbol, and one of her cheesecakes for dessert. She was cheerful and looked less tired. She said Dad was making progress and was less sleepy all the time. He had joined a class they ran at the Rehab Centre, making things out of wood. Apparently this was one of the things they did to help patients get better.

After supper, we cleared up and watched a long police thing on television. I went to sleep in the middle of it and was surprised to wake up in my bed with the sun pouring through a crack in the curtains. Mother had to leave straight after breakfast, so I cleared everything up, then let myself out, locked up and put the spare key through the letter box.

It was only a short ride to our old house. It made me feel really funny to see the board outside which said 'Sale Agreed.' Mother had already told me that a nice family wanted to buy it. I pushed the bike along the narrow track which goes behind the gardens and leads to the marsh. Mother had paid someone to keep the back garden tidy, so it looked just as it always did. I could see the bird feeder and there were some blue tits and great tits on it. I left my bike propped up against our back fence and went on to the stile. Beyond that the path dips down quite steeply to the marsh. I sat on the stile for a while looking through my binoculars over a scene that had been so familiar. It was one of those days when the clouds seem to sit on top of the trees. Then I saw a figure moving in the distance and recognised Pete straight away. I was just about to jump down from the stile and shout and wave, when I saw there was another figure. Pete turned and held out a hand to the second figure to go over another stile. It didn't take me long to work out who it was: Jane.

I told myself there was no reason why she shouldn't go bird watching with Pete, but it didn't stop me really minding. The fact is that I didn't think she was the bird watching type, which meant she had probably taken a fancy to Pete. Come to think of it I hadn't heard from him for a while. Then I thought she might be having her own back because Dad had made her look silly at that party, but I realised that was stupid because now that I was living with the Grampies, she wouldn't think I'd find out about it. Rachel had pointed out that I seemed to want to take the blame for everything – even for Dad's drinking. In fact my head was in a big muddle.

Anyway, when I saw Pete and Jane together, something caught in my throat, and I gulped. Then, after a moment, I turned back to get my bike and started the long ride back to the Grampies.

That was the evening I switched on to Junior Connect and had my first encounter with Baz.

October 2003 – April 2005

1

Our first contact was mega frosty. Well, I wasn't in the best place to start with. On the threshold of my teens I'd lost my home, my Dad was on another planet, and the favourite - well, *only* boy in my life had, as far as I could see, dumped me. And now here was this clown with a fancy name talking about birding as if it was a Big Joke. He had posted a one-liner on Junior Connect's birding section: *First UK sighting of the bright breasted rubylip* - and he'd been stupid enough to put his email address in case anyone was interested.

I was so angry I emailed him without stopping to think: *I suppose you think that's funny. Why don't you keep your sugestive comments for some playschool website.*

I was gobsmacked to get a reply in minutes: *Hey, who's been rattling your cage? By the way suggestive has two 'g's.*

That made me mad at myself as I knew very well that suggestive has two 'g's, but hadn't noticed the wrong spelling. So I sent him a l-o-o-ng email, explaining about birds, and telling him some of the stuff I had learned from Pete, about migration, about how they looked after their young; how important they were in the food chain. It took me ages, and when I'd finished I realised I hadn't thought about my awful life for nearly an hour.

It was a bit disappointing that he didn't reply, but when I got back from school next day there was another email. *Hi Nikki. I'm sorry I upset you by being stupid. I didn't know any of that stuff you told me, so maybe I'll try and identify some of our garden birds and perhaps you can help me.*

So we started this on-off email correspondence. He would email me a description of a bird and I would tell him what it was. I usually knew because they were fairly common birds, until he started going to some nature reserves, and then he started telling me about the less common birds he saw. We found we had the same taste in a lot of things, like music and books. We both preferred Pullman to Potter, though Baz understood all that parallel universe stuff better than I did.

Most people put their photograph on Junior Connect; mine was one that Mother took of me, reading in the garden. I'd got rid of the ponytail now, in fact gone through several hair styles before settling for the gamine look. The one of Baz made him look quite dishy if you like dark ruffled hair and a smile like a toothpaste ad. Sometimes there would be a long gap between our emails because one or other of us would be swatting for exams. He went to an independent boarding school in Devon. Then in the holidays, he would go off somewhere really exciting, like Africa or America, with his parents. In the meantime, our house was sold, Mother moved into a bigger flat where Dad joined her eventually. He got a job at a local factory, and seemed OK for a while, but he started drinking again and after a time went back to Rehab. I couldn't understand how he could be so stupid. This happened several times, until Mother threw him out. She was too upset to talk about it for a long time, but in the end she explained she couldn't go on and she'd told him to get himself sorted out. That didn't seem likely as Dad pushed off to stay with some of his drinking friends somewhere in Devon.

It was around then that Rachel invited me to her home for a week-end. I'd been to her house before, but not to stay. And I'd met her Mum, but not her Dad. I thought he was dire. Not in the way mine is but very bad tempered, especially with Rachel.

They'd put a camp bed in her room for me, and that evening we sat up talking. She said, "Don't take any notice of Dad, he can't help it."

"You mean like my Dad can't help it?"

"No. Well, in a way, yes. He has terrible arthritis and is in pain a lot of the time, except when he is on very strong painkillers and he doesn't like taking those. It's the pain that makes him like that."

Then I understood why she had never asked any of us home, and why she was more tolerant about my Dad than I was. It was that evening I told her about Junior Connect and meeting Baz. Rachel hates computers, but she tried to be interested, only warning that you had to be careful about meeting boys that way. Well, I'd already been through that with Mother.

At that stage there didn't seem much chance of our meeting. By then more than a year had passed and I was over fourteen. Baz was in his first year at Uni. Then I had a breathless-sounding email from him: *I've just found out something amazing. My cousin goes to your school. She's called Emma Woodward and is the daughter of my mother's sister. I found out because she came to our place and showed us some photos of her school sports day. And there you were in the relay. I recognised you from the pic you have on Junior Connect, even though your hair is different. She wants to meet you - my mother I mean - and wonders if you and Emma could go for tea one week-end.*

I read it several times before I could believe it.

Emma was in the Sixth Form and was, like, in a different hemisphere from me, but we were in the same art history group so I found a way of quizzing her about Baz as soon as I could. She said he was all right, a bit bossy, and yes, we could go and see her Aunt Fiona, Baz's mother, any time. Emma actually could drive and had a little car. How cool is that! So we fixed up to go on a week-end in November.

Baz's mother lived in a really nice house about twenty miles away. She told me to call her Fiona too, which felt weird, but otherwise I took to her straight away. We had sandwiches and chocolate cake and talked. She explained how her husband, Geoff, travelled a lot for his engineering company, so I said that my Dad did, too. Of course she wanted to know why he travelled and the only thing I could think of was computers. "I don't really understand it exactly, but something to do with computer chips."

Later Baz emailed that his mother had really taken to me and was glad he had a nice sensible girlfriend. That was a shock because I didn't realise I was his girl friend. Then I thought he probably meant that I was a girl and a friend. After that I saw quite a lot of Fiona. She drove over to the Grampies to see me and meet them, which pleased Mother who hadn't been keen on me meeting strange males on the internet. So I pointed out that I hadn't actually met him.

And then at last I did. By then, I knew a lot more about him than he did about me, thanks to listening in at all those tea parties. Apparently since he'd met me on the Internet, he taken up bird watching and walking and that sort of stuff, and did much less partying, so I was considered a Good Influence.

We met at his home a couple of days after he got back from Uni. Fiona invited me over to supper, only she called it dinner. When I got there, she took me into the living room where Baz was waiting, looking rather smarter than I expected. I explained I didn't drink alcohol and they gave me a yummy peach and mango mix. Baz had a shandy. I didn't know what to say, and he didn't either, so Fiona did most of the talking, telling about the Grampies. I'm sure it was a lovely meal, but I wasn't very hungry. Then Fiona had to go to some meeting and said she would be back in an hour and drive me home. When she'd gone, we sat looking at each other until Baz suddenly said in a dramatic voice "Wasn't that *awful!?*" His expression was so funny that I burst out laughing and after that everything was all right.

Like Emma, Baz could drive and was allowed to use his mother's car. He soon came over to meet the Grampies and they all liked each other, and so it was with Mother too in due course. What a relief. To my surprise Baz had taken up birding seriously. Because he could use the car, he knew much more about all the nature reserves in and around the Midlands, and now he took me to them whenever he was back from Uni. While he was away he emailed most days. Once or twice he mentioned that his parents had asked when they might meet my Dad, but I kept up the story that he was still travelling the world installing machinery and helping companies to programme it. As autumn turned to winter, we started going for country walks because this is the time you can see a lot of different birds that come here for our warmer winters. Then one day, after a particularly long walk, he was helping me over a stile, and as I jumped down on his side of it, he said in a funny voice, "You really are special, Nikki." He still kept hold of my hand, and bent down and kissed me. On the mouth. I'd often wondered what my First Kiss would be like after all the amazing accounts other girls gave. To be honest, it wasn't a great deal, though I thought about it a lot afterwards. And over the coming weeks, it got better with practise.

2

It was towards the end of November when he was home from Uni for the week-end that Baz said that his Dad really wanted to meet me. It was fixed for the first Sunday lunchtime in the New Year at the Good Shepherd, a pub near their home.

Baz picked me up and things got a bit involved. Gramp wanted to show him some new patio tubs she'd just planted with winter pansies and by the time she'd done that and he had moved them to where she wanted them, we were late. When we got to The Good Shepherd, Baz's parents looked as though they had been installed in the bar a long time.

Fiona cooee-ed and waved. "Over here darlings. Did you get held up? Geoff this is Nicole."

"Sorry," I said, "It was Gramp's fault."

"Nicole's grandmother," Fiona translated.

"Never mind," Baz's Dad said in a voice just like Stephen Fry's. "You're here now."

He was awesome, Baz's Dad I mean. And not just because he was a dishy older version of Baz. He had Presence. I knew he did stuff with buildings and bridges, but just then he was so-o-o relaxed in an amazing Calypso shirt worn loose over a pair of chinos.

Baz gave me a dig. "Dad is asking what you want to drink."

"Oh, sorry, Mr. Winters. Could I have a tonic please?"

"You'd better call me Geoff. Tonic coming up," Baz's Dad said as he got up to go over to the bar. He came back with the drinks and a clutch of menus. "So," he said. "Where exactly did you two meet?"

"Oh Geoff," Aunt Fiona said in that how-many-times-do-I-have-to-tell-you voice. "I told you, they met on the Internet."

"Oh, that Facebook thing?"

"Something like it," Baz said.

"We didn't have the Internet in our young days. We met at dances or parties."

"Or on holiday," Fiona interjected. I knew that she and Mr. ...Geoff had met in Austria, ski-ing. She raised her glass. "Here's to many happy days for you young people."

"Happy days," we all murmured

Then we all studied the menus. Fiona said the Cassoulet was good, so I settled for that.

Geoff went off to give the order, then he settled back in his chair and said, "And what does your father do, Nikki?"

My heart dived. I could hardly say 'well, you see my Dad's a drunk, so he can't actually hold down a job.' But I'd forgotten I'd already had that conversation with Fiona who now broke in with "Geoff dear, I told you. Nikki's father travels the world marketing chips."

"As in fish and ....?" Geoff queried, grinning broadly at his own joke.

"As in computers," Baz said. "Very specialised."

"Way above my head," his father said. "Anyway, when he's back from his travels, we must all meet up."

I sipped my tonic, relieved that it had all passed so smoothly and wondering why I had got myself in such a state over meeting Geoff. He was really nice, and I felt a pang of sorrow that I knew I couldn't introduce Baz to my Dad. The others started talking about plans for Christmas which they were spending in Nepal.. They were going to a place called Pokhara and do some trekking. I sat listening to them, feeling relaxed, firmly squashing another pang - this time of envy - that there was never likely to be a chance that Mother and Dad would ever find themselves in Nepal. I must have daydreamed a bit because suddenly Baz was giving me another dig. "Wake up. You're being offered another drink."

I looked at my empty glass in surprise.

"So I guess you enjoyed it," Geoff said.

"Oh yes, it was fine. A bit different from the kind I usually have, but fine."

He looked a bit odd. "Well, I did cheat a little and asked them to put a small gin in it."

Fiona said sharply, "That was not clever, Geoff. Nikki doesn't normally drink alcohol and she's only fourteen." Well, I knew heaps of girls both at the High and my new school who had got tipsy and thought it was a huge joke, but I knew better.

"Oh Lord, Nikki. I *am* sorry." And he really did look it. "I'll get you another - pure, unadulterated tonic this time."

"It's all right, honestly," I said, embarrassed by the fuss.

"I'm sure it is, and I don't think you'll go of the rails on one small G and T. But Fiona is rights, as so often."

"An unadulterated tonic would be very nice." Saying that made me feel better. My head was buzzing with dismay that, after all my obsessing about never taking alcohol, I'd done just that without realising it. I felt good that I'd made a decision not to have another. In fact, I didn't want another, though truth to tell the nice warm feeling I had was rather pleasant.

"Thanks for being such a sport," Geoff said.

"It's all right," I said again, but heaven knows what made me add rather primly, "but please don't do it again."

Fiona and Geoff looked at each other, then burst out laughing.

"You're a natural, Nikki," Geoff said, still chuckling.

A natural what I wasn't sure, but I liked the feeling of being it. In fact I was feeling unusually chilled out and I thought perhaps there was something to be said for alcohol. As long as you kept it under control.

3

During the meal Uncle Geoff asked me what career plans I had. It seemed feeble to say I hadn't actually got any yet, so I admitted to being keen on writing.

"There you are then," he said.   "You're a natural communicator."

That's what Rachel had said, so perhaps I was.

Then he asked about my interests, and I told him about the birding. I kept thinking of new interesting things to tell him, until I noticed that everyone had finished their Cassoulet and I was only half way through mine. It was a nice feeling having other people interested in what you had to say, especially when they are your boyfriend's parents. I think that was the first time I consciously thought of Baz that way.

On the way home. Baz said, "My parents loved you Nikki. Thanks again for being a sport over the gin, though I'm not sure why you're so against booze."

I shrugged. "There's someone near us who drinks too much, and it's put me off."

He patted my knee. "Well, as Dad said, I don't think that one drink will send you off the rails."

It really made me feel good to have got on so well with his parents and I was more determined than ever to sort out what I wanted to do with my life, and do it. The first thing was to make sure I got good results in my GCSEs which were only a year away now, and think hard what A levels I wanted. Thinking about what Geoff had said about being a natural communicator, I began to wonder about media studies.

Mother looked pleased about it when I told her. "Choosing something you really enjoy, as well as being good at, is so important. If only…." Then she stopped.

I knew she had been going to say something about Dad, who had always hated his job as a salesman. As far as I knew it was months since she had heard from him. All we knew was that he was somewhere in the West Country, staying with friends and doing odd jobs.

"I don't know how good I am at it, but I enjoy writing stuff more than anything. You know, making up stories. I thought perhaps I could get a job on a paper."

"Mmm. I'm not sure you're tough enough to be a journalist. Nor am I sure they'd want you making up stories. Still, there are a lot of other opportunities - magazines, TV, radio."

"The internet," I added, my enthusiasm growing. "I guess Media Studies is the way to go. I'll need to check what the entry requirements are."

Before Baz went back to Uni we spent a lot of time together and I really looked forward to those days when I woke up and knew we would be meeting. Mostly we went for walks, bird watching. Baz was better at it than me now, though I had more patience. If something interesting didn't appear soon, he wanted to move on while I was happy to wait as long as I'd seen the smallest movement. Perhaps impatience is a boy thing. I was better at recognising bird song too. Once or twice when we had been waiting for a while he would put his arms round me and give me a very big hug. I was aware of feelings that were both a bit exciting and disturbing and supposed this was something to do with sex. Once he cupped my face in his hands and said, very seriously, "I can't imagine any thing better than spending a night with you, Nikki." I felt myself go scarlet, partly because I wasn't sure precisely what he meant and couldn't ask him. For the first time for ages I wished that Dad was around because he would have explained about boy feelings.

Until I remembered how useless he was.

So I just said to Baz, 'well, perhaps one day', and he grinned, gave me another hug and seemed okay to leave it at that.

April 2005 – April 2006

1

Over the next few weeks I set myself a timetable. I talked it over with the Grampies who thought I was being too hard on myself, but then they couldn't know how important it was to reach the goals I was setting myself for the first time. I suppose up to now my goal had been for Dad to get sober, and I hadn't scored very high there.

Now I was going to take control of *my* life. At school I checked with some of the teachers the areas that I need to concentrate on. I got myself a pile of A4 scribbling pads, cleared a couple of shelves of ornaments for my books, and set up the table in my bedroom with the scribbling pads and a neat rows of coloured markers on one half, and my laptop on the other. Then it was all systems go.

We established a routine that after supper I would spend some time with the Grampies, watching some programme, or having a chess lesson from Grump. He usually fell asleep in the middle of it. Then I went upstairs to study. Around half-past nine, Gramp brought me a hot chocolate on her way to bed. And then the house was mine. The trouble was that by the time I'd finished the hot chocolate I was feeling pretty sleepy, but I made myself a rule that I wouldn't turn the light out until eleven. It was so annoying. I really slaved my way through that summer term, and then into the summer holidays. It felt really odd not to be at home in the holidays though Mother came over as often as she could. Baz was away trekking for a whole month in Scandinavia.

Then suddenly he was home, looking healthy and tanned and gorgeous. It was almost time for him to go back to Uni but he said he wanted to give me a special treat. So he drove me all the way over to Slimbridge where Sir Peter Scott runs a fantastic reserve for wild fowl. Peter Scott's Dad was Captain John Scott who went to the South Pole only to find someone else had got there first. I think I would have died. Well, he did die and that was terribly sad.

Baz had been there before so he knew the best places to go. I've never seen so many swans before and a few of them had yellow and black beaks which meant they had come from very cold places because our winters are milder, and then decided to stay. There was a book explaining that each swan has a different pattern of yellow and black so, if you're really good, you can get to know individual birds.

Later Baz and I went to more distant hides and I saw wildfowl I had never seen before. It felt like the best day in my life and when I said so to Baz he turned and gave me a big hug. We were having such a good time that we forgot about lunch, until I started feeling hollow inside. When I pointed out there was a good cafeteria, Baz said he thought we should celebrate with something a bit more special, so we drove out of the reserve and found a country pub he knew.

By now I was ravenous and ordered a big fry-up. Baz watched me gobbling it down with a grin on his face. I'd already had two tonic waters when he said he would get me another with a small gin in it as I'd had enough food to soak up the alcohol and never notice it. That wasn't quite true. Perhaps because I knew it was there this time, I was more aware of the warm feeling inside and a slightly light feeling in my head.

"It makes me want to giggle," I said.

"Never mind, it's a giggly sort of day."

When we got back to the car, which was under some trees at the back of the car park, he suggested we should sit in the back for a while. I wasn't sure why, but then he started to kiss me, and it felt very nice. After a while, his hands moved away from holding me round the back and started wandering about.

"What d'you doing?" I started but he kissed me so hard I couldn't think of anything else, until his hands began to creep up under my tee shirt. Then I wriggled free and protested "I don't want any of that..." And he let me go and said coolly, "I keep forgetting you're just a kid."

It didn't seem the right moment to point out I was nearly fifteen.

He didn't say anything more on the way home, and I felt great lumps of misery shifting about inside me. But that evening, he sent me an email apologising and saying how much he really liked me. Then he sent me a couple more messages when he got back to Uni. So everything was all right. I hoped.

After Baz had left for Uni, I thought a lot about that day with him. Even thinking about it made me feel a bit wobbly. Part of me wanted to know what happened when the petting got heavy so I would be like everyone else – or like everyone else said they were. But I knew I was a bit scared of finding out and that I had a great big Thing about staying in control of whatever happened.

47

This control thing was equally important when it came to my studies and the goals I had set myself. Maddeningly I still had the problem of managing to stay awake long enough to do all I wanted to do.

When I mentioned it over supper one evening, Grump said, "What you need is a pick-me-up to give you a second wind."

Gramp said sharply, "Good Heavens, Charles. Don't encourage the child to drink."

Grump grumbled, "Good Heavens, woman. What a suggestion." All the same he seemed determined to prove a point and while he and I were playing chess, he asked me to go to the dining room cupboard and get him a brandy. I'd never seen where they kept their drinks before and noticed they had quite a lot, including a bottle of gin.

The brandy certainly livened Grump up but he wasn't allowed to have another one, and soon after I went off to think about my essay on the Romantic Poets in the 19th century. It was several evenings later, and I was really struggling with a particularly tricky maths problem when I thought of Grump and his pick-me-up. I didn't do anything about it then, but after a couple more evenings of tricky problems, I crept downstairs and went to the cupboard in the dining room.

I looked at the gin bottle for a long time, then rinsed out the mug in which Gramp had brought the hot chocolate, and poured the smallest amount of gin in. When I had a sip of it, it tasted disgusting. Of course that's why people put orange or tonic in it. I couldn't see any tonic, so I put a splash in from the cold water tap, and it wasn't quite so bad, though it was difficult to think of people drinking it for pleasure. Presumably the one I'd had at the Good Shepherd had been awash with tonic. I'd get a bottle of that.

When I had crept back to my room, I was panting and realised I had been holding my breath. But the great thing was that the whole experience, probably helped by the gin itself, seemed to give me a new lease of energy and I suddenly saw a beginning to the solution to the maths problem. It was well past eleven and I'd done quite a bit more when I got into bed, not forgetting first to go to the bathroom and rinse the mug thoroughly. It was magic that so little could have such a good effect, though I did feel a twinge of guilt and made up my mind I would only repeat this if it were really necessary.

2

Then something happened that put my studies and Baz and Dad and everything right out of my head. Some time at the beginning of July, Rachel came with her parents. I was rather surprised her father had agreed to come, but an amazing thing happened. After a while, he and Grump discovered they had both been somewhere called El Alamein in the last World War. They hadn't actually met, but they knew some of the same people, and there were soon 'do-you-remember-old-so-and-so's filling the air. Rachel's Dad had been taken prisoner and sent to a big camp in Germany where he was stuck until the war ended years later. He had some amazing stories about those times. Grump was never taken prisoner but he had some bad experiences fighting in what they called the Battle of the Bulge near the end of the war. While the two men chatted, Rachel and her mother looked astonished. Rachel and I left them to it and went up to my room for a game of Scrabble. She was pink with pleasure to see her Dad enjoying himself like that, and by the time they went home arrangements had been made for the two men to meet and go to London to see some War Museum. I wished like anything that Dad had been there, until I remembered he would have probably ruined the whole day for everyone.

To make the day perfect, there was an announcement that London had been chosen as the city in which the 2012 Olympics would be held. Though it seemed a lifetime away, we could feel the excitement of all the people shouting and waving their arms on the television screen, and Mr. Blair looking very pleased with himself as though he had won an armful of gold medals. So the awful things that happened next morning seemed even more terrible. I was having breakfast when Grump suddenly yelled out as though someone had hit him. I rushed into the living room to see him sitting on the sofa, leaning forward, staring at the television as though his life depended on it. Gramp was standing behind the sofa just as shocked.

When I looked at the screen, there were people rushing in all directions, some of them with blood all over their clothes, some of them looking desperate.

"What's happened, what's happened?" I yelled.

"There have been some bombs let off in London," Gramp said quietly. "In the Underground."

I'd been on the Underground a few times, and I had this sudden picture of the darkness rushing past the windows and then .... And then I couldn't think beyond it.

49

"Why?" I yelled.

"Because there are some very wicked people in the world," Grump said, and I saw he was still staring at the screen with the tears streaming down his face. It was terrible to see my Grump crying. Then I remembered some of the stories he had been exchanging with Rachel's Dad, and understood that he knew how terrible it would be to be in such a situation. So I sat down beside him and hugged him. He took my hands in his and, after a bit, calmed down. "I can't understand why God lets it happen," he said sadly.

"You leave Him out of it," Gramp said crossly. "What's the point of His giving us free will if He interferes all the time?"

One of the problems seemed to me that there were too many Gods, but I thought I'd better keep that to myself for the moment.

We were glued to the television for the next couple of days. There were terrible stories, but also wonderful ones of how some very brave people helped those who couldn't help themselves. Then Mr. Blair came on the television and told us we must not let anyone try and change of our way of life and we must all carry on as normal. And that made me realise that I had not been carrying on as normal and it was time I started.

It took an evening or two to get back into the swing of it, and then I went back to the gin bottle and before long I was 'back to normal' like Mr Blair wanted, though he probably didn't mean it like that. Although I did not take much and not so often, by early December, the bottle was noticeably emptier, and with Christmas approaching there was a greater risk it might be noticed. Then out of nowhere I remembered hearing one of the girls from school talking about how she and her friends had nicked so much of her father's gin that they'd had to top the bottle up with water, and then went into fits of giggles because he apparently never noticed. So I filled a small jug with water and very carefully refilled the bottle to the level I remember it had been. It was a big relief a few evenings later when the Grampies had visitors one of whom had a gin with apparently no suspicion of anything strange. All the same, with the holidays approaching, I decided I would ease off on the studies and the gin.

Baz arrived back from Uni really pleased with life and happy to see me. So that was one worry over as I thought once he got up there with all those students he might go off me, especially after the car incident. On the contrary, he told me I was refreshing, and made it sound as though it was a good thing to be. But he added, "Though I have to say you don't look quite as refreshing as when I last saw you. The Grampies said you were working late a lot in the evening."

"Only to make sure I get good grades. And not every evening."

Baz said "Hmmm. Well, we don't want all work and no play making Nikki a dull girl. Where do you fancy going for a bit of fun?"

"How about a meal at the Good Shepherd?"

Baz looked a bit surprised, but said "Right."

We went on a mid-week evening about mid-December, before everywhere was packed out with Christmas parties. In fact, that evening it was rather quiet. We settled in the bar first.

"Drink?" Baz asked.

"A tonic," I said make a consciously sensible choice.

"With or without the gin?"

Well, it was nearly Christmas. "Oh well, just a small gin."

It definitely tasted better with tonic water. I made a mental note to get some before the next term began. Baz had a half of lager and we lifted our glasses. "Here's to Christmas and a great 2006."

They already had a Christmas menu, so we both decided on that and once he had ordered, Baz began to tell me about life on Campus, and how very, very different it was from being at school. "Suddenly you are in charge of yourself," he explained. "No one on your back telling you what to do with every minute of your time. Though of course there's a tutor breathing hard down your neck if you don't produce your work on time. Now tell me about you."

"Not a lot to tell," I said. But suddenly there was. I told him about my new work schedule - though not about the gin of course - and how it had all paid off with the encouraging comments on my report. "Mother's really pleased too," I added.

Baz looked thoughtful for a few moments. "I'm not sure that I am," he said at last. "You look really peaky."

"I thought you'd be pleased that I'm doing well."

He put one of his hands over mine. "Of course I am. I just don't want you ruining your health."

It gave me a nice warm feeling that he really seemed to care. I said "Baz, it's really important that I do well with GCSEs and then with A levels, so I can go ahead with what I've chosen to do."

"Which is what?"

"I told you, I must have done in my emails. Media studies."

He nodded. "Yes, you did. I guess I didn't take it seriously enough. You wouldn't believe the amount of mind-changing that goes on among the freshers." He went on looking at me more seriously than he usually did. "Tell you what. You promise not to work so many late evenings, and we'll arrange for you to come up to Liverpool for the half term, and we'll go to every nature reserve I can think of."

Well, there was no way I could resist an offer like that.

But there were other things to think about. Especially Mother. It would be our first Christmas without Dad, and though it was true he had messed up all the earlier ones, it would be very odd for him not to be there. I talked about it with the Grampies, and we decided to have a quiet family celebration here.

3

Baz and his parents went off to Nepal the week before Christmas. The Grampies did the best they could for us. They set a Christmas tree up in the conservatory and delegated Mother and I to decorate it. She'd kept the decorations we had from previous years and we had a great afternoon doing it together. It was the first time for a while that we had spent much time together, and as I watched her draping the tinsel over the branches, and looping the coloured balls over the tips, I realised what a change there was in her. It wasn't just that she looked younger - the Grampies had already commented on that - but she looked *happy*. I felt a pang as I thought this was the direct result of Dad not being around. I hadn't meant to say so aloud, and Mother stopped what she was doing for a moment, then took my hand and drew me over to a couple of basket chairs.

From there she surveyed the tree for a moment in silence before saying "It's looking really pretty this year, and will look prettier still when we have put the lights on." Then she said, "Look sweetheart, I'm not looking better just because your father isn't here for me to worry about. I'm also enjoying my work and getting out more."

The terrible thought struck me that she had found someone else, and I blurted "Is there someone else?"

She took my hand in both hers and laughed, and then stopped laughing and said quietly, "Oh darling, I'm not laughing because anything is funny - though I can't ever imagine going through that business of a new relationship again. No, the thing that has helped me most is that I have made some new friends and they have helped me to see how much I have to be thankful for."

Was I hearing right? "How do they make that out? Do they *know* about Dad?"

"That is the point," Mother said surprisingly. "They do know about Dad and they all have similar situations and have learned to live with it. Perhaps in the New Year you could meet some of them."

I was surprised how angry I felt. There was no way I was going to sit around with Mother's new friends slanging off Dad. I asked crossly, "So where did you meet these people?"

"It's a group that meets in Greenley once a week. Dr. Waring told me about it. He said other patients had found it helpful."

I was still digesting the fact that there were other families with the same problem. "What did you do - just walk in and say my husband's a drunk?"

Now Mother was angry. "No, I did not, Nikki. I sat down and listened to other people who had members of the family with the same illness - might be a husband, or son or wife or mother. I didn't say anything at all for a long time, but then I met one of the women for a coffee and it was such a relief to be able to talk openly."

So she was still thinking of it as an illness; and then I felt a bit ashamed of myself because if anyone knew how much Mother had worried over Dad then it had to me, and I suppose I minded that she was turning to other people for help. So I said, yes, I would go with her in the New Year, and we hugged and got on with decorating the tree.

Baz and his parents got back from Nepal only a few days before he went back to Uni. He came over to see me the next day, saying he felt jet-lagged. I didn't know how that felt but it didn't sound pleasant. He took me for a bar snack at The Good Shepherd. He wouldn't drink because he was driving but I had a gin and tonic. I'd forgotten how nice it was. Baz told me all about their holidays and how wonderful the people there were, and how he had a view of Annapurna from his bedroom window. Then he showed me some photographs of Annapurna and I understood why he was so enthusiastic. When he finished, he held my hands, his eyes still shining, and said "I'll take you there one day, Nikki, that's a promise." It felt so good that he wanted to do that.

I felt miserable when he had left for Liverpool but he texted me as soon as he got there. Because I had done so little over the holidays, there was a lot of work ahead, so I spent a few days making myself a timetable and getting all the books I needed. After all, the GCSEs were only a few short months away. I'd taken the bus into Oxford for these and while I was there I drifted into a supermarket. One of my uncles had sent me some money for Christmas, and I noticed there was a special offer for various drinks, including gin. So I bought a bottle and some small tonics. It would save that awful business of creeping downstairs and then having to top up the bottle with water. Well, I couldn't go on doing that indefinitely.

Right up to the Easter holidays, I *slaved* away. I got through an unbelievable amount of work. Even the teachers were amazed, including Miss Bilham and I certainly wasn't her favourite.

Just before Easter, Mother arranged for me to meet one of her new friends, Sally.

"Is she a Miss or a Mrs? What do I call her?"

"You call her Sally. We don't go in for surnames."

How weird was that?

We met this Sally in a coffee shop on Greenley market place. She had long blonde hair and a rather sulky expression. I was surprised that she was much younger than Mother, in fact not that much older than if I had an older sister.

"Hi, Anne," she greeted Mother, and that sounded odd for a start. "So this is Nikki?"

While Mother went to get the coffees for them and a juice for me, Sally said "Anne tells me you're getting ready for your GCSEs and you're planning to do Media Studies."

I wasn't sure how keen I was that Mother was discussing my future with a complete stranger. Then, as if she had read my mind, Sally went on, "I found it very helpful when she told me. I made a right mess of my GCSEs. My boyfriend Tom and I were going through a bad time just then."

I was still trying to think of how to reply when Mother came back with our drinks. As we settled down round the table, she asked Sally "So how's the new job going?"

Her face lit up with enthusiasm. "The first couple of days were really difficult. I didn't see how I'd ever fit in. Then I remembered what some of you said about everyone feeling like that and why not just say so and ask for help. So I did, and a couple of the girls seemed really keen to help. Then at the end of the week, the manager called me and said did I know there were some day classes that would help me get some of the subjects I flunked at school, so I'm going to check those out."

They went on chatting about Sally's job potential, and Mother's new interest in calligraphy (that was a new one for me, too). I waited for them to start on how awful Dad or Sally's boyfriend Tom had been, but they didn't. I asked Sally what kind of job she was doing, and she said she was a junior in an advertising agency but hoping to train up to designing lay-outs because art was the one thing she loved doing. Because of her job she knew just a bit about the way everything was spreading wider and wider, over television and the internet, so she was able to give me some new angles on the media business.

Then Mother said, "Sorry, ladies. I have a dental appointment. Sally, see you at the meeting on Friday. Nikki see you back at the flat later." And she went.

Looking after her, Sally said, "She's been such a help."

I couldn't help asking, "What happened to your Tom?"

"He was in and out of a rehab unit, but just couldn't crack it. I just hope he does one day."

"That sounds like my Dad. Once he starts he can't stop."

Sally nodded. "It's the first drink that triggers it." But she said it as though it really had nothing to do with her any more.

Anyway, she was wrong. It wasn't the first, but the fifth, sixth, seventh, that was the problem.

April - August 2006

1

Rachel's Dad was coming over to see Grump, so he drove me back from Greenley the next morning and there wasn't much opportunity to talk to Mother. I'd decided to concentrate on biology that term, so got everything set up to start on my study programme next evening. That was the day Miss Carter, our new Biology Teacher started. She was quite old but leathery as if she had just come in from the playing fields and she took us all by surprise by referring to bodily parts like vagina and penis as casually as you would an arm or a leg. A subdued giggle sort of rippled through the class, and Miss Carter stopped in the middle of a sentence, looked round the class and said, "Would you like to share the joke?"

After that we were as quiet as mice, even when she started on a summary of some of the stranger antics of different species.

I had a feeling biology was going to be a lot less boring than it had been before, but I was still way behind with knowing all the stuff I should about bones and muscles. That evening I made a systematic list of them all in alphabetic order, with a brief note in brackets after each saying where they were or what they did. By the time I'd finished I could have fallen into bed, but I got the gin bottle out and topped it up with a lot of tonic water. In fact I rather overdid the tonic as you could barely taste the gin, but I had a biggish gulp and felt the glow hitting my midriff and nudging my brain into a welcome little spurt of wakefulness.

As my eyes were tired I lay on the bed with them closed and my list beside me. Then I started memorising it. I must have got about half way through the bones when I dropped off and woke up with a start to see my bedside clock showing two o'clock in the morning, and there was the bottle of gin on the floor, and my list still beside me. And the light on. Just suppose Gramp had got up, seen the light on and investigated? I'd have to be a lot more careful in the future.

Still, it wasn't going to be a problem. I didn't have gin every night, only when I needed a bit of encouragement, or to celebrate if I'd done particularly well. I put the bottle at the bottom of the cupboard, tucked behind my suitcase. The tonics slipped in a drawer with my underwear. The only problem might be when I finished the bottle as I didn't have the sort of pocket money that ran to bottles of gin. Then I found the local village shop was looking for staff on a Saturday morning. Four mornings there, I calculated, would cover a bottle a month nicely. Problem solved.

As good as his word, Baz arranged for me to go to Liverpool for the half term. I could see Mother was worried.

"You don't imagine I'm going to get pregnant, do you?" I challenged her. "I do know about the so-called Facts of Life, and from the little I know sex is no great deal. Anyway, a whole group of them share a house, and there's a spare room as two are away." No point in adding that there would no doubt be quite a lot of bed sharing too.

The Grampies, bless them, funded my rail fare, and Baz was there at the station in Liverpool to meet me. The house was amazing. It belonged to the parents of one of the girls, Zoe ,and there were strict rules about keeping the place clean and tidy, replacing anything that got broken, and looking after the garden. They had a rota so everyone took their turn at various jobs, though they let me off as I was a visitor. There were four girls and three boys, and they all seemed to get on like a family. Zoe was especially friendly, as well as very pretty. The room I was using was next to hers and belonged to one of her friends who had gone down to London for the week. I thought how marvellous it would be to have a place like that myself in a few years time. Whether there was any bed sharing I slept too well to notice; the main thing was that Baz didn't suggest it. In a way I was a bit sorry. How weird is that?

Baz was obviously very popular though they teased him all the time about his untidiness and said it was because his Mother spoilt him at home. For most of my stay we were out a lot of the time, going to different nature reserves like Martin-Mere and Leighton Moss, two big reserves near the coast. It wouldn't be so long before the first of our autumn visitors started to arrive, including the distinctive Whooper and Bewick swans with their yellow bills. I found this whole business of migration was magic and, what with global warming that everyone was on about, it was also gradually changing. An increasing number of so-called 'new' species were coming here to breed - in some cases coming *back* after being wiped out by chemicals or hunted to extinction. We also looked up all the places associated with the Beatles as Baz knew I thought they were special.

In the evenings we took fish and chips or a balti back to the house, and a couple of times went out for a pub meal. Zoe came with us on one occasion. She had us in stitches as she was such a good mimic. All in all I had such a good time that I forgot my good intentions to get some reading done. With the GCSEs only weeks away, I was going to have to stick to a rigid timetable.

2

Over the next weeks, things went really well. Some weeks I didn't have any gin at all, and I have to say I felt good about it as, if I needed any proof, that just showed I didn't have a problem. Well, of course I didn't think I had a problem, but with Dad as part of my history I was really anxious that it should stay that way.

"You seem to be getting hold of the right end of the stick," Miss Carter told me after marking some of my homework. She'd obviously seen my earlier reports. "Let's see if you can keep it up."

So it seemed OK to have a bit of a celebration that evening. Remembering the last occasion when I'd fallen asleep over bones and muscles, I was very careful: just a small one with lots of tonic. It tasted good, too, after a break. I realised then that control was what it came down to. I puzzled for a while why I could see that and Dad couldn't. Perhaps we'd have a chat about that one day, though that didn't seem likely any time soon as we hadn't heard directly from him for ages. Just a call from one of his friends saying that they were now in Yorkshire, he was doing all right and sent his love. At least it showed that he cared, though it would have been nicer if he had telephoned himself.

In the meantime, Mother was continuing to look better and going out quite often for a meal or film with Sally and others from her group. One of them called Brian cropped up in the conversation quite a lot, so it wasn't just for women as I had thought. When I asked about him, Mother said she didn't discuss other people's problems outside the group. But from odd facts she dropped, I gathered this Brian's wife had The Problem.

All round though, after those dire happenings the previous year, things were much better. It still felt odd not being a proper family living under the same roof, though the Grampies were lovely and I loved being with them. I also learned some amazing things about them. Apparently when they were young – well, not exactly young, but younger than now – they had a really ancient campervan and travelled all over Europe in it, sometimes staying away for months at a time.

Gramp kept a diary and let me borrow it. Now that was real history. It was at the time of the Cold War, which we were told about at school. Europe was divided into East and West and there were all kinds of regulations if you went into the East. Gramp said in her diary that she had to keep an eye on Grump because he wasn't very good at following rules and would try to do things he shouldn't and get into arguments with the border control people. It was hard to imagine, because now Grump was getting a bit worrying in other ways, as he forgot things and dozed a lot of the time. Once when I came home from school, he said, "Nikki, lovely to see you. Have you come to stay?" Gramp explained it was his short-term memory. He could remember the big war as though it were yesterday but couldn't remember a visit to the doctor he'd had that morning. Rachel's father still came over quite regularly, and then there was no stopping the old memories.

Most of the time I just worked and worked, keeping to a special timetable. And by a miracle when the exams came, I seemed to get all the right questions. Well mostly. Then suddenly the exams were over, there was no more prospect of late-night study slogs, clandestine tipples, and gnawing anxieties that one day surely someone would find me out. There was a stomach-dropping sense of anti-climax: until the following evening Mother said, "Sweetheart you really deserve a special break after such a difficult few months. Perhaps we both do. So how do you fancy a couple of weeks coach cruising through France, Switzerland and Belgium." Then she spoilt it all. "Sally – you remember Sally? Well, she and Tom are going. I think I told you Tom is out of rehab and doing well?"

I could think of every reason against it. The last time we'd gone abroad was with Dad and over time this had turned itself in my mind as the best holiday anyone could possibly have. True we would be travelling by coach, not campervan. True we would be staying in small rural hotels rather than campsites. But why should I want to go on my second trip abroad with one complete stranger and one mere acquaintance? In fact, why should I want to go anywhere with my mother's new friend and her partner?

Mother arranged for us to meet up with Sally and Tom for a balti. I largely agreed to this out of curiosity to see what an ex-drunk looked like. I'd decided to dislike him, but then found I couldn't. He was a slightly older and thinner version of Madge's brother Adrian, with a similar dry humour and engaging ability to find himself very funny. He also had a rubbery face and teased me like an older brother. In fact he didn't look at all like a drunk, which made me wonder what I expected a drunk to look like. Like my Dad?

After we'd ordered, Mother and Sally went off to the loo. Perhaps they thought it would give Tom and me a chance to talk more freely. I still can't work out why adults do some of the things they do.

"If I were you," Tom announced, "I wouldn't want me tacked on to a well deserved holiday after the enforced slavery of studying for GCSEs."

I opened my mouth, shut it, opened it again. "Don't think I have much choice."

Tom nodded. "Probably not. They want to keep me on the rails and haven't yet realised the only person who can do that is me."

I was curious. "Is it that difficult?"

"Perhaps I'll tell you about it some time." He talked to me as though we were the same age. I liked that.

3

The journey out was weird, mainly because I kept waiting for things that didn't happen. I thought Sally would be glued to Tom so that she could watch everything he did. But no, she sat with Mother on the coach, and Tom sat with me. On the ferry crossing Mother and Sally stood out on deck with the wind flinging their hair about. So it was me who followed Tom into the bar and watched him order a coffee.

He seemed to have eyes in the back of his head. "Keeping an eye on me?"

I said, "No. Well, yes. I was a bit worried. May I have a coffee too?"

We sat at a table near a window. A couple at the next table were getting through a bottle of wine rather fast and talking ever louder, but I didn't mean to say, "Being a bit woozy can't hurt, can it?"

"You've tried it?"

"Only to keep me awake when I was studying. But please don't ..."

Tom interrupted, "Of course I won't tell anyone. I don't recommend it though."

"Well, it did help increase the amount of studying I could do. Anyway that's over now."

"Mm." Tom peered over the rim of his coffee cup at me. "There are A-levels ahead."

Yes, there was that. I rather wished he hadn't mentioned them

But, hey, they were way ahead. Now we were on holiday and I was enjoying myself more than I had expected. The itinerary started with two days on the coach followed by three nights in Paris, another day on the coach, three nights by Lake Geneva, a further day on the coach and a final two nights in a region called the Ardennes before crossing home.

The first day in France felt very much like being in England, except for the architecture, the road signs and driving on the wrong side of the road. Tom said it was Napoleon's fault that Europe drove on the right because he was left handed and needed to keep his right (sword) arm free when riding in case of attack. Tom was full of odd facts and once I asked if he had learned them in Rehab. He made an amazing grimace with his rubbery face and said "Good Lord, I wish. No I've always been a great reader. At Rehab our main purpose was to Learn About Ourselves." I could hear the capital letters.

Then I found myself wondering why a great reader should become an alcoholic, though come to think of it, Dad had been a great reader once. I was about to tell Tom that when I saw he had fallen asleep.

Paris turned out to be a bit boring. Mother decided to give me a crash course on the Impressionists. I liked them well enough, even if I did mix up Manets and Monets, but not enough to look at them for several hours a day. Tom rescued me on the second day and we escaped to explore the Metro. When we got back to the hotel, Mother told me off. Sally had been really worried and after a bit I realised it had been unkind, even though Tom hadn't had as much as a cup of coffee.

On the last morning we went up the Eiffel Tower and I found I didn't much like heights, which is annoying. Tom said it was better than claustrophobia which he had and meant he couldn't travel in small lifts without windows. He was good at looking at the positive side of things. Perhaps he learned that in Rehab, but I didn't ask him.

The day we left Paris for Lake Geneva, Mother said, "You're obviously good for Tom, but I think you should sit with me on the coach now." Good for Tom? Like medicine?

Then I thought, *yes, after all Tom is Sally's partner. Wonder why they haven't married. In fact, why Mother married Dad if he was a drunk?* So I asked her as we approached the Swiss border.

"He drank quite a lot, but it wasn't a problem. The drinking started getting heavier when I was pregnant.

"So it's my fault," I interrupted.

"No, it was *not* your fault," she began and then stopped. And that was when I first learned she'd had a miscarriage before me. A baby boy!

So I'd had a brother!

"How long did he live?"

"He was still-born, sweetheart."

I tried to visualise this tiny unmoving being who by now would have been several years older than me, And if he'd lived perhaps Dad wouldn't have started drinking more. And perhaps if I'd been a boy he wouldn't either.

We were silent for a long time. I asked, "Did he have a name?"

"What? Oh yes, Alex."

We didn't talk much after that and once we had settled in our pension in Vevey overlooking Lake Geneva, I went to find Tom and blurted, "Just discovered I had a still-born brother."

He was leaning over a rail overlooking the lake. "Mm. I had a still-born sister. Younger than me."

How amazing that there should have been so many dead babies. "Do you think that's why you drank?"

Tom looked astonished. "Don't tell me you're into psychobabble! Why should that make me drink? In fact, that way I got more attention."

Yes there was that. I had begun to notice Tom's self-centredness.

I looked out across the lake. The light was fading and there was a distant twinkle of lights. Tom said, "That's France over there."

When I looked up the valley, the skyline was dominated by mountain silhouettes beginning to merge into the darkening sky. One group was sharp as teeth. When I commented as much, Tom said, "Those are the Dents du Midi – it means the Teeth of the South, or of Midday."

After a culture overdose in Paris, I enjoyed Vevey with the mountain flanks of France rearing up from the opposite shore. Behind

Vevey were vineyards and next day we went for a walk through them until we reached the forest rim. From then on Tom spent most of his time with Sally. They laughed a lot, and occasionally cuddled but not in an embarrassing way, and I tried to imagine having that sort of relationship with Baz, but didn't quite succeed. On our second day in Vevey we visited an old castle on the Swiss side of the lake.

It's funny how the beginnings of holidays seem to go quite slowly, and then suddenly time speeds up and before you know it you're on the way home. May be it was partly because I spent quite a lot of time thinking of Alex, the brother I never knew. And from that I tried to imagine what Dad must have felt. And what about Mother? I eventually asked her, and her eyes went sad and she said it was a terrible time and she still did something special every year to remember his birthday, which was in April. I asked why she hadn't told me about Alex, and she said it seemed too sad a thing to share with a child, then as I got a bit older there was the growing problem with Dad's drinking.

I liked the Ardennes, but don't remember much about them. But I do remember the old town of Bruges where we spent the last two nights. It had lots of canals and churches which rang out their bells. I loved walking around the old streets on my own and watching the life on the canals.

It seemed the next minute we were home, and it was early August and nearly time to go to school for my GCSE results. Mother offered to come with me, but this was something I knew I wanted to do alone.

August-October 2006

1

I'd done even better than I dared hope, getting an A* in English, Geography and Art, A in History, French and Science, and B in Maths, for starters. Everyone was either jumping around or moping according to their results, hugging each other or commiserating. Then my mobile jingled, and it was Rachel hardly able to speak for excitement, because of course she'd done even better. And no doubt without gin.

That week-end, she came with her father. While he and Grump went into their shared memories, Rach and I nipped up to my room for our own 'do-you-remembers'. It was then she said, "How would you feel about a Classmates reunion at your old school. I gather there's to be a Seventies Disco to launch the Autumn Term, and celebrate our GCSE successes. It's the first one ever. They want to get old pupils to keep in touch with the school, perhaps mentor one of the kids. Or something like that."

"You're joking!" was my first reaction. "You won't catch me dressing up in Mother's old gear. I'm surprised you're interested."

"You can dress any way you want as long as it reflects the Seventies," Rachel said. She seemed unusually persistent. "And you can bring boy friends."

Since when had Rachel been interested in the presence of boyfriends? "Ah!" I said. "You have a boyfriend."

"Well, it's not a criminal offence," Rachel parried defensively. "Anyway, so have you."

Yes, but why did it seem so odd that Rachel had one? Come to think of it, the reunion was during the Uni vacs, so Baz would be able to come if he didn't think it was beneath him.

"Where did you meet this boyfriend? And what's his name?" I wanted to know.

" Remember Adrian, Madge's brother who was at your party that time?" That ghastly party – how could I forget? How could Adrian forget? "Well I met him in the library the other week, and we've been out a few times." Rachel gave an uncharacteristic giggle. "He was skulking in South India while I was checking out the Mahabharata."

"The *what?"*

"It's one of the main bases of Hindu philosophy which is one of Adrian's subjects."

"Good Lord," was all I could think of saying. But I was thinking perhaps this Classmates reunion might be interesting since, after all, a lot of the pupils concerned were well into their teens. And I might see Pete if he didn't consider it beneath his dignity.

Once I had decided it was not such a bad idea after all, I gave it quite a lot of thought. I sent a text to Baz who replied enthusiastically that he'd love to see if my little girl friends had turned out as well as I had, as long as he did not have to dress up too. Gramp and I discussed possible costumes with funny contributions from Grump on how he had dressed up for Cowboys and Indians when he was young. Gramp and I settled on a Serious Student outfit, which we could make out of a combination of my wardrobe and Mother's. Actually some of the styles were quite cool. I settled for a Granny maxi dress with high neck and a pair of enormous spectacles. Rachel thought it was great, and showed me her own amazing outfit: figure-hugging hot pants. I'd never noticed what great legs she had or registered how pretty she had become. Of course the Seventies music was fine by me as it still featured the Beatles, as well as Pink Floyd and the Bee Gees.

It did cross my mind more and more that at this Reunion I would be meeting, face to face, some of the girls that Dad had so embarrassed at my parties. But, hey, that was a lifetime ago. I had moved on so far from that, and they must have done too. And I would be proud to go in with a companion like Baz. But supposing one of them mentioned that awful party in Baz's hearing? For a few moments I had a wild panic. Then the answer came quite simply. Why pretend it didn't happen? Just agree how awful it was that Dad had made a bit of a fool of himself on that occasion. I don't suppose he was the only adult who had ever made a fool of himself in this way.

There were still a few weeks before the reunion and in the meantime I'd given myself some tougher study targets for a project that our English teacher, Miss Bilham, had set us. In fact, I was quite interested in it. It was to select an Oxford-born writer and write a paper on how their work reflected their environment. I wanted to get well ahead with this so that I could take time off to be with Baz when he was down from Uni. I decided to spend time researching a selection of Oxford-born writers carefully so that I had all the facts at my fingertips on which to base my arguments. But then I hadn't realised just how many Oxford-born writers there were.

So after a session on the Internet, and another in the library, I came home with bagfuls of books.

Gramp looked at them in alarm. "You surely don't have to read all those, Nikki?"

"Not exactly read; just study them," I said, and fortunately she didn't ask me what the difference was.

I set myself the task of researching one author a night: making notes on their lives, styles, choice of subject. I also decided to cut down on the gin. The Saturday job had packed up so supplies were short. I had also discovered that alcohol wasn't a great help in taking stuff in that you were reading. Where it really helped was in coming to conclusions and triggering ideas once you went through your notes. And in going to sleep afterwards. Again, I wondered why Dad hadn't been able to work that out.

2

Baz hadn't seen me in my outfit before, so when he came to pick me up his face was a study in disbelief, amusement and admiration. Then he pulled me towards him, gave me a long, lingering and very enjoyable kiss and said, "You're a mega star."

He didn't look so bad himself in one of those designer denim suits, and his hair rather longer than it usually was.

.   "You make a very handsome couple," Gramp said, quickly covering up Grump's "Nikki, aren't you going to introduce me to your young man?"

All the same, I was nervous as we drove back along the familiar lanes to Greenley. So much had happened since I was last there, even apart from that awful party. And not forgetting my distance glimpse of Jane with Pete.

The reunion was being held in the Assembly Hall, which you reach across some lawns on which we were never allowed to play. As we were quite late, there were already quite a lot of people drifting about, and I could hear excited greetings and breathless "Is it really *you!*"s. The range of outfits was incredible from maxis to minis, hot pants to flares.

The first person I saw was Jane. She looked *so* grown-up and sophisticated with her hair short one side, long the other and the most amazing blue-grey eye shadow. In fact she saw me first. *"Nikki!"* she shouted. "You look fan-*tas*-tic. Is it really you?" The eye shadow matched the floaty material of her drop waist miniskirt.

And then the question was repeated and very close at hand: "Good Lord, it really is *you*, Nikki."

I turned and found myself looking at Pete. Except that he was taller and his hair was a bit longer, he looked just the same.

"I wasn't quite sure at first," he said. "What was behind those enormous specs? You look great." He looked questioningly at Baz.

"Hi, and thanks. This is Baz. Just down from Uni. Baz, this is Pete who was the first one to get me interested in bird watching."

"Hi Pete. Well, you did a great job. It's even rubbed off on me now."

"Good, good. So, Nikki, how is your - how are your parents these days."

"Fine, fine. Dad is working in the north of England at the moment, when he's not abroad."

"Abroad? Is he …?"

I interrupted, "As I said, he's fine. And what are you doing these days?"

"I decided to stay with the birds and the bees. Or rather trees in this case. I am doing a course at the School for Forestry."

"That sounds perfect for you. Well, I suppose we had better go in, hadn't we?" I tried not to notice how Jane was draping herself over Pete's shoulder. Baz took my hand; it felt good. We walked away and I managed not to look back.

They had done a good job of the Assembly Hall, which had a stage and was also used for pantomimes. I had hideous memories of us putting on Snow White and the Seven Dwarfs. I wanted to be Prince Charming as my then best friend was Snow White, but a hateful girl got the part and I was stuck with Doc and had to have a pillow stuffed into my knickers to make me a suitable shape. Now there was a bar up one end of the hall, and up on the stage I could see they had set up a music centre and sound system. In charge of it was a young man of chunky dimensions wearing rimless glasses. He looked vaguely familiar and then I recognised him as Madge's brother Adrian. And beside him was ….

"Rachel !" I exclaimed, dragging Baz in that direction.

We went up the steps on to the stage and as soon as I was within reach, Rachel gave me a hug. "Adrian, remember my best friend Nikki?"

How on earth could he forget me after that dire party, I wondered? But he just beamed at me, came over clasping a tangle of cables and plugs and held out a large hand. It was a firm grasp. I said, "I certainly remember you." But I didn't mean to add, "Rach said you're a philosophy student. You're not quite what I imagined."

He looked rueful. "I know - you were expecting someone lean and ascetic and interesting-looking. I'm working on it." Then he twinkled at me, and I thought he was just the right person for my friend.

From the stage there was a good view over the Assembly Hall and I stood watching everyone milling about, seeing who I could pick out. I spotted Madge and Laura straight away; they had barely changed except for rather more rounded figures. I went on looking round, gradually sorting out most of my own old classmates, but of course there were quite a lot who had been in lower classes when I was there and changed beyond recognition. There was no further sign of Pete.

Then Madge was up on the stage beside us, giving me a hug. "Nikki you are looking absolutely terrific. Is that your boyfriend over there? He's a dish." She stood grinning at me, and I realised her memories of That Party had quite faded. Baz looked round and came over to join us.

"I didn't realise Nikki had so many gorgeous friends," he said.

"You wouldn't have thought so a few years ago," Madge said, laughing. "Remember that party of yours Nikki, when your father came back and...." So she hadn't forgotten. She stopped, embarrassed.

"And what?" Baz was intrigued.

Remembering my earlier decision, I turned and faced him. "Oh Dad came home drunk and made a bit of a fool of himself," I said.

Baz laughed. "I guess that'll happen to us all sooner or later." I could have hugged him for passing it off so lightly.

"Right," Adrian suddenly announced. "Would all those who are not concerned with tonight's entertainment please now vacate the stage."

Laughing and chatting we all left the stage and went to find a table among those that had been set up round the open space of the dance floor. Madge and her boyfriend joined Baz and me, and in due course so did Rachel and Adrian.

In fact, I was a bit worried about the dancing even though style didn't seem to matter much by the look of it. Baz said there was nothing to it and he'd soon teach me the basics, but before he had a chance, Adrian stood up and said, "I insist on having the first dance with Nikki." And it was one of those slow melodies that sounded really old fashioned.

My head went into a panic. Then Adrian put one arm round me, his hand resting lightly on my back, and the other hand holding mine out, and proceeded to lead me round the floor as if we had been dancing together all our lives. I couldn't believe it. Why did it seem so strange that a philosophy student could be such a natural dancer. In the end it did not go quite so smoothly with Baz, who wasn't such a natural leader, but who didn't seem to mind me stumbling over his feet a few times.

Then it did go smoothly. Suddenly the mood went back into old-time.

"Slow waltz," Baz said, holding out his hand. "This is a doddle." I laughed out loud because 'doddle' was a favourite word of Dad's. Then I felt sad because I didn't know if he used it any more, or even for sure where he was.

Then I forgot about Dad, because the slow waltz was dreamy. We started off in our usual stumbly way, but very soon Baz had drawn me close so that I could feel the pressure of his leg against mine and the movements were so natural that we seemed to be moulded into one figure flowing with the music. Then Baz bent his head and nuzzled into the crook of my neck. And I thought I'd burst into flames. I'd had feelings before that I knew were stirrings of arousal, but this was something else. I wanted to wrap myself round him and never let go. I grunted and tried to push him gently away, but he just held me closer. Then he said in my ear, "If you knew how I want to make love to you, Nikki...."

"No," I whispered.

"No, you don't want to? Or no, it's not allowed."

"No ... well, yes I want to. But not yet."

He sighed and held me a little less close, but it was still magic. So magic that when Peter danced by quite close and I saw that Jane was looking up at him as though they belonged to each other, I barely felt a quiver of dismay, even though I swear there was a glint of triumph in her expression as she caught my eye.

I stayed on a bit of a cloud for the rest of the evening. Baz drove me home, and we parked outside the house. He turned to me. "Well...?"

Then he kissed me and it was longer and deeper than usual, and all those stirrings started taking over. And so did the fear of what was expected of me and whether I'd get it right. I extricated myself from his arms.

"You're going back at the week-end," I said in as normal a voice as possible.

"Mm. I'll miss you Nikki."

"I'll miss you. Text me when you get back."

"Don't I always?"

Up in my room I removed my enormous spectacles and studied myself in the mirror. I was flushed and my eyes sparkled, and the stirrings were fading inside, though when I thought back over the feel of Baz's arms round me and his mouth on mine, I could feel them returning. I don't remember getting out the gin bottle, but the next moment I was sitting there holding it and taking a swig from it, because I hadn't got anything to pour it into. I sat staring at it for a moment, then screwed the cap on and said angrily. "What *are* you doing?"

But I knew very well what I was doing. There had been no alcohol at the Reunion, except for light beer which I hated. The glow of the gin circled round my midriff and settled in my mind in a warm mist. That was all I needed, I told myself, as I put the bottle back in the cupboard, noting that there was not a lot left in it and thinking I'd better start looking round for a Saturday job again.

3

That was an unforgettable night. Because my mind was full of the excitement of the evening, I lay in bed for a long time, staring up into the darkness. And then I heard quiet sounds and saw a light showing under the gap of my door. After a few more moments a voice said quietly outside my door, "Nikki, Nikki. Are you awake?"

I swung my legs out of bed and opened the door. Gramp was standing there, her woolly dressing gown wrapped tight over her nightie. She looked shrivelled and worried and old.

"Gramp whatever is the matter?"

"Grump has gone."

"Gone? What do you mean gone?"

70

"Gone means gone. In other words he's not here." Suddenly she was tetchy and that seemed better than the shrivelled worried look. "I got up to go to the loo and he wasn't in bed beside me. So I went downstairs and he's not there, but the back door is open."

Without stopping to think, I pulled a pair of jeans and sweater over my pyjamas.

"What are you doing?" she demanded.

"I'm going to look for him, of course. I'll take my bike. You ring 999."

"You're not to go out alone....." But I'd already gone, grabbing my bike from the shed and wheeling it out on to the road.

I decided he was more likely to have turned right out of the house as the road went downhill. It wasn't completely dark as there was an almost full moon, but the view of the road was restricted as it soon bent out of sight. I switched on my lights and set off. In fact it was a beautiful night and under other circumstances I would have enjoyed the silence of it and the darkness of the hedges and their shadows sent sprawling across the road by the moon. In the distance an owl hooted, and the thought of Pete briefly crossed my mind.

I had gone about a half a mile when I caught up with Grump, moving quite slowly with a shuffling walk and looking very frail, still in his pyjamas.

"Grump!" I called quietly.

He stopped, turned round and in the moonlight I saw his broad smile. "Nikki!" he said. "How lovely. Have you come to stay?"

I got off my bike. "Yes, I've come to stay, but what I'd really like is a cup of tea."

"That's a good idea," Grump said. "Let's go home and Gramp will make you one."

It took us a while to walk back as Grump kept stopping to tell me some story that he'd already told me before. I explained that Gramp might worry if we didn't get back soon, but he was quite sure he had told her he was going for a walk. When we rounded the bend, I saw there was a car by the house with a flashing blue light.

"Good heavens," Grump said. "There's a police car."

When we got in a burly police sergeant was having a cup of tea with Gramp who greeted me with a huge smile and Grump with "Where have you been you silly old man?"

71

"I told you I was going for a walk," Grump said. "And look who's come to stay with us, dear. Nikki! And she's dying for a cup of tea."

While this was being poured out for me the policeman said in a hoarse whisper, "Well done, Miss. I understand your grandfather does this quite often?" Which was news to me.

"It's the first time he's done it at night," Gramp said, tiredly.

"And it's a beautiful night," Grump chipped in.

The policeman nodded, then turned to Grump. "So you're all right, sir?"

"Fine, fine, officer. Thank you for finding Nikki for me."

The policeman winked at me. "In which case, I'll leave you to get back to sleep. Many thanks for tea, Madam." Still looking at me, he added, "You did a good job, Miss, but I do suggest that next time you wait for one of us to arrive before you become a one-person search party." He smiled so that I would know I really had done all right.

After Grump had been tucked up in bed again, Gramp and I had another cup of tea and she told me a bit more of what had been happening. Apparently he had taken to wandering away some time earlier, but during the day. Now it was the first thing I asked Gramp when I came home from school. These days he was sleeping a lot, so mostly it wasn't a problem, but two or three times a week he'd slip out at night when she sleeping. Usually she found him before he had gone many yards and she kept assuring me that everything was OK, but I could see how tired she was looking. Grump's wanderings had become more frequent, or at least I became more aware of them and I made Gramp promise to wake me up if it happened again..

And I began to sense that something in my life was going to change soon.

4

In the meantime, I was pleased with my own study programme, based on the Miss Bilham's Oxford authors project.. After a lot of reading and note-taking, I'd decided to do my project on Lewis Carroll. It was Baz who triggered the decision. We are both Philip Pullman fans and one day he happened to ask didn't I think that in a way *Alice in Wonderland* represented another form of parallel universe. I can't say that the thought had occurred to me, but I got the book out of the library and read it through very carefully. Then I sat thinking about it and I began to see what Baz meant. Obviously the techniques were completely different: Alice disappeared through a rabbit hole and Myra happened to find a fault in the fabric of space-time as she wandering down the Banbury Road in Oxford. But the principle was similar.

I must say that a little gin helped to free the imagination and I wrote reams and reams of notes from which gradually I extracted something of an acceptable length putting forward a reasoned argument. I emailed it to Baz, and he thought I had put up a pretty good case, just raising one or two points which I agreed needed more thought.

It was the day after my 16th birthday and I had nearly finished the project when Gramp woke me at about three in the morning. I must have had a bit more gin than I intended, for it was quite difficult to come out of a deep sleep, but as soon as I saw her worried face, I was wide awake.

She had already rung the police, and looked so frail and anxious that I followed her wish and stayed with her rather than haring off on my bike. As luck would have it, it was the same police sergeant, and he suggested I might like to go with him, so that when we found Grump there would be a familiar face for him.

It was awful. We seemed to drive round the lanes forever, and this time there was no moon so it was much more difficult to sort out the shadows. The Sergeant, who told me to call him Brad, asked me about my studies and what I wanted to do, though I realised he was just filling the silence. I've noticed that people don't really like silence. My generation fill it with music or visual distractions, and the older generation can't seem to stop chattering. I answered him as best I could, but my intention was focussed on the roadsides

I suppose he's used to looking for things, for suddenly Brad said, "Ah!" and stopped the car. I would never have noticed what looked like a bundle of clothes heaped on the grass verge. I jumped out of the car and followed Brad. It was Grump all right, curled up in a ball. He had a brown blanket wrapped round him.

Brad was really gentle, squatting down beside Grump and just gently touching his shoulder, saying quietly "Hello there, Grump. I think it's time to go home."

After a while the bundle stirred, Grump nudged the blanket down so that his face was clear. He opened his eyes and looked at me, though he couldn't really have seen me in that light. "Is that my Nikki?" His voice was a bit quavery.

"Yes, Grump," I said, my voice all hoarse and raspy because I was finding it difficult not to cry. "We've come to take you home."

"I couldn't find you," he said. "Then I got tired so I thought I'd have a rest."

Brad helped him to his feet. It took a while. Then we got him into the front passenger seat of the car, and tucked the blanket round him.

He was almost asleep again in the short time it took to drive home. I went in first to tell Gramp we had found him. She was huddled in an armchair in the living room, looking so small and frail.

When I said, "He's OK Gramp, just a bit sleepy. He seemed to think he was looking for me," she didn't smile, only went on looking helpless. At last she said, "I can't go on, Nikki. I can't look after him properly any more."

And then I knew something would be changing pretty soon.

October – December 2006

1

It did, about a week before I was due to go back to school. During that week, I concentrated on the parallel universe aspect of my project. I didn't think Miss Bilham had a very high opinion of me, even though my English results were so good, and I was afraid my ideas might be classed as 'pretentious nonsense', a favourite expression of hers.

But all that went right out of my mind when Mother came over one evening with that Serious Talk expression on her face. We went into my room, and she sat on my bed beside me, holding one of my hands.

"I'm sure you've realised," she said, "that poor Grump isn't at all well. It happens to some old people. They stop remembering things and get very muddled up about time and events and even where they are."

I muttered, "Yes, I had noticed. In fact, he seems quite happy, but it must be a worry for Gramp."

She squeezed my hand. "It's clever of you to realise that." She was silent for a while. I could feel her trying to find the right words. At last she went on, "It's going to mean some big changes for us all. Gramp can't go on taking care of him, so she is looking for a nice place for him to live where he will be well looked after. This sort of place costs a lot of money, so Gramp will sell the house and buy a little house or flat near Grump's new home."

I nodded. The tears were pressing hard at the back of my eyes because I loved the Grampies an awful lot and hated to think of them being parted. "So where will I go?" I asked, because clearly I wouldn't be able to stay with Gramp any longer.

Mother smiled. "That's the one good thing from my point of view. You'll move back with me. I'll have to get somewhere bigger because you will need your own space. But Sally has a sister who has a big house part of which is being turned into self-contained flats. I think one of these will be ideal."

I didn't ask the next obvious question, because I knew the answer. Obviously I wouldn't be able to stay at my school, and would have to go back to Greenley High, which had a Sixth Form where I could do my As. The hugeness of it was too much, and tears burst out, pouring down my face.

"Oh darling," Mother said, and put her arms round me holding me tight. Then she sat back and went on with a smile, "but it won't all be quite as abrupt a change as you may think. I've arranged for us to talk to Mr. Pearson, the deputy head at Greenley High. But you won't actually go there until Gramp's house is sold. In fact, you can be a great help to her in packing up." She shook her head. "Oh dear, you're having to take on so much for your age."

I gave a noisy gulp and said, "Mother I'm six*teen* for heaven's sake." And she hugged me again and said indeed I was and that the one good thing was that at least I'd be rejoining at least one of my old friends, Rachel. And that nice boy Peter. In fact, that nice boy Peter had left to train at some School for Forestry, even if he hadn't dumped me long ago.

But yes, Rachel – that would be good, and some of the others with whom I had caught up a bit at the September party.

For the following few weeks, it was like living in a whirlwind. With the help of the local council and one of the charities for old people, Gramp found a nursing home just outside Banbury. It was in two parts, so if you were reasonably all right you could stay in the part where you had a room to yourself but they provided all the meals; but if you got worse you could move into the part which gave day and night care. For the moment Grump was considered in the first category and, when they went to visit and he found an old school friend was already in residence, he was quite happy about it, though he just couldn't grasp that Gramp wouldn't be with him.

Then came the business of putting their house on the market. I could tell Gramp hated it, but she didn't say anything and I helped as much as possible clearing out cupboards and boxing up books to go to auction. By the time I got down to some studying in the evening, I thought I had really earned my gin. All the same I wasn't drinking as much as before, and I thought of Dad and wondered if he would have been all right if only he had had more things to think about.

In the meantime I was getting on at school. To my surprise Miss Bilham was OK about the parallel universe business and turned out to be a fan of Philip Pullman too. I was also going with Mother to see different flats, and being interviewed by the deputy head at Greenley High. Mr Pearson seemed a pleasant man who had clearly been primed about my situation and said that under all the circumstances I had done very well. I told him about my Oxford authors project and though he seemed a bit mystified by my parallel universes, he said there was no reason why I could not make that one of my English projects for A levels. He said he'd have a word with Greg, the English tutor. He also knew that I had several friends at the school. He said, "That's good because you will find it very different from your previous school."

Well, I was aware of that, thank you.

2

The Grampies' cottage sold very quickly, so the next thing that happened was moving in with Mother. We'd been several times to see the flat in Sally's sister's, Amy Lewis', house, and I had to agree it was quite special. Just the approach down a long drive was impressive. We had our own separate entrance and the flat was on two floors. Mother had her room on the ground floor next to the small living room and kitchen, and I had mine upstairs by the bathroom. Mine was quite a big room, which I guess was Mother being nice and letting me have more space; and being alone on the first floor gave me a sense of privacy. I had a great view looking out over lawns to the edge of a wood.

And then I was back at Greenley High. I hated it. Mother said I was spoilt and should stop making comparisons. I suppose she was right but I couldn't help comparing the relaxed atmosphere of my previous school, which had been like a rather posh country house, with the long corridors and all the clatter, shoving and pushing that was Greenley High. Not to mention the size of the classes. Before I had been one of twenty, now there were thirty-five of us.

That sounds snobby, I know, so I stopped going on about it after Mother ticked me off. And of course I didn't say anything to Rachel. Thanks to her I made one or two new friends who were not of the shoving and pushing kind. We sat together in class when we could, but of course we weren't all doing the same subjects. Actually I rather liked Greg, the English tutor, who seemed to think my parallel universe project was quite cool. Rachel and Moira were doing Philosophy, Neil had chosen Maths. Only one of them was doing media studies like me, and that was Tracey who was the bubbliest of our group.

One good thing was that the school ran a lot of clubs. This meant that you got the chance to meet other people with the same interests as you, so I joined the birding group. Not that I'd done much of that lately, but now one lot of exams was over, I could take some time off. Anyway, it would bring nice memories. My first attendance also yielded some very interesting information. Everyone remembered Pete who had been one of their best birders – indeed their Secretary until recently. Of course he was now at that School of Forestry and currently doing work practice somewhere up north. When I casually enquired whether Jane had come to the meetings, there was the odd smirk and someone said, "Oh, she dumped him – couldn't cope with all the mud."

That was the best news I'd heard for a long time.

And then a miracle happened. One morning in November I found an envelope addressed to me on the doormat in handwriting that was half familiar. In it was a £50 note, and a scrawl on a piece of paper: "Proud of you Tuppence." And signed *Dad.* I couldn't believe it, turned the enveloped in every direction, peered at the postmark – a smudgy *Yorkshire* – and turned it round and round again. And put it in my pocket to show it to Mother. And took it out again. It would be too cruel to raise her hopes … for what? I still did not know where he was, nor could I tell what state he was in. I didn't even know whether she would be pleased to hear from him any more.

But I knew what I would do with the money.

"I think I'll go and spend a week-end with Baz before I start school," I said to Mother, very casually. "I've been saving up, so I have enough money." I felt quite shocked at how easily the lie slipped out.

Mother's doubt only lasted a moment. "Well, you've certainly earned a bit of fun. Call me when you get there. Baz meeting you at the station?"

"Yup," I said, another lie coming all too easily. He could hardly be meeting me at the station as he didn't know I was coming. It was the first time I'd done anything so daring as turn up somewhere unannounced. I wasn't exactly sure why I wanted it that way. Baz had called since his return from trekking in Scandinavia and knew I'd done OK with the GCSEs, but not how much OK. He didn't know I'd decided on my A-level subjects, or that I had a half-promise of a placement for work practise on the local week-end paper. OK, so it was as messenger girl, but it was work and it was on a paper. It was the first time I had really important life changing news that I'd sorted out for myself, and I wanted to hug them to myself for a while longer.

On the rail journey north I made another life changing decision. All this time I'd refused to have full sex with Baz. I knew it was difficult for him, and it was pretty difficult for me even though I didn't know yet what I was missing. "Old fashioned little thing, aren't you?" he teased, but after a while he stopped going on about it. I was grateful for that because I knew I wouldn't need much persuasion. For several months, all my friends seemed to talk about nothing else but who had done what with whom. I don't know why I felt differently, but I did: that it was something precious, not to be given away just to be like everyone else. But now, on this brink of adult life, here was something precious that I could share with Baz..

It felt really weird when I arrived at Liverpool, not to be looking for Baz. He had always kept on about what a marvellous station it was, so now I gave it a bit more attention. He had pointed out the soaring steel superstructure of the roof and now I stood gawping at it, feeling myself shrink in size. On a late Friday afternoon, it was very busy and that made me feel pretty small, too.

I took a taxi. After all, this was a defining time in my life, and Dad's £50 had given me a rare sense of riches. I told the taxi driver to drop me at the entrance to the campus, which he did. I always like strolling through it, the sense of purpose that the place buzzed with. But I didn't stroll too slowly. Baz's hall of residence was only five minutes' walk, and I entered it, went up the stairs, headed down the long corridor. And outside his door I hesitated. So much had changed since I last saw him, with Grump's illness, helping Gramp to pack up the house, going to the new school, while he had been having heaven-knows-what adventures in wild Nordic places.

Before I could change my mind, I tapped firmly on the door. There was silence, then a series of grunting sounds and a light giggle that certainly didn't belong to Baz.

"Dammit," said his voice. "Go see who that is, sweetie, and tell whoever to go away."

I heard light footsteps and fled.

I heard the door open, a voice call "Hi?" in a tone that ended with a question mark.

I turned and gasped "S-sorry. Wrong door."

She had short reddish hair and a clutched towel covering between armpits and thighs. What she had been doing did not need much imagination.

She waved an arm. "No probs," she said. An Aussie accent.

79

I got out of the building as quickly as possible, then started walking and walking without any plan or purpose except to get away from that brief glimpse that in seconds destroyed the only relationship I'd had.

3

Eventually I found a seat in a bit of a park. Dusk was falling and I let myself sink into its shadows.

Someone hurried past, paused. "You OK?"

"Fine," I said. "Just recovering from the day." Meaningless phrase but it seemed to satisfy the person who hurried on.

So that was why Baz hadn't been too bothered about sex; he had simply gone elsewhere for it. How could I have been such a fool? A tear trickled down my nose, then another, and soon they were an uncontrollable flood, interrupted by horrible choking sounds. The knowledge came slowly that there was no one in the world I could really turn to: not Dad, not Baz, not the Grampies because they had enough problems, not Mother.

Why not Mother? Yes, she had a lot of problems too, but they had always shared problems, hadn't they?

Someone sat down beside me. "Can I help?"

I glanced up. She wore glasses, had long straight hair, a concerned expression.

"No, not really. I've been d-dumped."

A hand came round to rest on my shoulder. "Oh, you poor creature. That's terrible." Irish accent. Gentle. "And haven't I been dumped enough times? Sure, but aren't I dumping material? You, though, you're gorgeous."

A flicker of self esteem returned. I straightened up. "Thank you. And you're much too nice to be dumped." I sniffed, blew my nose. "I suppose I'd better head for home."

"Where's home?"

"Oxfordshire. I'll get a train from Lime Street."

"Isn't Oxfordshire a terrible long way! I'll take you to Lime Street. I have a car, a very little car. I'm Bridie by the way." It did turn out to be a very little car, an ancient Robin Reliant, bright red. Someone in our street in Greenley had had one: a rather serious young man called Tommy, and it had become known at Tommy's tin can.

Bridie's kindness and the memory of Tommy's tin can helped a bit. The train was crowded and the carriage soon unbearably stuffy, so

I soon escaped to the restaurant car, which turned out to be more bar than restaurant. I was just wondering whether I could get away with ordering a gin when a middle aged man asked if the young lady would like a drink. It seemed 'the young lady' was me, and he had a round, cheerful and unthreatening face, so I said yes. Talking to someone would take my mind off the awfulness of the day. The round-faced man said his name was Bill. He asked me about my studies and said he had two daughters a bit older than me. Then he asked if I would like another one, and I realised I had finished my drink rather quickly. I muttered it was all right, I'd got some money, but he wouldn't hear of it and this time he brought me a large one.

After that Bill started getting a bit friendlier – I mean, swivelling round in his seat so his knee touched mine. I thought it was accidental at first, but then he started moving his knee up and down so it rubbed against mine. It took me a while to realise what was happening. After all, the man had two daughters older than me. This time I sipped my drink very slowly and when I was quite sure what was happening, I moved my knee away and said, "Would you like someone doing that to one of your daughters?"

"No," he said. "But I wouldn't have expected her to be drinking under age either."

Well, he was right, wasn't he? I felt the tears pricking behind my eyes and got up, leaving most of the drink, and made my way back down the train, finding a carriage that wasn't so crowded, and squeezing in between two old people.

If this was what was meant by growing up, I didn't think much of it: finding out people weren't what they seemed, having to pretend to be someone you weren't. At that point I must have drifted off for quite a while, because I became aware suddenly of something heaving about under my head, and found it had dropped off on the shoulder of the old man next to me. Outside it was black as anything so we must have been going through countryside with just the occasion pinprick of light whizzing by.

"Sorry to wake you, my dear. I was getting cramp." He had blue eyes and a benign expression.

I felt myself blush. "Oh, I'm so sorry. How awful ….."

From the other side of the carriage, the old lady interrupted. "Don't you worry your pretty head. My husband thoroughly enjoyed being your pillow."

They reminded me a bit of the Grampies. My faith in humanity felt a fraction restored. They started asking me about my studies and were really nice when I told them about my GCSE results, though looked a bit vague when I talked about media studies. I noticed that the old man only had one arm and he saw me noticing and explained he had lost it in the war. "World War Two," he explained. "That'll be history for you."

So I told him about Grump's experiences which made me realise that I didn't know all that much about it so I decided I would ask him next time I went to the nursing home. Time passed amazingly quickly and I hadn't thought of Baz or that Bill person for ages, when the old lady started shuffling about and saying, "Not far to go now, John. Banbury next stop."

That brought me back to the awfulness of the present with a jolt, and the terrible aching emptiness that was life without Baz.

4

I helped the old couple with their luggage at Banbury station, and down the steps to get a taxi. When I had waved them out of sight, I stood in the ticket hall wondering what on earth to do. Then I fished my mobile out, flicked through the numbers stored and found my solution. Rachel. I glanced at my watched. Ten o'clock. It was just not too late. It was a huge relief when she picked up. I told her everything was terrible and the world about to end, and she said calmly, "Right, you'd better come and tell me about it. There's a late bus about now, you may be lucky. Mum and Dad are out until about midnight. I'll check the spare room. Do you want me to call your Mum?"

No, I didn't. I thanked any God there might be for a sane friend.

I did make the late bus, and was with Rachel in half an hour. Theirs was a modernised cottage in the village next to Mother's. Rachel opened the door in her dressing gown with a hood with rabbit ears, surprisingly frivolous for someone like Rachel. Once we were in and the door closed, I started to laugh at how funny she looked, but the laugh turned to sobs and then I was howling and snuffling and sobbing like a toddler. Through it all I told her about Baz and by the time I'd finished, she had made a hot drink and we were both sitting in her living room while she said, "Nikki, you've really had an awful time recently. It's not surprising you are upset." Rachel is sixteen coming on thirty. "And Baz never was right for you."

That stopped me mid-snuffle. "How can you say that?"

"Well, I grant that he was very good looking; but you have to admit he was superficial."

"How can you say that?" I repeated. "First of all, good looks don't come into it." (Not true.) "And second if he were so superficial, he wouldn't have gone to all that trouble to get interested in bird watching."

Ignoring the point about looks, Rachel said calmly, "Of course he would. He was obviously very attracted to you and wanted to please you. Anyway, maybe he even did get interested in bird watching." She put a hand on my shoulder. "The last thing I want is to upset you more than you are. But if you are realistic about it, it won't be so painful in the end." As I said, she's sixteen coming on thirty.

I thought back to that giggle and Baz's voice saying *Sweetie tell whoever to go away.* Could that ever stop being painful?

"What will I tell everyone?"

"How many people do you think care? Or even know? Yes, there are Madge and Laura, but we don't see much of them these days. Oh, and Jane." I didn't want to think about Jane, except that she reminded me of Pete and I suddenly did care what he thought.

Rachel stood up. "I don't know about you, but I'm starving. How about a bacon sarnie?"

You weren't supposed to feel hungry if you had a broken heart, but just the mention of it made my mouth water. We went into the kitchen and Rachel assembled the appropriate ingredients and tools. We were in the middle of preparations when we heard a key turn in the front door and a moment later Rachel's mother's voice calling "Hellooooo! Helloooo?." A moment later her head peered round the kitchen door. "What a heavenly smell! Enough for two more? Oh hello, Nikki."

Rachel put on more bacon and toast while her parents took off coats and bustled about putting plates on trays. It was taken for granted that I was staying the night and no one questioned why I was there.

Next morning I rang Mother to say I was coming home, muttering that Baz and I had broken up. She made sympathetic noises but did not interrogate me as to the reasons. I'm not sure I would have even told her, but then quite soon after that Life took over again. The first thing that happened a couple of days later was a call from Baz.

"Hi, Sweetie!" (Did he call all his girl friends Sweetie?) "I thought it was time we got together before our respective studies take over."

I'd spent two days practising what I'd say when the occasion arose. "I'm glad you rang Baz. I've been doing a lot of thinking and now that I've got some good GCSE grades, I'm going to go all out on my As. So, I thought it might be better for both of us if we, like, eased off a bit."

"Oh?" Amazing how such a little word could convey such taken-abackness. "Well, that's a bit of a blow. Are you sure?" I noted there was no great attempt to make me change my mind.

"Quite sure," I said firmly. "Perhaps when you come home we could meet up and catch up."

"Yeah, that'd be good. Though this coming year I might get posted anywhere on work practice." So he was beginning to distance himself now.

"Never mind, just get in touch if you're in the area." That bit hadn't been practised and I felt really proud of it.

December 2006 – April 2007

1

After I put the phone down, I burst into tears. Mother hugged me and went to put the kettle on, then I told her everything that had happened and she hugged me again. While she was doing that she told me about a boy called Ginger she had fallen in love with at college. They had been out a couple of times and she'd had her first kiss, and he had sent her a poem he had written about it. Soon after she had found him kissing another girl behind the bicycle sheds. I found I could almost feel her devastation, and leaned back to look at her through blurring tears, not sure whether to laugh or cry.

"I always thought he was a bit superficial, that Baz," Mother said.

"That's what Rach said."

"She's got a good head on her shoulders," Mother added. As I said, sixteen coming on thirty.

That morning Mother and I agreed we would have the best Christmas possible, without husbands or boyfriends, but keeping close to the people most important in our lives. So we bought a Christmas tree and got out all the old decorations. The flat was a bit small for a tree with candles, but Sally's sister said we could put it in a corner of the conservatory as long as we only lit it when we were there to keep an eye on it.

For Christmas Eve, we invited Rachel, her parents and Adrian. On Christmas Day, Mother fetched the Grampies; and on Boxing Day, Sally and Tom came. Predictably both Adrian and Tom made comments about warning the Fire Brigade when we lit the candles, just like Dad always had. But once we got that annual ritual over, the tree looked more magical than ever, its lights reflecting in the conservatory windows so that twenty candles turned into a myriad points of light that seemed to stretch in every direction. And the only time I thought of Baz was when I saw Sally and Tom kissing under the mistletoe they had insisted on bringing with them. I wondered whether Tom minded everyone having Christmas drinks around him, though we limited our offerings to wine, but he looked quite relaxed. As I'm not that keen on wine, I didn't bother either. And we grinned at each other and raised our eyes to heaven in complicity as voices got louder and jokes less funny.

On New Year's Eve, I cycled over to our old home to visit the marshes. This was usually a great time for winter visitors. To my dismay, it was full of heavy equipment and looked like a building site. One of our old neighbours was walking his dog and told me the land was being drained to make it suitable for more houses. The neighbour was clearly upset and I could imagine what Pete would have thought of that. What would happen to the nesting lapwing, and some of the rarities that paused here on their way to the Wildfowl Centre at Slimbridge? When I got back to the flat, Mother agreed with me that it was awful, though for different reasons. She pointed out that if you built too many houses on low-lying areas, they would be likely to flood. But I must say my sympathies were with the lapwing. If people were stupid enough to buy houses in the wrong places, that was their problem. When I expressed that opinion, I was told I was getting intolerant. I wrote to Pete to see what he thought, but there was no reply.

Then it was time to go back to school and life was suddenly very boring. Mother said it was the anticlimax after slogging for my GSCEs and that Baz business. And though Greg, my new English teacher, was quite keen on the Oxford writers project, and so was I, I'd suddenly had enough of swatting and at that stage A levels seemed a long way off. Anyway, it meant I stayed off the gin. At that stage I still associated gin with work.

Rachel wasn't a lot of help. I really liked her but she wasn't what you'd call a fun person, with her nose always in a book. I was probably noticing this more now that my nose wasn't always in a book, too. Also her interests always focussed more on some remote part of the globe than what was happening in our street. And, of course, there was Adrian.

Once I asked her, "Have you done it yet?"

"Done what?" Then she understood. "*No,*" she said firmly. "And we both agree that it's something we'll explore when the time is right," by which I assume she meant when they were married. Compared with the way other people went on about sex, this was pretty amazing.

This made me wonder how I would feel about it if I was going steady with Baz. I remembered how I had been ready to present him with the great gift of my virginity and cringed when I thought what would have happened if I'd succeeded then found he was cheating on me.

But you're not going steady with Baz, I reminded myself. And found it didn't seem to hurt so much any more.

Anyway Rachel's social life revolved entirely round Adrian, not least because even their studies were similar. I had wondered what Rachel's Dad made of it all, and found out when she invited me round one evening. Clearly he thought Adrian was the best thing since sliced bread and once or twice they even went together to visit Grump in Freshfields, the residential home where he was living. In fact, Grump seemed a bit better these days, perhaps because he didn't have to pretend any more that he was better than he was. He was a favourite among some of the nurses and, of course, he loved that. Gramp had settled in a small bungalow and she could still drive so visited Grump most days. I went to have supper with her once a week and play Scrabble.

So my social life wasn't exactly riveting.

2

I was clearly going to have to do something about it. There was a group in our year that always went around together, so one evening when Rach was again 'sorry, I'm meeting Adrian,' I accepted their invitation to join them at a Teens Club. They were noisy and some of them a bit weird. One of the boys had that woolly hair that was fashionable, and a small ring in his nose, and one of the girls went in for multi-coloured streaks in her hair. But I must say they seemed to have a lot of fun. One afternoon after school I noticed that Tracey had joined the group, all sharing a joke as they headed into town.

"So where were you all off to?" I asked next morning as we met at the school entrance.

"To suss out a great new coffee shop just off the High." Tracey sparkled with enthusiasm. "We're going there again after school. You should come with us. They're great fun."

"Yeah. Shall I ask Rachel?"

"Rachel's a gem. Just wish she'd chill out a bit."

I'd been thinking the same myself.

So I did join them, and hadn't laughed so much for a very long time. The girl, Zoe, with the coloured streaks, was a natural mimic and so was Matt, the guy with the woolly hair. Zoe was the one enthusing about a rave she'd heard about the following Saturday. She turned to Tracey and me. "Are you up for it?"

I was up for anything. "You could stay with me that night," Tracey said, "if you're worried about getting home late."

It was the wickedest evening I'd had. It was in a converted barn out in the country. A couple of the boys ran a bar at one end, and they'd rigged up some fab lighting. The only thing that went a bit wrong was that when Matt got in the first round of drinks, I asked for a tonic, but when it came I knew from the first sip that it had gin in it. I hesitated and then thought, so what? I hadn't had any alcohol for weeks except for that wine at Christmas, so didn't that prove I couldn't have a problem with it? After that I had one or two – may be four or five more. I felt absolutely terrific, as though I could do anything I wanted in the world as long as I put my mind to it.

On the way home I felt a bit sick and when we got to Tracey's I threw up, but at least got to the loo in time. Fortunately her parents were away for the week-end, so we could sleep in, but I felt rather rough in the morning.

"You need a bit more practice," Tracey suggested.

But I decided I'd better watch it. When I thought about it, it was the first time I had drunk for fun rather than for helping me with my course work, and that did make it seem different.

Still, I enjoyed being with that crowd, so when they suggested another gig I was up for it straight away. This one was run by a friend of Matt who had a farm and an unused barn about ten miles away. I'd started calling him Woolly Bear because of his hair, and he seemed to like that, pretending to be a bear and catching me up in a bear hug. I was a bit curious about him because, although he played the fool and seemed to like to draw attention to himself some of the time, he also quite often sat in the background looking thoughtful.

On that occasion I decided to stick to plain tonic water.

"What's the matter with you?" asked Zoe, once she had noticed.

"Nothing," I said. "I just like to show who's in control." Then I wished I hadn't because it sounded so smug. Zoe clearly thought so too, because from time to time throughout the evening, she would drape herself round my shoulder and say in an exaggeratedly posh voice, "Are we still in contro-o-o-o-l Nikki?"

To tell the truth, it was getting a bit boring, not just Zoe, but the whole evening with everyone larking about and me feeling as though I was on another planet. In the end I gave up, and asked one of the boys to put a splash of gin in. Then I had a couple in quick succession to sort of catch up. Then I started enjoying myself.

So the weeks passed. My new group went out about every second week-end, and on those occasions I would stay overnight with Tracey. She had come to our flat and Mother seemed to like her, but for the moment I avoided bringing Zoe or Matt home as I thought she might think they were a bit o.t.t.

Out of classes I didn't see much of Rachel and felt guilty because it didn't seem to matter. So, if we bumped into each other in town, I made a point of suggesting we went and had a snack and once we went to the cinema together. She never made any comment about the fact I went out with the other group, but then she was completely involved with her plans with Adrian. They'd started saving for a house. She was seventeen by then, but *really!*

Perhaps she was so involved in her own affairs that she didn't notice. I'd also got into a better routine with my own studies, putting so many hours for them each week and keeping to a timetable. This didn't include gin. I was still determined to show that I had this under control.

One evening in the middle of supper, Mother went to answer the phone and came back holding the cordless, her mouth twitching. "There's someone called Woolly Bear for you," she said.

"Hi Matt," I said into the receiver. After all, there is a time and place for Woolly Bears.

"You're having supper," he said. "I can hear you chewing."

"It's not illegal,"

"May be it should be. Most of us stuff too much," adding before I could, "including me."

Mother had started removing plates. "Look, Matt, I'm sure you didn't ring to discuss the state of the nation's obesity."

"No, I rang to see if you were free for a game of bowls, as in the Superbowling Alley."

"I've never tried."

"Never tried?" I imagine his broad face twisted in amazement. "Is there something seriously wrong with you?"

Mother came with the dessert. "Mother, Matt wants to go bowling."

"Run along then," she said, and I hoped Matt hadn't heard that.

He had. "I'll pick you up in ten minutes," he said.

It was quite a surprise when he turned up in an old Morris Minor he had restored himself and proved to be a really good, careful driver.

3

At the Superbowling, I watched Matt a few times and, seemingly out of nowhere, a memory emerged. Dad was at the far end of the garden, bat in hand, looking back at me – it seemed such a long way away – and calling, "Straight as you can, Tuppence; straight as you can." And then there I was, crouching down, frowning, concentrating on that distant figure and the effort of sending that ball down straight. I was four or five at the time. Dad had adored cricket, played every weekend, sometimes taking me, so that the peculiarities of googlies and leg breaks were as familiar as nursery rhymes. Until the drink took over, and he rarely saw the ball let alone hit it.

"Nikki, *Nikki,* **Nikki!!"** My name was being called ever louder. I shook my head clear and turned to see Matt watching me quizzically. "You were miles away," he accused.

"I was thinking of Dad. He played cricket and I threw balls for him."

"Daddy's little girl were you?"

"No," I said. Then more forcefully, "**No!**"

He came over, put a hand on my shoulder. "OK.OK. It's just that I've never heard you mention your Dad."

Don't go there. "Oh, he's away much of the time now. Something to do with computer chips. But way back I went to cricket matches with him."

"Mine's away a lot, too." Matt pulled me towards the start of the lane. "Come on, let's see what you can do."

I got all ten skittles with two balls. Matt watched in silence.

"I expect it was beginner's luck," I said at last.

We went to have a beer – or at least, Matt had a beer, and I had a spritzer because I thought wine might taste better if it was watered down. It did, though it didn't match gin. We sat on a sort of balcony overlooking the lanes.

"So why is your Dad away so much?" I asked.

"Well, you could say he's into computers, too," Matt said, and I was just about to say *well, what a coincidence,* when he added, "Only he nicks them and doesn't even do that properly so he's in and out of prison."

After a few moments he went on, "Your mouth's open."

"I don't know what to say," I said before I shut it.

"Mm, yes, it is the sort of comment that kills conversation. But I've got used to it. Though Dad hasn't done me many favours. Mum visits regularly, but always comes back miserable. In fact, she's miserable most of the time."

"Have you brother or sisters?"

"Sister ten years older. She got out, went to Devon, married a farmer, has two kids. Sends money when she can. Brother Bill is three years older, and probably going the same way as Dad."

I thought about it. "So why didn't you?"

"Didn't I what? Go the same way as Dad? Chrissake I don't know, Nikki. Perhaps I inherited my genes from a Woolly Bear!"

"Sorry," I said. "I didn't mean to upset you. I really like you."

He peered at me over the rim of his glass, "That's the best thing I've heard since forever." He put his beer down and stared into it for a while. "Hey, would you be my girl friend for a bit? You know, go out, have fun?"

Why not? Baz had gone, Pete wasn't interested. Perhaps I could save Matt from going the same way as his Dad.

"OK," I said.

"Wow," Matt said. "Let's have another drink."

We got into a routine of twice a week, either a film, or bowling, or some new place that had opened. Then at the week-end we joined up with the rest of the crowd.

"Don't forget your studies," Mother murmured from time to time.

Well, I hadn't forgotten them completely, but I'd certainly slowed down. Matt was going to study engineering and occasionally, if Mother was out with Sally or other friends, Matt would come over and we would have a study session. It was a fact that Matt on his own was very different from Matt in a crowd. But I'd noticed that when boys got together they tended to get competitive, which often meant stupid. Mother quite took to him, merely commenting that it was a pity he didn't look after himself better, which I have learned is adult-speak for a boy with shaggy hair, baggy jeans, a gap of midriff showing between jeans and tee-shirt, and probably a not very clean tee-shirt.

Anyway, she showed no hesitation in leaving us alone in the flat together, and interestingly, Matt showed no inclination towards getting me into bed. I was probably a rather worse influence on him

91

than he was on me, because I started keeping a small store of beer and wine in my room. By now I'd acquired a taste for wine, even without water.

At New Year, Matt had made a resolution to take more exercise. I didn't think for a minute he would stick to it, and after a month at the Leisure Centre in town, he did give up. But he got a taste for expanding heart and lungs as he put it, and after school began jogging, or running as he preferred to call it, starting with half an hour and gradually extending to an hour or more. I'd join him in a coffee shop after he'd showered and changed and we'd either go on to bowling, a film or back to my place for some study. It began to feel quite comfortable.

April – November 2007

1

In February, I started swimming while Matt was jogging. I wasn't very good at it, but liked the feeling of my body moving through the water. The coffee shop overlooked the pool and Matt was usually there waiting for me with a glass of juice. "You looked great in that swimsuit," he greeted me once.

It was the first time he had commented on my appearance. I thought *if I were Tracey I'd say something like 'I look even better out of it'*. But I'm not Tracey. In fact she had recently commented to me, "You and Matt are cosy these days. Have you – er – you know, have you …?"

"Done it?" I finished for her. Why is everyone so interested in each other's sex life? "Well, I think that's between Matt and me," which probably infuriated her and led her to the wrong conclusion. In fact, we didn't go with the gang as much as we once did. Matt didn't drink much and found them a bit boring, and we had got into our own routine.

Towards the end of March, a trip was organised for the engineering students to go north to visit a special steam museum and have a ride on a vintage train. They were away for three days and I was quite surprised how much I missed Matt. On the first evening, Mother was out, so after flicking through the TV remote control several times, I went up to my room and checked my most recent notes on *Alice in Wonderland.* And was quite surprised. I'd forgotten I had done so many notes from research on the Internet and that my conclusions had at some point taken on a life of their own. For example, there were a number of suggestions that the strange worlds that inhabited Alice's dreams might have their origins in drug taking. I wasn't convinced by this. After all, the extraordinary size or shape or behaviour of many of *Wonderland's* inhabitants, could just as well have come out of a fantasy world as out of drug inducement. And perhaps those fantasy worlds were not so fantastic, but merely waiting for us, quite close, in some parallel universe.

What a pity there was no longer Baz to discuss it with. But how about Matt? Even engineers must acknowledge worlds beyond material construction.

Feeling rather pleased with myself, I fished the remains of a bottle of wine from the back of a cupboard. There was not much in it, and it tasted rather disgustingly acid, but I drank it away. And probably would have opened another if Mother had not come home just then.

The second evening, I started earlier on my notes and the opening of a bottle. Mother had announced she was going to bed early and I said I would check everything was locked up. It's much easier to go into fantasy worlds once your mind has loosened up a bit, so I started making a list of the features shared in common by both fantasy and parallel universes. I became so involved with this that I only drank a couple of glasses and in due course went to asleep well pleased with my progress.

It was the third evening that things really went wrong. At breakfast Mother said she would be staying away over night, and 'would I be OK on my own?' As I raised my eyes to heaven, she said before I could, "Yes, I know you're sixteen...."

"Sixteen and a half," I corrected. And that was the end of the conversation.

That evening, I was on my third glass of wine and feeling restless when the phone rang.

"I'm told," Zoe's voice said, "that your shadow is away on a college trip, and that it might even be possible to extract you from purdah,"

If it hadn't been my third glass, I would probably have said I was in the middle of an essay I must finish. But I wasn't and didn't. The idea of joining the gang and doing something silly was very appealing.

"I've just called a cab to pick me up to join the others. I'll call by yours on the way."

The others were at a brand new bar with amazing décor and flashing lights that swirled round the ceiling in a changing combination of colours. I didn't like to say they made me feel slightly sick. Zoe hung an arm round my shoulder and studied me carefully. "You're not wanting to be in contro-o-o-l tonight Nikki?"

"Not really," I said.

"G-o-o-o-d. And with Matt away, mice can play."

"Wha' d'ya mean?"

"Come on Sweetie. A nice guy, but not exactly a bundle of fun. I couldn't believe it when Tracey said that you and he … you know. Well, of course, we all thought he was gay."

"Matt is absolutely great." I jumped to his defence. "He just doesn't think it's necessary to go off the wall."

But Zoe was not listening, already off on to the next interesting thing, which was a group of young men at the other end of the bar, clearly intrigued by our presence. In minutes our two groups had merged, and a blonde young man had his arm tightly round my waist.

An hour later both groups had thinned out and we were six couples, some of them in positions I did my best not to notice. The blonde young man had given up on me, but I was relaxing on a bench seat with my feet in the lap of a dark, sleek chap. He'd taken my shoes off and was stroking my soles with results that were distinctly disturbing. He had just reached across to pull me up closer, when someone sat on the other side and a familiar voice said, "So that's what happens when I go away."

I spun round and found myself looking into Matt's sad, brown eyes. "How did you know where I was?"

His grin had no humour in it. "I know my Nikki. When I found your place empty, I knew you wouldn't be far from the latest flash joint in town."

Matt grabbed the shoes from the sleek young man, gripped my arm and hauled me away. The sleek young man looked as though he might come after us, then changed his mind.

Outside the cool air was like chilled water. "Sorry, Matt," I said, hanging on to him for support. "Sorry. I was bored, and wanted to do something stupid."

He pushed me down on a bench, put my shoes on, sat beside me. "Well, you certainly achieved that. I've never seen you in such a state."

And of course he hadn't.

"I didn't expect you back until tomorrow."

"Clearly not."

"Did you have a good trip?"

"It would have been better if you'd been there."

I fished out a handkerchief and started snuffling. "That's nice. I don't really know what you think of me."

He took hold of my shoulders and looked at me steadily. "You're my best mate, Nikki. You must know that." He paused,

95

grinned and added, "Though I must say I'm not into stroking soles of feet."

"I don't know what got into me."

Matt raised one of his hands from my shoulder and stroked my head. It felt nice, and I said so. He caught me up in a hug, a really Woolly Bear Hug. "That's even better," I said.

He leaned down and plonked a kiss on my forehead. "All you have to do is ask, Nikki."

He took me home, but didn't come in. "To answer your question of about an hour ago, it was a good trip, but I missed you so decided to miss the last night booze-up."

I went on tiptoe and kissed him gently on the mouth and felt his lips quiver under mine. "In the end, I'm glad you did. Am I forgiven?"

Matt said, "Best pals are always forgiven." He turned away, and then said over his shoulder, "Or almost always."

2

We slipped back into our old routine, though I started swimming more, gradually increasing the length and speed of my swims. I'd settled in well at college and was enjoying my studies. Greg had become quite hooked on my parallel universe project, even if he thought some of the conclusions were far-fetched.

Matt and I rarely went out with the gang now. With the lengthening days, an evening walk rounded off by a drink at a country pub seemed more attractive and usually I settled for a glass of wine. I also still found it was helpful if I was on a study drive, though limited it when Matt was around. Mother had quite taken to Matt and encouraged his visits.

From time to time I remembered what Zoe had said about him being gay and wondered about it, but I couldn't bring myself to ask him, and anyway I didn't really care. Any petting I'd experienced had usually been after a few drinks and my recollections weren't encouraging.

Then one day, Matt said he would like me to meet his parents. They were farming folk and lived in a small village called Clapham in the Yorkshire Dales. By now Matt had invested in an old Robin Reliant. It did rather feel like driving in a tin can and juddered every time anything big overtook it, but Matt had Mother's seal of approval, so we decided to go up during the summer vacation.

Of course I'd seen documentaries about Yorkshire and I'd read some of those dark stories by the famous Yorkshire women writers. But the reality came as a surprise. The size of the skies nearly blew me away – so huge and dominating as though the clouds marching or scudding or just feathering above the land were in complete command of what went on down below. Matt's Dad (he told me to call him Jake) was just what I expected: a bit stern and talking in monosyllables, though his face lit up when he saw me which made me feel special. His Mother, Angie, was round and homely and looked as if she had been wearing an apron and a smudge of flour on her face all her life. She had put me in a small room overlooking the farmyard and the fields beyond, which sloped down to a river then swept up the other side to bare fields touching the sky. The fields were criss-crossed with stone walls and there were sheep in some of them.

On that first evening, we had what Angie and Jake called high tea, which was a massive amount of food that seemed to combine features of breakfast and tea. Afterwards we went for a walk round the farm. The sky was a deepening blue, and as the sun went down there were all kinds of golden streaks that deepened through orange to red.

"They call this God's own country," Jake said, in the tone of voice that indicated he entirely agree with them. Then we all went down to feed the sheep and as soon as they saw us by the feed troughs they all came heading towards us as though answering a signal. Later we had a hot drink and watched the news on television, and Angie nudged Jake and said, "Let's go up and leave the young folk to themselves."

As soon as the door had closed behind them Matt said quickly, "They really like you," to cover his embarrassment.

And to cover mine, I said "And I really like them." Then I sat on the sofa, patted the place beside me and said, "It's OK Matt, I don't want you to stroke the soles of my feet," and he laughed and sat down and we started planning the next day.

It seemed quite odd to be sleeping under the same roof. Matt was in the room next to mine and soon after I had my put my light out, I could hear the rumble of his snore through the wall. And quite soon the rhythm of it sent me to sleep.

Over breakfast next morning, Matt said, "I'm taking you for a drive, secret destination."

"Oh dear," Angie said. "And I'd planned to show her how to make a proper Yorkshire pudding."

I was quietly grateful to Matt. Making Yorkshire puddings sounded a bit domestic to me and sowed the question in mind of how committed Angie thought our relationship was. It didn't help when she added, "Matt has spoken so much about you in his letters and phone calls."

As he obviously wanted to keep our destination secret, I didn't ask questions but just leaned back and enjoyed the scenery, mostly wide and sweeping, rising higher to the north. Quite a lot later we reached water and I couldn't resist asking "That the sea?" and Matt nodded and looked pleased with himself. And then I became aware of occasional familiar features, especially the names on the signposts, and in particular one with the sign of a bird on it pointing towards Martin-Mere.

I couldn't spoil it for Matt by even hinting that I had been there before, especially as it had been with Baz. But I managed to do it all the same. We went into the information centre to get tickets and I said, "Just going to the loo," heading straight for it and realising too late that I'd given the game away.

3

He was flipping through an identification book when I came back and said without looking up, "I suppose you came with that Baz."

"Yeah. Sorry."

There was a board that told us what species had been seen on the reserve that day.

I followed him out on to the reserve and the main path that led across limitless hectares of reeds.

"Was he good at identifying them?" Matt asked.

"Mm. He became quite good." I told him the story of how we'd met on the website and I'd started teaching him, and then he'd got interested.

"I expect he wanted to get inside your knickers." Matt was hunched, his hands thrust into his pockets. For him that was really unusually crude.

"Well he didn't succeed."

Matt flicked a glance at me. "Good. Is that why he dumped you?"

"*I* dumped him."

"Why?"

"I found he was cheating on me."

Matt stopped and looked out over the reeds, letting a chattering group go passed. "I won't do that," he said.

"Nor will I."

"Is that because you love me?"

This must be the oddest conversation ever witnessed by Martin-Mere, I thought. "Not sure about love, but I feel very comfortable with you."

Matt turned to face me, and went on looking at me for what felt like a very long time. At last he said, "Do you think I'm gay?"

What sort of a question is that? "Don't you think you'd know that better than me?"

"I never feel right with girls, women. Especially the flirty ones in the gang. But you're not like that."

No, I wasn't. Well, not normally. Was that good? Matt seemed to be happy with it. And what about him? Was I missing the touchy-feely side of a relationship? Not really. It was a bit like having that brother who never survived. I must have said something aloud, for Matt said, "You never told me that, about your brother."

"He was called Alex. I've never mentioned him to anyone else before."

He reached out for hand, squeezed it. "Let's go and you teach me about birds."

Mid-August is not normally the best time for birding: too early for the winter visitors and too late for viewing the more unusual summer visitors. Martin-Mere is also known for its waders, not the easiest family of birds for a novice to start with. But there are a lot of ducks too, so I kept my fingers crossed we'd get a good cross-section of those. We started, though, with among the most difficult of all.

"Stop," I said, "and listen."

Matt stopped and listened. "You mean that stuttering sound in the reeds?" That was a good way of describing it.

"Mm. It's a Reed Warbler. Or a Sedge Warbler."

"Would it help if we knew whether these were reeds or sedges?"

"May be, but do you know the difference?"

"No, but I can see a bird flitting up and down whatever-they-are."

It took another ten minutes before it stopped long enough at the top of a reed for me to say with certainty, "Sedge Warbler. See the stripe over its eye."

"Mm, I think so. Stay still, damn you. Yes, *yes,* got it."
Matt's face was shiny with triumph.

I patted him on the shoulder. "That's pretty good: a sedge warbler as your first identified bird."

After that we had a great day, clocking up six species of duck, five of waders, a kingfisher, several grey herons, a harrier quartering over the marshes and….

"What's that booming noise?" Matt asked.

"Terrific. That's a booming bittern. You're more likely to hear than see them." I riffled through the book to find the illustration so he could see why.

It was about a week later that Matt rang me after school to say he couldn't meet me for the next few evenings as he had an extra assignment to complete by the end of the week. And when I met him that week-end, he seemed preoccupied.

"What's up?" I asked. "Difficult assignment?"

"Mmm. I thought I'd cracked it, but old Doc said he was expecting more originality."

"Oh *him.*" Most of us had had our ration of Doc Masters sarcasm at some time. "Forget it."

"Yes, except he's presented us with another assignment for next week."

"Oh well half-term is coming up soon."

Matt shuffled around looking uncomfortable. "That's another thing. Mother's decided we ought to go and visit the grandparents, you know up in Yorkshire."

I was surprised. Matt was not known for fitting in graciously with family plans. I missed him over half-term. Of course we weren't an item in the usual sense, but being with him did fill up a lot of my time.

"What's happened to Matt?" Mother asked one evening.

"Gone to see grandparents," I muttered.

"You could do worse than going to see yours. Or go and see Rachel. You're a bit like a headless chicken."

By then half-term was almost over, but it was a good idea. I hadn't seen Rach, not properly, for weeks. But of course she was just on her way out with Adrian. For some reason I didn't feel like catching up with Zoe or any other members of the gang. It was one of those miserable November evenings, so I wrapped up and stomped off, calling out, "Just out for a while."

I caught the bus into Greenley centre. On a Tuesday evening, there was not a lot going on and I scuffed about for a while, looking into shop windows. Then I noticed a pub I hadn't been in for a long time. I didn't usually go in to pubs on my own nowadays, but it felt as though I deserved cheering up, so I pushed open the door. There was a lot of noise and thumpy music, but I ordered myself a glass of wine at the bar, and stood looking round. There were a lot of men, but that wasn't unusual, though something felt different.

Then with a shock of recognition, in a corner table well away from the bar, I saw Matt's head. I didn't recognise it immediately because it wasn't woolly any more, which made him look younger and more vulnerable. I was about to call out when I saw he was with a young man. Their heads were close together in deep conversation, and they were holding hands. Stupidly it had never occurred to me that Matt might find a male partner or to wonder how I would feel if he did.

It was the following morning that I picked up an envelope from the doormat, addressed to me in familiar writing.

November 2007

1

"*Nikki, my darling,*" my father began. "*I want you to know I am much better. It is three years since I had my last alcoholic drink. You may remember that two years ago I sent you a small amount of money, and that was to celebrate my first year of sobriety. Mostly I give any spare money to the charity which helps to support us, but it felt appropriate to send a little to those that suffered at my hands. I sent your mother flowers.*"

I had brought the letter up to my room and was sitting on the edge of my bed. I put the letter down and stared at the pattern on the carpet, remembering the flowers and thinking they were from some new admirer. I picked up the letter again. Dad continued *I'm aware of how much I hurt your mother, perhaps less aware of the damage to you and your sense of security. You were a little girl then and now you are a young adult, and I have missed all those years.*

Through a contact, I know about the Grampies and your change of circumstances and, of course, these are also down to my behaviour. It is a relief that your mother has made new friends though probably doubtful that she would ever allow me back into her life, and it is probably better if she does not know about this letter. But you? Would you consider it?

It's far too big a question for you to answer yet, but I hope you will think about it. Perhaps we could begin by exchanging letters like old friends who have not met for some years. What do you think? Your loving Dad.

It wasn't just a big question, it was mega-huge. I read the letter through more times, each time coming to a different conclusion. Should I tell Mother about it? Clearly Dad wanted this kept between him and me, recognising that I was now old enough to make my own decisions. Did I want to keep in touch with him? Of course I did. Did I want to do it in this secret fashion? No, but see answer to question one. And what did he mean by 'through a contact'?

It needed talking through with someone. Matt would be the best person.

But Matt had a new friend. Did same-sex partners have the similar feelings of possession where a heterosexual friend was concerned? I hadn't a clue.

I grabbed my mobile and punched in Rachel's number. "I need to see you," I said, and before she could make any excuse, added, "It's urgent."

We met an hour later at our favourite coffee shop in the market place. Rachel was already there and said, "Adrian will join us in ten minutes," adding, before I could protest, "We'd already arranged it and there's no way I could get hold of him to change it."

OK, so I was being unreasonable. I asked, "Do you think Adrian knows any gay guys?"

Rachel laughed. "You do come out with the oddest questions. Is this something to do with Matt?"

"Why should it be anything to do with Matt?"

She laughed again. "Dearest Nikki. I think you're the only person I know who could go out with Matt for quite some time and not suss out he's gay."

It sounded like criticism and I felt piqued. "I had sussed it out. But there are other things in life than sex," I said, and then had to laugh too as it had came out so primly.

Rachel leaned over and gave me a hug. "I wasn't laughing *at* you Nik, but with you. But you do have this way of being quite unaware at times of what is going on around you."

"Well." I said. "You may remember about the time you and Adrian were getting mutually obsessed, I was getting down to some **really** serious study. *And* it paid off. Is still paying off."

"You're right. It has and is. And since you and Matt have started combining your study programmes, it's been great. Before that you were sometimes completely lost in your own little bubble."

"You're exaggerating."

"Who's exaggerating about what?" Adrian asked, sliding in to the seat next to Rach.

"Your lovely wife-to-be," I said grumpily. "Says I used to live in a bubble."

"Well, how would you describe answering the phone with *uh-huh* and switching off again."

"I never did that!"

Rachel put in, "Well, sometimes it was more than *uh-huh.* Sometimes it was *hi, nice to hear you. Busy at the moment.* But the effect was the same."

Then I remembered why I wanted to see Rach. "Anyway, what I wanted to talk to you about is Matt being gay."

"We all know that. So?"

"Well, I saw him in a pub earlier. He was with another boy."

"So?"

"They looked quite – quite friendly together. And *please* don't 'So?' again."

There was a silence that went on for rather a long time. Adrian was stirring his coffee, looking down at it. Rach was staring at me, her mouth open.

"What?" I asked.

"You don't mean," Rach said slowly, "that you begrudge him another friendship?"

Put like that it sounded awful. I said defensively, "Well, this is different isn't it? I mean there's something I want to discuss with Matt, and I don't know if this new guy will change things."

I had to admit it still sounded awful.

"I knew you were a bit self-centred," Rach said. "But not that you could be so *mee-e-an.*" She drew the word out so that it really did sound mean.

"Steady on, Rach," Adrian said. "We don't know what it is that Nik wanted to discuss."

"It was about my Dad," I said and burst into tears.

Rach was up and round the table, her hands gripping my shoulders. "Oh Nikki, what's happened?"

I said tartly, "No, there hasn't been any tragedy. In fact, he sounds as if he's much better."

She drew back looking bewildered. "So what's the problem?"

"He wants us to write letters, get to know each other again." I could feel the shake in my voice.

"And?"

"And he doesn't want Mother to know."

Adrian said, "Ah, that would make things tricky for you."

I blew my nose and looked at him gratefully. "I don't know what to do."

Rach sat back on her side of the table, reached across and took my hands in hers. "Grown-ups can be very insensitive at times. You must write and tell him you want to keep in touch, but there's no way you are keeping this from your mother."

Seventeen going on thirty had just become nearly-eighteen going on forty.

"Do you realise, Adrian?" I asked, "that you are marrying a middle aged woman?"

He smiled at Rach affectionately, "I think I can live with that. But you know, you still haven't explained what this has to do with Matt being gay."

"Nothing, except I wanted to talk to him about it, and wasn't sure how OK that would be if he's found a new friend."

"How about asking him?"

2

That evening I sat at the table in my room and started: *Hello Dad, I was amazed to get your letter,* then I stared at the nearly blank sheet for a long time before continuing *and very pleased to hear you are better. Thank you very much for the money you sent me two years ago. I didn't know how to thank you then. As you know I did all right with my GCSEs. Now I'm in the second year of A levels and taking four subjects...*

I stopped again and read through what I'd written. It was like writing to a stranger. And, of course, that's what he was. The fact was that I didn't know how to write to my father.

I crumpled the piece of paper and started again: *Hello Dad – I was amazed to get your letter, but I'm finding it difficult to reply. The first thing I must say is that I can't keep this contact a secret from Mother. She's had a hard time, so it wouldn't be fair. Anyway I'm awful at keeping secrets and she would be sure to find out. If you can agree to this I would love to write to you and get to know you again.*

He answered by return of post. *What a wise young woman you have become, Tuppence* he wrote. I smiled at his use of that childhood name. *It was stupid of me to suggest you didn't tell your mother as though I haven't brought enough deception into her life.*

*Just tell me the basics of your life and I will tell you mine. I can't remember much detail of my drinking life, though I am aware that I must never forget it if I want to keep the new life I have. One of my most vivid memories is of your appalled little face when I barged into your party. What happened to that nice boy, Peter? After your mother threw me out (and I **don't** blame her for that), I lived in a squat*

105

for a long time. There were five of us, and we got jobs when we ran out of booze. We moved round the country quite a bit, finally ending up here in Yorkshire. Then a long, long time later, I got knocked down by a car (my fault) and ended up in hospital. In the day room, I met this guy who asked me if I wanted to go on living like that, because he had found a way out. He told me about this group and after a lot of ups and downs I started going, and found a new life.

I have a small flat over a newsagents and work delivering the papers and doing odd jobs. It's enough to manage on. Most of my friends are ex-drunks. Basically we're quite a nice lot once we've kicked the habit.

Perhaps that will do as an opener. Can't wait to read yours. My love – Dad.

I was lying on my bed that afternoon, looking at the ceiling and thinking of my reply to Dad, when Mother came in and said, "Waste paper baskets," meaning that she had come to collect mine for emptying. She stood with it in her hand, looking at me lying on the bed.

"I don't suppose there's something you have to tell me," she said.

Then I saw it, sticking out of the top of the wpb – the envelope in which Dad's letter had arrived, addressed in his unmistakeable hand. *How could I be so stupid?*

"I was going to tell you," I said. "Honestly."

Mother put the wpb down and sat on the edge of the bed. "I believe you. How about now being a good time?"

So I told her about both letters and how Dad had agreed I should not keep our correspondence from her. She nodded and said, "That's good. There's only one thing: I really, really don't want to know what he says."

How odd can parents be? And why was it that, because she had said that, I really, really wanted to tell her how well Dad was doing.

"Nor," Mother went on, "do I want plans for surreptitious visits. Though if you want to go and see your Dad wherever-he-is, that's fine." Then she picked up the wpb and went out.

So there I was, lying on my bed, left to make my own mega decisions and to ponder on Mother's uncompromising stance. Of course, she had been hurt more than I could possibly imagine, and had to keep up a brave face so we had as normal a family life as possible. I remembered how embarrassing it was that everyone – absolutely everyone knew about Dad's drinking, and most of the time I had been able to escape that in the bubble of my school world. Mother had probably protected me countless times from knowledge of the consequences of his drinking. And she had had no one to share it with.

I thought of Baz and how devastated I had felt when I found he was cheating on me – and he was only a boyfriend. It was impossible to imagine what it would be like if someone you loved and planned to spend the rest of your life with, gradually changed into someone quite different.

I was still mulling it over when the phone rang. Mother got to it before I did and yelled up the stairs. "For you Nikki. Matt."

I rolled off the bed and picked up the cordless extension. As Mother hadn't put the receiver back, I could hear her clattering in the kitchen. "Hi Matt. Good trip?"

"Yeah. Nikki I need to see you." *Need?*

"Any time."

We arranged to meet at our favourite bar near the canal, and I put a cold flannel over my face to get rid of all that soul-searching before heading into town. And I did not get around to writing to Dad that day.

3

I found Matt sitting in the darkest corner away from the bar, as though he was trying to avoid being seen. He glanced up and gave a small smile of acknowledgment as I sat down beside him. He took a sip of his beer.

There was a longish silence before he said, "Something to tell you."

The silence resumed for what seemed an age. "Matt," I said, "you're beginning to worry me."

"Yeah, sorry. It's that you know I was wondering whether I was gay?"

"Mmm."

"Well, I am."

"So?" *Heavens, I was beginning to sound like Rach.*

"I've met someone. He's called Neil. And it feels like – like I've met my soul mate. We met when we were both running."

"Ah, all that manly sweat…" I didn't mean to mutter aloud.

Matt stopped and looked sad. "Don't laugh at me Nik."

"Sorry." I really felt contrite. "Truth is I suppose I'm a bit jealous. Not of the manly sweat, but of the soul mate thing. I thought we were soul mates in a different way."

He nodded. "That's it. In a different way. You've kept me sane for months, Nikki. And I don't want to stop seeing you, but it might be a bit more difficult....."

I made a mega effort not to react too quickly and finally said, "Yes, I imagine if I had a boyfriend, he wouldn't be too keen on me seeing you." I created a grin. "By the way you look quite different with your hair sort of normal."

"Yeah, what do you think? Neil hates that woolly stuff."

"I did too." I did manage to stop myself from adding *perhaps I should have been a gay boy too.* Because it wasn't funny. It just felt lonely.

"Of course," Matt said, "I told him all about you." *Well, that was something.* "And he'd like to meet. But, like me it's taken him a very long time to get here, and I don't want to make things more difficult."

"Nor do I." Instinctively I put a hand over one of his big paws. "By the way is Neil at college?"

"No, he's doing work experience stuff in Coventry."

"So, why don't you and I give each other a break for a month or so, then arrange to meet up?"

He put a second big paw over my hand. "Nik, you're a star. That would be perfect. Only one thing. If you have some problem you want to chew over, you'll get in touch before. Promise?"

I knew I wouldn't, but it was nice that he wanted me to. So I told him about the new contact with Dad, making it sound like a really Good Thing that would keep me happily occupied in the coming weeks, and he looked pleased for me, and somehow that made it all seem easier.

For a while.

Mother read my mood as soon as I came through the door. She put the kettle on and I watched her make tea while I told her more or less what had happened.

"It's good for Matt, but it will be hard for you," she said. It helped that I didn't have to explain that.

Over a second cup of tea, Mother went on that she knew I wouldn't want to hear this, but I had been neglecting my studies a bit and there were only about six months left to A levels. She said, "That doesn't mean I want you to repeat that manic episode of study you went through at one stage when your light was on half the night, but there's probably a case for making a study plan and working out on which subjects you need to concentrate." *Though clearly I must be much more careful concealing the light.*

We had a cosy evening, Mother and I, watching a documentary on Big Cats followed by a cup of hot chocolate. Then I went to bed, but not before pulling a bottle of wine out of my wardrobe, then putting it back. It wasn't a very good night.

The next couple of weeks weren't much fun. I did work out a quite detailed study programme, concentrating on certain aspects of English Lit and Maths about which I felt far from confident. After Mother's comment about noticing my light had been on half the night at one time, I also had to work out a plan for not causing her unnecessary concern. Gone were the days when the Grampies left me to my own devices. Mother had lived alongside deception too long herself to be easily fooled. But in the end, it wasn't so difficult. While I had been living with the Grampies, she had become accustomed to her own kind of freedom, and really liked to spend odd nights away, either with Sally or others in her group of friends. We settled on a routine where she was away mid-week for a couple of nights and from time to time for the week-end.

Then she said to me, "Sweetheart, I worry about the fact you're not having any fun these days. Why don't you go out with the old gang as you used to?"

So I did. I just turned up at the club where I knew they still met. There was a chorus of *"Hey, look who's here!"*, and someone called Geoff got me a gin without being asked.

"We've missed you Nik," several people said, and sounded as though they meant it.

I'd forgotten what fun it was to talk nonsense and make extravagant plans and act more sophisticated than you felt. Geoff drove me home, and I asked him to drop me at the top of the road so I could compose myself. He made a half-hearted pass at me, but I think read the situation accurately. I had to throw up in a garden several doors from us, but it helped, and I was reasonably OK by the time I let myself in.

"Have a good time, Love?" came Mother's sleepy voice from her room. "Want a hot drink?"

"It was great," I said. "And no thanks. Just now, all I want to do is sle-e-e-e-p"

"Sleep tight," she mumbled, without knowing how apt that was.

December 2007 – March 2008

1

"You've got a hangover," Mother stated rather than suggested next morning over breakfast.

"Yes, sorry." I don't think I had ever felt so dreadful, and my reflection in the mirror wasn't pretty.

Mother poured herself another cup of coffee. "I suppose it's not that surprising, given all that's happened in the last few days. Just as long as you don't get used to it."

I was aghast. "I *couldn't!* I never ever want to feel like this again." And I meant it.

We were approaching Christmas. I made a huge effort to get the control back in my hands, and somewhere from the past came the memory of someone saying, "It's the first drink that does it."

It had seemed absurd at the time, and in a way still did but I could see if there wasn't a first drink there couldn't be a second, third or tenth. There were three unopened bottles of wine left in my wardrobe and they were looking for prizes to give away at the forthcoming Church Christmas Bazaar. At the first opportunity, I smuggled them out of the house and took them down to the Church. Tony, the vicar, was in the vestry.

"That's very generous of you , Nicole," he said, not quite able to hide his surprise for I was not known for my church-going. "That will provide three very acceptable prizes."

"That's all right Tony," I said, feeling rather pleased with myself, though the warm glow had worn off by the time I was struggling with sample A-level history papers that evening and trying to remember why Winston Churchill had lost the first election following World War Two. It was momentarily a shock when I went to the wardrobe and found the cupboard bare.

I headed downstairs to the kitchen calling out, "Feel like a hot chocolate Ma?"

"No thanks, darling. And *don't* call me Ma."

The hot chocolate did the trick and I became quite addicted to it in the coming days. It didn't quite come up with all the answers to my questions, but it did direct me towards the right sources for the information. In fact, as far as Churchill was concerned, I thought the

British public were an ungrateful lot. Though, as Mother pointed out when I said so, I wasn't alive at the time and didn't know what life was like without social welfare.

It made me feel good that I could work, and work well, without the prop I had come to rely on. Life was busy in other ways, too, as we had decided to have a proper Christmas celebration, spending Christmas Eve afternoon with the Grampies at Grump's home, and then inviting Sally and Tom over for Christmas Day itself. Rachel and Adrian had gone on a walking trip, so they would have to wait until the New Year.

Mother's idea of celebrating Christmas properly requires mega organisation. We still put live candles on our tree, which means it has to be trimmed accordingly so the candles are all safe. Mother gets really mad if we go to one of those posh outlets for trees where they have already trimmed the tree for you, so we usually go to a nursery and buy a bushy one that we can trim ourselves. Each tree is studied from every possible angle before the decision is made. All the trimmed bits are strewn at the foot of the tree and scattered amongst them are all our favourite souvenirs of trips away or family mementoes. The process of decorating it has always been an enjoyable ritual. Mother would start off with a theme in her head and we'd sift through our treasures picking out items to fit in with it, but before long we 'couldn't possibly leave this or that' out so it usually ended up as an intriguing hotch-potch.

Christmas Day at Grump's home was difficult, mainly because a lot of the residents clearly did not know who they were or anyone else. Then Gramp pointed out that at least they were happy, and if they could be then why couldn't we be happy for them? She had this way of turning things round so that things never seemed quite so bad. I guessed I hadn't yet had enough practice at doing this, but I felt quite pleased when Grump smiled at me, and said, "You used to come and stay with us, didn't you?"

"That's right Grump."

He thought for a bit and widened his smile. "Would you come and stay with me here? You make me happy", and just then it felt like the nicest thing anyone had ever said to me.

I said, "That's an interesting idea, Grump. Tell you what, I'll finish my exams and then we'll talk about it again."

His smile widened even more and I glanced across at Gramp, and she nodded, and I knew I had got it right this time.

112

In spite of that, and a really nice afternoon listening to carols and the distribution of presents from under the tree (though this one had electric lights of course), I felt sad when we got home. Mother wanted to listen to a Midnight Service on television, so I went upstairs and wrote to Dad, telling him about the day and how I felt. And the sadness gradually lifted.

2

On Christmas morning, Mother and I went to church. That's one of the few days of the year I do church, the others being Remembrance Sunday, the nearest Sunday to the day Dad left (I haven't told him that yet), and the nearest Sunday to my birthday (I don't know why).

Before we went, we got all the veg ready and put the turkey in a slow oven. Sally and Tom were picking us up after church and we were going to have a drink at a canal-side pub. I ordered an apple juice and Tom raised an eyebrow at me (he really can do that).

"On the wagon?" he asked.

"She overdid it recently, and learned her lesson," Mother chipped in. "Or I hope she did."

"I remember them well," Tom murmured, "those learning of lessons."

Otherwise they were full of news of their latest combined project. Sally had gone on a creative writing course and found she had a talent for kids' stuff, especially semi-fantasy stories, and Tom had finally decided to scale down his ambitions to be the next Rembrandt, and discovered a skill for illustrations of a caricature kind. They'd gone into Print on Demand and produced the first two of a series devoted to the adventures of an unlikely duo: an elderly cat and a young mouse.

By the time we got home, the smells from the turkey were irresistible. We settled Sally and Tom in the conservatory with a drink to admire the unlit tree while we did the necessary with the veg. It was a great meal and we took a long time happily, all agreeing to keep the Christmas pudding for later. By then the late December dusk was falling and we allowed our guests to clear the debris of lunch and wash up while we made final adjustments to the tree and lit the candles.

It looked so beautiful that even Tom forgot to make his usual remarks about forewarning the Fire Brigade. Mother put on some quiet music and we all sat watching the candles in silence. I felt quite tearful for a bit, then traced it to a nostalgic wish that Dad could have

113

been with us not as his disruptive old self but as he had become. And then there was Matt and wondering how he was getting on with … with that Neil. The candles had already been lit once, so it didn't take so long for them to burn low.

"That one will be the last one to go," Tom said pointing to a candle on one of the lowest branches, and when he was proved right demanded to know what his prize would be.

"No prizes for those who already know the secret of success," I said firmly. "It doesn't take rocket science to know that one of the lower candles will last longer than the ones above being quietly toasted from below."

Once the candles were out, we got out the scrabble board and wrangled happily over whether certain words did or did not exist. Only one incident spoiled an otherwise perfect day. Mother and Tom were arguing over whether 'alkie' was or was not an acceptable word, when the phone rang.

When I answered it I was so surprised that I blurted out "***Dad!***" before I could stop myself.

"Happy Christmas, Tuppence. It's such a long time since I said that, or are you too grown up for that name now?"

"No, it's OK when you say it."

"Good." I could hear the smile in his voice. "What are you doing?"

"We're playing Scrabble with some friends of Mother's." I glanced across at her and she shook her head gently. I put on a pleading look, but she went on shaking her head. The silence went on for rather too long before Dad said, "Well, I'm having a good time with some mates here, and in case you're wondering, I'm as sober as a judge."

"That's good to hear." I hated to put the phone down on him. "Hey, give me your number and I'll call you some time in the New Year."

He gave it to me and said, his voice slightly shaky, "I would really love that. Love to your Mum. 'Bye."

I could feel the tears pricking and said, "Need the loo," and disappeared long enough to pull myself together. As I got back I heard Sally ask, "You really can't talk to him, Anne?" and Mother's reply "Thin end of wedges 'n all that."

Tom said, "You can use a wedge to prop a door ajar. You don't have to push it wide open," and Mother said, "Well, you

114

wouldn't know what it's like to be on the receiving end." And no one could argue with that.

Apart from that incident, it was a good Christmas. Matt rang on Boxing Day and we swapped news. He'd gone to Neil's family for Christmas Day. Apparently he, Neil, had come out with them some time back and they were OK with it, but not keen on the rather wild social life he had been leading, so as a friend Matt was regarded as a great new asset. I didn't ask whether Matt thought his parents would have the same reaction to Neil. After all it was none of my business and I was too busy being disappointed that he didn't suggest we should meet up.

The week after Christmas felt like an anticlimax, so it seemed a good idea to start planning stuff for the New Year. The first good thing that happened was that Rach and Adrian returned from their walking holiday and invited me round for New Year's Eve. It was a great relief as I'd already had an offer from Tracey to join the gang on their usual celebration and I could imagine what that meant.

We had a really lovely evening. Adrian brought out maps and they took it in turns to interrupt each other recounting the events. Long distance walking isn't my thing, but it was great to hear them. It wasn't just that their account of cold-weather camping was hilarious, but they gave out such an impression of togetherness, including the way they managed their disagreements on quite a lot of things.

"And by the way," Rachel said at one point, "we've done it. And we're not going into any details."

For a moment Adrian looked puzzled then said, slightly shocked, "*Really*, Rach."

I said, "It's a bit of a relief actually. I was beginning to think you must both be frigid!"

Later I told them about Matt and Neil, and they agreed it was bound to change our easygoing relationship, though ever-optimistic Rachel suggested, "Perhaps when you meet this Neil you'll hit it off so well that you'll have two mates instead of one." No harm in hoping.

Before I left we had a quick forward look at 2008. Adrian still had a year to do in Edinburgh for this Ph.D. If she were accepted, Rachel was aiming to join him in Edinburgh for the Librarianship degree she was planning after A levels.

"And you?" they asked.

"I'm sticking to media studies, probably with a leaning towards e-zines. But I wasn't actually thinking so much of careers."

"What then?"

It was difficult to explain. Some time back I had turned away from a fun-orientated life style in exchange for the quieter companionship of Matt combined with studying. Somehow I wanted to keep on that path albeit without him. I said, "I was thinking of taking a course at the leisure centre."

"The one where Matt goes?" Perhaps Rach knew me better than I knew myself.

"If he still does. Anyway I'm not thinking of anything so athletic. I was wondering about yoga."

"I think some yogis might question your assessment of their athleticism," Adrian commented. "But I think I know what you mean."

Stifling giggles Rachel said, "Do you remember when we had a school visit from that Swami-someone who talked about getting in touch with our inner selves?"

After a few moments I thought I did remember. She had beamed calm over the whole class, rather like some sci-fi contraption in *Doctor Who.* "You thought she was funny?"

Rach stopped giggling and looked surprise. "No I didn't think she was funny any more than I thought you were serious. But why not? One's inner self is a pretty mysterious being."

3

They clearly were not going to take me seriously, so I changed the subject. Then I checked on-line for details of the courses and on enrolment day duly lined up to book myself for eight-sessions that said they focussed on pranayama, which means breathing. Well, most of us think we know how to breathe, but apparently we don't. To prepare myself, I went into our main book shop and had a look at the books listed under *Philosophy and Spirituality.* There were several on breathing, so I bought a couple which had lots of diagrams.

My first instinct was to ring Matt and suggest he came over to try some of the exercises out, but of course that was a no-no under our present agreement. I turned my attention to a section called The Whole Breath. Well, you wouldn't want a less than whole breath, would you? I did not attempt the Lotus or even Semi Lotus position, but found a straight-backed chair and followed instructions: feet slightly apart and flat on the floor, spine upright but not leaning against the chair back, neck upright to form a continuous line with the spine, and hands resting on thighs.

Take a couple of easy breaths, the book suggested; so I did. *Now allow your stomach to swell as you breathe in. As the breath rises, expand the rib cage. As it continues to rise, let the breath fill the upper lung as your chest rises.* By the time I had reached that stage, I had run out of air and needed to take a gulping breath. After several more attempts it began to develop as a continuous movement instead of a series of jerks. I thought, *with his heavier frame Matt might find it quite difficult. And why had Rachel and Adrian thought the idea of meditation so funny? What would Mother think?*

These intruding thoughts did not help. I found myself running out of breath again. After a while I picked up the book again. Somewhere it said *you may find that thoughts entering your mind distract you from your meditation, like a monkey chattering in a tree.* Yes, just like that. *Bring your mind back to your breathing and if thoughts intrude, allow them to pass through your mind and out again, all the time returning your focus on your breathing.* Dammit, there was more to this breathing business than met the eye.

I practised a few times over the next few days and in the second week in January went to my first class. Most of the other members of the class were around Mother's age and seemed to know each other. One of them explained that several of them had done Sam's beginner's class the previous year and thought she was very good. So Sam was a woman. It turned out that she was Mother's age too: not particularly slim, but very upright and serene in her movements. Unlike Mother she didn't tint her hair, and wore her grey-brown mix in a ponytail.

Sam started off by getting us to sit in the position that "was right for each of us". Some of the others could produce what seemed to me a pretty impressive lotus position, but Sam had other ideas and suggested that one or other of them sat on one or two blocks in order to get their knees on the ground. My knees stuck resolutely up in the air. Sam lowered herself into a squat beside me.

"Don't worry," she said. "It's not essential. In any case I can give you some poses to practise that will help with the lotus position. In the meantime just sit back on your heels like this." She gave a demonstration, adding, "Remember to keep your spine straight and your neck in line with your spine."

There were a dozen of us and while Sam went round the rest of us, I sat very straight and still trying to remember the instructions for The Whole Breath. Then Sam's quiet voice interrupted with "Now think carefully round your body. Are you aware of any pockets of tension?"

I thought carefully round my body and found, in my efforts to be straight and still, much of it was rigid with tension. There was the audible sound of twelve people letting go of tension.

The hour sped by. I could hardly believe it when Sam said, "Now I want you to spend the last few minutes sitting on your mats, ease any tensions, and then concentrate on the breathing exercise we have just done."

We shuffled ourselves into position and began to concentrate. In fact we had not done The Whole Breath, but something called Nadi Shodhana, whereby you breathed in through one nostril and out through the other, counting mentally for each inhalation and exhalation. The idea was gradually to increase the length of each.

"And remember this is not a competition," came Sam's voice, just as I was wondering how my performance was comparing with anyone else's.

While everyone was collecting up their things, she showed me a couple of poses to practice that would help me with the Lotus position, adding, "While you are practising, do remember to breathe."

Gradually, my weekly class and almost daily practice became part of the routine of the first term of 2008, along with quite frequent letters to and from Dad. From time to time Matt and I emailed each other, and a couple of times he rang. I told him about *pranayama* and he was quite impressed. "I think Neil has been into that sort of thing," he said.

"How's it going?" I asked.

I thought there was a slight hesitation. "Wonderful. I miss you though," but he didn't suggest we meet.

I started going out with a boy called Robert, a Uni student who was the brother of one of my mates and doing work experience in Oxford. He was rather serious, but not too serious to get drunk one Saturday evening when we were at a party. That was the night I lost my virginity in a spectacularly unmemorable way. Apart from the build up, the final bit was painful, messy and a big anticlimax. After I'd stopped regretting it had happened, I wondered what on earth all

118

the fuss was about. Presumably Robert wasn't impressed either as the next I heard he had returned to Uni and that was the last of him.

When eventually I told Rachel, her first comment was that she assumed we had taken precautions which had not occurred to us under the circumstances. There followed an anxious ten days before my period started right on cue, but relief was tempered by a deep-down gutted feeling that such a major event had proved so unmemorable. I knew it wouldn't have happened if I'd been sober. I decided to take back control of my life.

Around a week later, Mother commented "You're looking great Sweetheart. That yoga seems to suit you."

"Yeah. And I decided to put all that Matt stuff behind me and get on with the rest of my life." I'd always thought that was a meaningless phrase but somehow it fitted with where I was at. I'd got a grip on my studies programme, too, especially the whole parallel universe thing.

Winter edged its way into spring. The clocks went forward and the days got longer. Sally and Tom invited Mother and me to join them on an Easter cruise, but I knew I couldn't take the time off with the A levels looming ever closer. Mother didn't need too much persuasion to agree to go with them without me. After all, she had seen how sensible I had become. It felt a bit odd, after seeing her off, to return to an empty house.

It was during those days of being on my own that I came to a decision. I had come to realise that my whole parallel universe project was developing into something much bigger and deeper than I had initially thought. Trawling the Internet I had come across a number of international contests based on original research, the prize for which was acceptance at this or that university. By now I must have enough material for my A level paper, but supposing I carried on with the research and had a go at one of those contests. I wouldn't tell anyone, I'd just do it. After all I didn't have to accept the prize.

The decision needed celebrating, but as I'd not replenished my own supplies it meant raiding Mother's. Never mind, there was plenty of time to replace it.

And then Matt texted me to say that it was high time I met Neil.

4

They were waiting for me in our favourite pub, standing at the bar. The last time I had seen Neil he had been sitting and now I saw he was tall and lean, and resting an elbow on Matt's shoulder. I had decided, of course, to be completely undemonstrative, so greeted him with "Hi Matt, how's life?" And he leaned forward and gave me a peck on the cheek and said, "Great, so much better having someone to share it with," which hurt because he could have shared it with me. Then he added, "And this is Neil."

I turned my full attention to Neil and smiled at him. It seemed absurdly formal to hold out my hand, but he did, so I took it and returned its firm grasp. He said, "Matt's told me all about you," in a drawl that had a hint of superciliousness in it.

"Well, this is the first chance I've had to hear all about you," I said and then wondered if that carried a note of criticism.

I saw they had a bottle of white wine and that Matt was pouring out a glass for me so said quickly, "No thanks, Matt. I'll have an apple juice."

"Oh, so he didn't tell me all about you" Neil murmured, "At least not that you were teetotal." He sounded amused.

"I am not teetotal," I said. "I just like to stay in control." And that seemed to amuse him even more. Oh dear, I was beginning not to like him terribly. Or perhaps nearer the truth was that I didn't know how to react naturally to someone who was in no way a rival, but who seemed to regard me as one.

Matt was quite oblivious of any tension, real or imagined. "Loo," he said getting up. "You two decide where we can all go next."

I looked at Neil cautiously. He had blue eyes and I tried hard not to see their expression as calculating. "I'm so glad Matt's found … found someone," I said, wishing it didn't sound even faintly patronising or as though Matt had recovered something that he had lost. "He said you're into running, too."

"Right, though old Matt is more dedicated than I am. I suspect he's more dedicated to most things than me." Neil watched me. I thought: *including friendship? Don't you dare let him down,* and could imagine Neil reading my thoughts. And I felt a wash of sadness at the thought that I was about to lose the least complicated relationship I had ever had.

Perhaps it was that regret that made me say, "Anyway I hope we can remain friends. He's always been a great prop in my wobblier moments." *Dammit couldn't I say anything without it being open to misinterpretation.*

Neil leaned forward to put a companionable hand on my shoulder. "Of course we can all remain friends. I look forward to it, and sharing all our wobblier moments together. And don't worry about Matt. He's the best partner I've had in a long while, and I don't intend to lose him." He waited while the implication sank in, then added, "But now I'm sure you're ready for another apple juice."

He had moved to a less crowded part of the bar to order it when Matt came back. "You two getting on all right?" he said anxiously. "Have you decided where to go for lunch?"

"Fine," I lied, because I didn't think I could do anything else. "But I really am dog tired. Neil is getting me another apple juice, but do you mind if I slip off – tell him I'm sorry, Matt."

I noticed that he did not try to stop me.

March-July 2008

1

When I got back to our empty flat, it had a silent, waiting feel about it. Up in my room, my desk was strewn with papers: my latest notes on *Alice in Wonderland* and a book on theories on time with a piece of paper marking the next chapter I needed to study.

"I don't think you're being very fair, God," I said into the empty room. If there were an answer, I didn't hear it. "You can't blame me if I have a glass to cheer myself up."

But the cupboard was still bare. I hadn't re-stocked since that unprecedented gift to the vicar at Christmas. I went down to the living room to check on Mother's stocks. No wine, but an unopened bottle of whiskey and a half full bottle of gin. I settled for gin and took the bottle back to my room. I'd forgotten how awful neat gin tasted and hurried back to the living room to retrieve a small tonic.

As I sat at my desk my attention was caught by the last sentence in my notes. I had been working on my original theme that children's books that extended into the adult reading world covered a much, much wider field than the area of Lewis Caroll v Philip Pullman where I had begun. My last note urged me to investigate medieval tales such as *The Golden Legend.*

I opened the tonic bottle, topped up my smallish glass, sipped it, then typed 'The Golden Legend' into Google's search panel and came up with over sixteen million entries. I took another sip and made a start. After checking a dozen or so entries it was clear that the great majority of them were exclusively concerned with the lives of saints and dated from the 13th century. Except of course, it wasn't as simple as that.

Apparently it was a collection of manuscripts dealing with saints' lives by a guy called Jacobus de Voragine and it became a medieval best seller. My first thought was that they must have been a bit short of things to read in those days, until I remembered that probably not a lot of them could read. For the purposes of my arguments it was complicated by the fact that they were based on hundreds of different manuscripts, mostly in Latin but also in medieval French and English. Of course this helped to make my point of how things can get distorted in translation, but trying to extract fact from fiction looked like a lifetime's work.

I leaned back, glanced at my watch and saw that over an hour had passed and I hadn't given another thought to Matt or Neil, or come to that the bottle of gin. I remedied the latter immediately, but my mind was still on those saints and how their lives had dominated the literature of the time. *Indeed, the Harry Potter of medieval times*, I thought, and giggled.

The phone rang. "What are you doing, Tuppence?" asked Dad's voice.

Better not mention the gin, for a start. "Would you believe it if I said I'm looking into a medieval account of the lives of saints?"

A pause. "Well, if that's what takes your fancy! A friend is driving your way on Easter Sunday and can give me a lift. Could I lure you away from the Saints and take you out to lunch? I gather your mother is away." *How did he know that?* "I was thinking of The Gourmet, if it still exists."

"It still exists."

"Good. How about I meet you there at 12.30?"

"Fine."

"I can't wait."

I put the phone down and sat staring at my computer screen. Easter Sunday was only four days away. I gazed at a section headed 'Fanciful Etymologies' which explained how Jacobus had worked out explanations for saints' names. The phone rang again.

Matt said in a gabble "Neil and I were thinking it was a shame we never had that lunch. How are you fixed for Easter Sunday? It was Neil's idea." *Bully for Neil.*

"Do thank him," I said. "But I'm having lunch with Dad."

"But that's great, Nik. Let's make it another time. Soon."

Suddenly everyone wanted to see me. Somehow 'Fanciful Etymologies' didn't seem so interesting any more. Nor did the gin bottle. Checking it, I thought no one was likely to notice the level was slightly lower. I took it back to the living room, watched the Ten O'clock News, then went to bed.

Over the next days, I divided my time between the lives of the Saints and trying to decide what to wear for my lunch with Dad. It felt rather like going out on a first date. In the end I settled for my latest denim suit and an emerald scarf of the kind that winds round and round.

I arrived at The Gourmet just a few minutes late intentionally, my stomach churning with anxiety just as if I were on a first date. At first I did not recognise him when I peered through the window. And then I did. He was looking at a menu with frequent anxious glances at the door. His hair was quite white and he had lost weight. Almost overwhelmed by a surge of affection, I pushed the door open. He stood up as soon as he saw me, and he was in a denim suit similar to mine. There was a brief mutual appraisal, then we both burst out laughing.

Several heads turned to watch as I hurried through the tables and we clasped each other in a bear hug worthy of Matt's. "They probably think I'm your sugar daddy," Dad whispered in my ear.

"I prefer you as a Dad," I said. And any possibility of awkwardness was shattered.

"What would you like to drink?" he asked, as we sat down, arms still interlinked.

"Same as you will do."

He grinned. "You won't catch me that way. I'm almost an old hand at this teetotal lark. It's tropical juice by the way."

We couldn't stop talking, though I did most of it to begin with because he wanted to know "everything" – my state of health, studies, yoga, .and finally love life. As we got to that, I wrinkled my nose. "Mm. I don't seem to be very good at men."

"I thought I was brilliant at women when I found your mother. And look what a pig's ear I made of that. How is she by the way? I was so glad she had gone on that cruise."

"Yeah, and how did you know about that?"

"Doesn't matter. Once I started getting better I was desperate for news of you both, and there are ways round everything if you want things badly enough."

He clearly was not going to enlarge any more on that so I said, "Now, you have to tell me about you."

2

It was a long and sorry tale whose details were blurred by time and alcohol. "The weeks immediately after your mother threw me out are very hazy. I had a few fellow alkie friends and we slept rough around the countryside – I think it was summer at the time. Then as the days shortened, one of them – Jacko I think it was – remembered an uncle with a farm in Yorkshire, so we made our way up there. Can't say the welcome was very warm, but he let us kip in the barn and gave us a hearty meal a day in exchange for some labour. We got money somehow for booze but less than we were used to and what with that and working in the open air, our health did improve a bit. Then we had a row over something stupid and split up, and the others went off while I stayed with Jacko."

I sat watching his every expression as he spoke, still not quite able to believe that these things happened to this man with the neat haircut and pleasant expression. Once I interrupted with "But why couldn't you just stop?"

He paused and took one of my hands in both of his. "Tuppence, if I could answer that I could save the sanity of millions of people and the lives of many hundreds of thousands. They call it a sickness of mind, body and soul. Still not quite sure about the soul bit, but I'll go along with it while life stays as good as it is."

"And what if it doesn't?"

He squeezed my hand. "That's why we do it a day at a time. You can do for a day what you couldn't contemplate doing for a life time." *Yeah,* I thought, *you could apply that to other things too.*

"Okay, so what are you doing a day at a time at the moment?"

"Well, we doddered along like this, Jacko and I, for months, years. Then one day Jacko was run over. I'd been on a binge and didn't register much for a few days. Then his uncle took me by the scruff of the neck, so to speak, and marched me off to see him in hospital. I hardly recognised him: not just because his leg was held up off the bed in a sort of cradle, and he was on a drip, but because apart from that I had never seen him look so fit. He'd met this woman – another patient – who was a recovering alkie and she'd talked him into meeting other people like her in a self-help group. And in the end I joined it, too."

"Just like that?"

"No, not just like that. It was hard, bloody hard. But we went to these meetings and members of the group came to visit us and gradually it got easier. For me anyway. Jacko couldn't crack it, kept getting drunk, and eventually his uncle threw him off the farm. I nearly went with him, but everyone persuaded me it wouldn't help him and it might be the end of me. So I started working for the uncle, then a newsagent, eventually broadening my scope until I rented the little cottage I have now." He paused, looking down at his tropical juice for several moments. "And that's it, my Sweet. More or less."

"Less rather than more," I suggested. The tears had been welling as I'd listened to what was, after all, the story of my Dad. But there he was quite relaxed, looking well. I asked, "Does Mother know all this?"

"I've written to her. I don't know if she's read it."

"I'll talk to her, shall I?"

Dad shook his head. "Don't blame her, Tuppence. She had an awful time, so many ruined occasions, so much money wasted, so many promises broken. I'm sure I couldn't have put up with me for half as long as she did."

"But if she could only see you now."

Dad shrugged. "It has to be her choice. But there is no reason why you and I can't meet. Anyway tell me about this problem you have with men in your life? Or shall we order some lunch first?"

We both settled for a duck salad, and while we waited for it I tried to find as honest answers as I could to Dad's question. No one had asked me that before. My friends were all wrapped up in their own relationships. Mum had taken Matt for granted, but didn't really understand what a soul mate you can have without sex being involved. And I hadn't dared tell her about Robert. Now I told Dad.

"Oh Tuppence," he said, looking sad. After a while he asked "Had you been drinking?"

"Yes, wouldn't have had the courage otherwise. But I've decided never to have sex or alcohol again." I really meant both at the same time, but the words were already out.

That made him smile. "Amen to the latter, but I wouldn't write sex off completely yet."

We paused as the duck salad arrived. Then I told him about Matt. He nodded. "That sounds like a real relationship, and it's a shame he can't manage to have a partner and your friendship."

"Oh I think Matt could. Neil, his partner, is the problem."

"Mm. That's probably a sign of insecurity on Neil's part. We have a gay guy in our group. I can't pretend to understand how that works, but he's the nicest guy. Probably the most compassionate of the whole group. But he seems to flit from one relationship to another, though I suppose that could be a problem whether you're gay or not. But you've never told me what happened to that nice young man of yours, Peter."

"Well, he never was mine for a start. Then I thought he'd taken a fancy to a friend of mine called Jane...."

"Yes, I remember Jane. I wouldn't have thought she was at all his sort."

"Yeah, well I was away with the Grampies for a while, then cycled over and saw them together and probably jumped to the wrong conclusion. Though they were together at a school reunion."

"And it was my fault that you were at the Grampies, so I've managed to ruin your life, too." I looked across at him and noticed the twinkle in his eye. "No seriously Tuppence, I do think you may have got the wrong idea. Where is he now?"

"Doing forestry somewhere in the Midlands."

"How about a call 'for old times' sake'? Then ring me up and tell me you've done it?"

"Supposing he fobs me off?"

"Then you'll have to accept a real situation instead of an imaginary one."

"You have become wise."

"Is that boring of me?"

"Just a little bit irritating," I grinned to show I wasn't serious. "Now let's talk about something else."

"Okay, well you can start by explaining why you're into the lives of Saints. Have you got religion?"

I explained briefly about my theories regarding parallel universes and some 19th century literature, and how this had led further back in time. Dad looked thoughtful, then a bit worried. He said, "I can understand how you've developed the first part of your theory, but not its extension to the Saints. After all, a lot of what is known about their lives is based on legend."

That took me by surprise. "I didn't know you knew anything about Saints' lives, Dad."

"I don't – well, not a lot. But when my brain began clearing, I started doing a lot of reading. And in the library where I was doing rehab, there were a lot of books on spirituality, including as it applied to Christian saints."

"Mm. You don't think the legends might have the same basis?"

Dad shook his head. "Seems unlikely that those guys in the Middle Ages had found the way to nip across into parallel universes, though I'll be happy to be proved wrong. In any case, even if they had, the legends vary so much a lot of people seem to have got their facts badly wrong. No, I think it's more likely the stories got distorted by word of mouth."

I was beginning to see strong reasons for reviewing my thinking. "Okay, I'll check it all over." And then I found myself telling him about my plan to go in for one of the contests on original research. He was as pleased as anything, and we talked about that for a bit before I said, "And now you tell me what has been happening to you since you stopped drinking."

Over the rest of lunch – lemon posset to follow the duck salad, then coffee – Dad told me about the various jobs he'd taken over the past three years, and how he had found he had a penchant for woodwork, followed a course, and was now making candlesticks that he sold through local shops. He reached into a bag and produced one "for you". He knew I loved candles, and this was special, a block of wood from which he had carved several candle sticks at slightly different levels. Each had a small glass ring to fit round the candle and catch the drips.

"I love it," I said. "How are they selling?"

"Steady. It's a newish line, so I'm waiting for Christmas."

"I'll do you a web page," I said. "Or Adrian will. That's Rachel's husband to be." Suddenly there seemed several things to be looking forward to. I added, "I do love you Dad."

He coughed, choked, and I saw his eyes were damp. "That is the very best thing I've heard since I had my last drink." He gave a wobbly grin, and I grinned back. "Will you tell your mother? Not that you love me, but that we met?"

"I'll have to. I'm no good at hiding stuff," I said. "She's back the day after tomorrow."

Dad didn't say he knew that, but I sensed he did.

3

Mother rang two days later from London Airport to say she would arrive at our local bus station at 3 p.m., and I made sure I was there. They all looked well and happy, Mother, Sally, Tom - and a man I hadn't met before. I gave Mother a bit hug, then stood back to admire her tan and new hair do. She took the strange man's arm and said, "Alec this is my daughter Nicole, who insists on calling herself Nikki."

He took my hand, nice firm grip, and gave a complicit wink, "Alec Chapman. Hello Nikki. I prefer Alec to the full-blown

Alexander." *Alexander like my non-brother, I noted, and where have you come from,* which was answered almost immediately by Sally. She said, "We met on the ship – such a coincidence that Alec lives near Banbury."

It turned out that Alec's wife Marion was in Rehab and making rather hard work of it. She had been due to come on the cruise, but apparently she had a relapse, so Alec was persuaded to go on his own. In fact, he lived the opposite side of Banbury, just over the border into Warwickshire, so we saw him off in his car before piling into Sally's that had been parked in a friend's yard.

I thought Mother looked very tanned and relaxed and hoped that this didn't have too much to do with Alec. It was bad enough trying to sort out my own relationships without having to worry about hers. She sat with me in the back of the car and swivelled round to observe me.

"So how's it been in my absence? Things sorted out with Matt?"

"In a way. Neil hasn't taken to me, so end of story."

Mother said quickly, "Oh I'm sorry, love. Perhaps he'll change his mind."

But I didn't feel like being on the receiving end of pity just then, so I said jauntily, "Yes, it was a bit of a bummer, but what cheered me up no end was having lunch with Dad a couple of days ago."

"Oh," Mother said, and that was all she did say until we had unloaded at the flat, bundled ourselves in and distributed her luggage.

"I've done a casserole," I said.

"Lovely, Sweetheart." And it was over the casserole that she quizzed me about Dad.

Any idea I might have harboured that I was going to act as confidante and go-between in a happy reconciliation was soon knocked on the head. Mother listened closely to my account of the encounter, to the details of Dad's life then and now (at which she nodded several times, so she had obviously read those letters), and his suggestions concerning my own. It went on through the casserole and then the apple crumble (can't do crumble so I'd cheated and got a supermarket one). Then she rested her elbows on the table and said quietly. "Nikki, my dear, I do have an inkling of how you feel, but in the last few years I have rediscovered who I really am -   well, rather like your Dad has. I could never go back to the hurt and betrayal that was part of living with him. I'm not sure I ever can."

And I knew by her tone that nothing I said would change her mind, though I did try on a number of occasions..

Over the coming weeks, I spent a lot of time rethinking my ideas on parallel universes in literature. I wasn't convinced that Dad had got it right. Who was to know what had been discovered and then lost or forgotten several hundred years ago? Who was to know that in some parallel universe you couldn't multiply loaves and fishes or cure the sick? Or that if you wanted to do it enough, you could, especially if you were the Son of God? I wrote to Dad about these matters. Sometimes he rang me but usually he wrote back. Our discussions were inevitably inconclusive, but it was good to have someone to chew them over with. Once he asked me if I had done anything about getting in touch with Peter, so one evening after a few glasses of wine I wrote to him c/o the Forestry Course.

In the meantime, I had a proper study plan and kept to it. And I stayed off the gin, though I did occasionally indulge in a bottle of wine or two. I still went to the yoga class each week and most days managed to fit in some practice, usually concentrating on the balance and breathing exercises. About once a fortnight I met up with Rachel and Adrian. Mother had started going out quite a lot, and a couple of times when I was in town I glimpsed her with Alec. From time to time I joined Tracey and the gang, but usually got so bored with their silliness I'd have a drink to join them on the same planet, which usually led to another and another, then regretted it next day.

Still this didn't happen often and by the time A levels were upon me, I was feeling OK and focussed. The exams extended over a two-week period and Dad emailed me almost every day to wish me luck. It felt really weird when at last they were over, like any reason for getting up in the morning had gone. As a reward, Mother and Alec took me out for dinner at one of the best restaurants in the area. I took the opportunity to tell them of my plan to continue with the parallel universe project, and Alec seemed really interested.

Then, just as I had given up ever hearing from him, I had an email from Pete. He had been on a several-weeks' course in Poland studying some forest that was about as primeval as it gets. Apparently it even harboured wolves that came and went across the border with Ukraine, presumably without passports. Pete attached a document about it and wrote: *The bird life is fabulous and once or twice I thought how much you would enjoy it. How's your birding getting on. Perhaps if you're up this way we could have a birding session together. And I'd like you to meet Denise who will become my wife in October.*

I felt suddenly still inside. So that was that.

I wrote to Dad to tell him about it. His reply was: *Reality never is easy to cope with. How about coming up to me for a few days? You can get me up to speed on your A levels.*

"If that's what you want," Mother said when I told her about the invitation.

It was a few days later that I came home at dusk. The light was on in the living room and Mother hadn't drawn the curtains, so there was nothing to stop me seeing her in a clinch with Alec Chapman of the kind you don't normally expect to see your mother in.

July 2008

1

I'd created a picture of Dad's cottage as quaint, untidy and him bumbling along on in it in a disorganised sort of way. It was quite wrong. I took a train up to Leeds and Dad had borrowed a car from a friend for the time I was there. To my knowledge he had never been of a DIY turn of mind so I wasn't surprised that the cottage looked a bit scruffy from the outside, though the door was newly painted green and the window frames white. A climbing rose clambered round the door, and I glimpsed leggy hollyhocks bowing over delphiniums and lupins.

"You and gardening, that's new," I said as we turned through the narrow gate, and I eased out alongside rampant geraniums.

"Friends give me stuff," Dad said. "I don't do annuals, though."

The front door opened straight into the living room dominated by a chintzy sofa and armchair and a fold-up dining table by the far window. Upstairs were two bedrooms and the bathroom. My room was small, with a stripy counterpane matching stripy curtains. Perhaps this was more stuff acquired from friends, but, no, Dad said he'd found the matching sets in M & S. My room looked over the back: more hollyhocks, delphiniums, lupins, and other things I couldn't name giving an unarguably cottage-garden effect. I gazed out at it, thinking back to our garden in Greenley and how Dad never did anything in it.

"Tea's up," he called from downstairs.

The kitchen had been extended and modernised and had a small breakfast bar near the back window. We sat at it looking out at the tangle of colour while Dad poured out tea and handed me a plate with fruit cake.

"Don't tell me you made this," I said.

"No, one of my women friends did." Dad watched my expression. "And you needn't look at me like that. I don't mean woman friend in that sense, but a friend who happens to be a woman."

It was good fruit cake. After a while, Dad said "I hear your mother has a new friend – Alec Somebody."

"How on earth….?" I let the question trail.

He shrugged. "I thought you might have guessed. But I do find this cloak-and-dagger stuff difficult, so I'll tell you, it's through Tom."

I stared at him. "Tom? Sally's Tom?" The penny dropped. "Oh, of course, he is, was an alcoholic."

"Yes, well I just ask you to keep it to yourself. We coincided at some convention of recovering alkies, got talking, found common acquaintances, and one thing led to another. So what do you think of this Alec person?"

Oh dear. I sipped tea and tried to think very hard. "Well, to be honest, he seems OK. Just ordinary really, though quite good looking in an oldish way."

Dad grinned. "No so much of the oldish. I gather he is younger than me. But if he's ordinary, that sounds all right. I wouldn't want your mother...."

"Hey!" I interrupted. "No one has said anything about this becoming a permanent relationship. She just seems happy and relaxed. You know, a normal relationship."

"Mm. She could do with a bit of that."

We were silent for a while. Then I couldn't resist asking, "And you? How would you feel if Mother wanted to make it permanent?"

"I'd mind," Dad said. "But she has every right to an ordinary, happy and relaxed relationship."

This wasn't turning out at all the way I had planned. I'd come to get to know my Dad again, and suddenly here we were talking about a broken home. As though he had read my thoughts, Dad said, "Let's get away from the subject,Tuppence. I wanted you here to share a bit of my new life with you and to be able to catch up with how you are progressing with that intriguing project of yours. My plan is to take you down to a nearby pub around six, when it's not too crowded ...."

"A pub ...?"

"Ye-e-e-s. I may not drink alcohol, but I do still drink liquid. And you'll meet some of my friends. Then we'll come home to lamb and dumplings with carrots, not prepared by me but by our excellent local butcher. And tomorrow I'll take you for a drive round my patch."

The pub was about ten minutes' walk away, along a lane, through the narrowest of ginnels and out on to the small market place. It was called The Ostrich, which seemed a little inappropriate for an almost-hill village and they were indeed greeted by a near-lifesize model of the bird at the pub's entrance.

"Hi Jim!" greeted a small chorus of voices as they entered, then "So this is the famous Nikki!" as I followed.

There were four of them round a table by one of the windows overlooking the market place. Maggie and Tod were the two that made the most impression on me. Maggie was sort of middle-aged, but really lively and pretty in an older kind of way. Tod was older still, his hair grey and worn in a ponytail that hung well down his back.

Maggie and I hit it off straight away. She was even more into flowers than I was into birds, and her excitement at the recent discovery of a rare orchid was infectious. It reminded me of the time I had looked out of our kitchen window and seen a sparrowhawk perching on our fence. And another occasion when some snipe settled on a neighbour's lawn, rhythmically probing it with their thin bills, like knitting needles.

"Ah," interrupted Tod. "But I bet you never found a robin in your oven." It was on a bitter winter's day apparently and he had lit the oven preparatory to lunch when he was distracted by a knock at the door and had returned to find a robin huddled on the lower shelf.

I looked round their laughing faces. Could these possibly all have been out-of-control drunks? I glanced at Dad and saw he was watching me, smiling. "It doesn't happen overnight," he said, confirming that he had read my thoughts.

"So are you a birder?" I asked Tod.

"I'm a Renaissance man," he said, which threw me a bit.

"He means he knows a bit about a lot of things, and not a lot about any one thing," Dad said.

"I think I prefer your daughter to you," Tod said in a mock huff. "So, Nikki, what do you do when you're not birding."

"Just finished A levels, but I've got a sort of project in mind. And I'm aiming for a university course in media studies."

"Mm. I wanted to be a writer. Still do. I wrote the most prize-winning rubbish when I was drunk. It remains to be seen what I can do sober." This presumably meant he hadn't been sober for very long, though looking round the group, they all seemed relaxed and comfortable in their own skins to use one of Dad's favourite expressions. "Anyway, Nikki, can you afford to waste valuable time with a group of weirdoes with an important deadline looming?"

"I haven't seen Dad for four years. Anyway I've brought some work with me."

"She's into parallel universes," Dad explained. "She's doing research so that she can go in for some international contest."

"Well," Tod said. "That's enough to put a stopper on any conversation."

I grinned at him, and thought: *these are good people to have as friends.*

2

When we got back to the cottage, Dad took me down to the shed at the bottom of his long narrow garden. He'd adapted the shed into a workshop and I was amazed. It was full of equipment and tools all neatly laid out or put on shelves or hooks. There were also shelves of his work: the candlesticks in various sizes and some new items – small carved figures, miniature rural scenes.

"Why didn't you tell me about these? They're marvellous. I could have tried some marketing for you."

"All in hand, Tuppence. You have enough to do. Your friend Adrian knows about them and has set me up with an account on something called Ebay. I'm doing rather well." He grinned at me. "Your mouth is open."

I closed my mouth and gave him a big hug, reflecting that it was surprising what went on without your knowledge.

Then Dad said. "Seriously, it's magic having you here, but there's no way I'm going to be a reason for you missing your deadline."

"The deadline isn't until 1st December," I pointed out.

"Never mind. You're not using me as an excuse for slacking. So while I'm doing my constitutional tomorrow morning, I suggest you get down to some studying."

According to him his constitutional lasted a couple of hours though I suspected this was a lengthened version in the interests of my work. I went along with it anyway.

And my musings went well. It felt a real luxury to have so much time for expanding my research, but Dad was right. I must not get complacent about it. Perhaps it was also the change of surroundings, the stimulus of new company, but some of my uncertainties began to crystallise into specific questions that stood a chance of being answered with some kind of method. I thought about them, drafted, re-drafted and re-re-drafted until I had six points for discussion. When Dad returned, he seemed singularly *not* out of breath.

"You smell of coffee and bacon butties," I accused.

"Well, the inner man has to be fed. Anyway, how have you got on?"

I handed him the sheet of paper with my questions. He read them through a number of times before saying, "I think you'll start floundering on the first question if you start trying to quote scientific sources for the bases of parallel universes. I suspect one person's parallel universe will be another's fantasy or dream sequence or even biblical parable...."

"You're brilliant," I said. "That's just where I was getting to."

He looked pleased and surprised. "Which means we're both brilliant. But I don't think it's your job to provide the scientific evidence. Your task is to make a convincing case for the examples you quote and how they fit into the different concepts of people's ideas of parallel universes. Do you really want to get involved with quantum physics?"

"No, thanks. Okay, so I'll keep it simple."

Dad smiled. "Good." He glanced back at my list. "Though I see you are part way there with your different categories: science fiction, fantasy, legend, parable.... So you are going back to the Bible?"

"I guess that's where it all started."

He shook his head. "I don't agree. It will have started round camp fires far beyond the mists of time when people tried to explain to each other why things happened the way they did, eventually leading to creation stories. A lot of those will still exist in places where descendants of the original natives survive, like Australasia and North America, before we all came along and confused them with science."

"You get more brilliant by the minute," I said enthusiastically, scribbling frantically as he spoke.

Dad got up, crossed to where I was sitting and gently removed the biro from my hand. "Recreation time for students," he said. "Now I'm going to show you a bit of my patch."

And a very nice patch it was. We drove over high bleak passes through the fells where the sight of a Norse raiding party would not have seemed out of place, then down alongside gurgling streams that burrowed ever deeper into woods and came out on rolling valley floors neatly dissected by stone walls, and passed farms and barns that looked as though they had been there for ever.

"God's own country," Dad said.

"What?"

"That's what Yorkshiremen call Yorkshire."

"Well, they would, wouldn't they?"

Dad drove on taking right or left turns that led up and over and then down and under, and finally alongside a lake. He turned into a parking place. "I want you to see this," he said.

"This" was a road-side monument with wreaths leaning against it. It commemorated an Old Pals Battalion – one made up literally of old pals: either all the young men from a whole community or workplace, who had signed up and gone out to fight together in the First World War, probably cheered on by the rest of the community. In this case they had all been wiped out at the Battle of the Somme. I looked at their names and their ages – most of them only a few months or a year or two older than me. It was easy not to be aware that our generation had avoided all that.

I must have said it aloud because Dad picked up with, "My generation too – though of course there has been Iraq and Afghanistan and Libya and…."

Soon after we stopped for lunch in a tiny pub crammed between a row of shops and the church. Over fish and chips, I asked, "Dad, why did you start drinking?"

He smiled. "I've been asked that question so many times, by friends, doctors, shrinks, other alkies. Most of all by myself. The initial answer is that it was for the same reason as most other people: to enjoy the conviviality, loosen up a bit, feel part of the crowd."

"And?"

"And then I realised how much I didn't feel part of the crowd when I was sober. So I decided it was all right to go over the top under special circumstances. But the special circumstances seemed to happen more and more. So staying gently topped up seemed a better solution. Only finding the right level and maintaining it wasn't as easy as I thought. So I suppose I got used to erring on the side of caution and didn't notice how much it was eroding my life – and your mother's and yours. And at a certain point I stopped caring. Taking the edge off reality became the Number One answer to every problem. And after I left home, there didn't seem any point in stopping."

There didn't seem a right answer to any of that.

"My turn to ask the questions," Dad said. "Let's get back to your parallel universes. I like the way you have sub-divided the possibilities of interpreting this, but I haven't yet caught up with the reasoning behind them."

"Yeah, well that's probably because the reasoning isn't yet very well developed."

"So how about we do some developing. The Saints' Lives, for example. How do they figure into the reasoning?"

"I haven't completely worked that out yet?"

"For a start, are they based on fact or fiction?"

The waiter came and removed our plates, then presented us with the dessert menu. I frowned at it. All this thinking was giving me a headache. I said, "I'll have an Eton Mess."

"So will I. Do you want a Madeira with yours?" *Good Lord, had he read my mind?*

"I'd prefer something drier."

"Okay." Dad signalled to the waiter. "Two Eton Messes please, and a glass of Côte du Rhone for the lady."

"Getting back to the Saints," I said. "The details of their lives seem to come from a whole range of sources...."

"Most of which," Dad interrupted, "would be hand written and copied with all the margin for error that implies."

"Added to which," I added firmly, "some were in Latin, some in medieval French or medieval English, so you have to take into account the reliability of the translators."

"Couldn't you have chosen a simpler project?"

"One that everyone else was doing?" I extricated a cream-covered titbit of meringue from among the forest fruits. "Anyway I've discovered I actually like the research and the red herrings that lead you further and further into the unknown."

"Mm. Time-taking. But what does puzzle me is why you're continuing with the research now you're A levels are behind you."

"You're right. I could do with a more disciplined mind. Perhaps I'll get that at Uni "

Dad nodded. "I envy you that, Tuppence. It was my choice to go straight into an office for what I called practical experience. Well, I got that all right." He licked a blob of cream from his upper lip. "By the way you put that wine away pretty smartly. Need another?"

138

I felt a flash of resentment at the implied criticism and the wording of his question. "No thanks, I don't *need* anything. But a coffee would be good."

For some reason, that comment continued to rankle. I was also aware that my thoughts arising from the conversation we'd had about parallel universes needed putting in order. It really was time to go home. When I said so that evening, Dad looked disappointed but said quickly, "You must do what you think is right."

It was also that evening when we had another conversation that was to revolutionise my life. Dad said, "It's amazing how much money you can save when you've not got much to spend it on. I've been thinking it would be really good if you learned to drive. I haven't given you a lot except anxiety in your teens, so how about I pay for driving lessons?"

I rushed over to give him a hug. He said, "I'll give you a cheque."

"I haven't a bank account yet."

"Then you can open one with this, and mind you spend it on the lessons. I shall want a regular report."

Next morning he drove me to Leeds. On the platform, we had a big father-daughter hug.

"I'm proud of you Nikki," Dad said into my hair.

"I'm proud of you. It can't have been easy." I stood back and studied his face and the steady expression in his grey eyes.

He nodded, gave me another hug, opened the carriage door, nudged me gently inside. "Let me know how …. everything… goes."

"I will." Then the train was moving and I was leaning out of the window and we began rounding a bend and Dad disappeared from view.

The journey was only taking just over three hours. After a while I went to the buffet car and ordered a gin. It seemed an all-right thing to do while I mulled over the events of the last couple of days, cherishing the warm feelings I had towards Dad. All the same I didn't go along with everything he said. I still thought that if he had *really* tried he could have stopped the drinking sooner and saved us all a lot of humiliation and difficulties. After all, if I could do it, anyone could. I'd stopped loads of times and, though I'd started again, I had stopped again too. The gin felt good as it slipped down and communicated warmth and power. I drank it rather more quickly than I intended, and it seemed sensible to have another. But I was in control, wasn't I? Another one could wait.

I enjoyed the journey back through the summer countryside and the long evening. After a bit I really wanted to go and have that second gin, but instead got my notebook out of my bag and started jotting down some of the ideas that swirled round my head. When I reached Banbury I decided to treat myself to a taxi. After all it was a celebratory sort of occasion, having completed a memorable first encounter with Dad on his home territory. As I paid off the taxi, I noticed Alec's car was in our drive. A pity. I wanted Mother to myself just then.

August - December 2008

1

Mother and Alec were in the living room, Mother on the sofa looking a bit dishevelled, Alec in the armchair though it didn't look as though he had been there very long.

"You're back early," Mother said.

"Yeah. There's some research I want to do in Oxford."

"So how was your father?" Alec asked.

"Amazing," I said. "Lovely cottage and he's into woodwork."

"He was always good at that," Mother said. "When he could be bothered."

"Well he's bothered now."

"Good."

There didn't seem much else to say, so I went up to bed soon after, and before long heard Alec leaving. For a long time I lay on my back staring up into the darkness, my thoughts all over the place, memories of the new relationship that was developing with Dad muddling with an awful sense of loneliness.

Over breakfast next morning, I told Mother properly about my visit to Dad. And about the driving lessons. She listened carefully, but there was also a sad look about her. When I'd finished, she came and sat beside me and put a hand over one of mine.

She said, "I'm so glad you had a good time with your Dad, Nikki. And, of course, I'm delighted about the driving lessons. But I do want you to understand that it's a part of my life I can't go back to. It happened so often, when you were younger – too young to realise. Promises made and broken – not always straight away, sometimes weeks, even months later, but always broken."

"But never after three years," I protested.

"No, may be not as long as that, but every time something else inside me died. I'd swear I would never put myself through it again, and then I did. And again, and again."

"I think it's for real this time," I said, not much above a whisper.

She squeezed my hand. "I hope it is, for your Dad's sake. But it's too late for me."

"You mean, because of Alec?"

"No, I don't mean because of Alec. I mean precisely what I said – it's too late for me. All the same, Alec and I have come to mean a lot to each other, partly because of the shared experience. But he'll never abandon Marion. We'll just have to settle for what we have."

She had to leave for work soon after, and I pottered about clearing up the breakfast things, thinking about what she had said. Because I'd seen how much Dad had changed, I couldn't accept that if only she'd agree to see him, Mother wouldn't change her mind. Or perhaps she would if Alec had not come on the scene.

In the end, it was going round in my head so much that I called Rach. She must have heard something in my tone of voice because she suggested straight away that I should go round that evening. I left the flat just before Mother came home. Adrian was there, of course, but as soon as I arrived he disappeared 'to meet a mate at the pub.' Then I burst into tears and Rachel hugged me and I told her the whole sorry tale, finishing with "I never thought I'd end up being the product of a broken home," and cried some more.

"On the contrary," Rachel said. "Your parents have each discovered their importance as separate individuals, so you have the rare choice of being able to participate in two lives instead of a combined one."

There she went, eighteen going on fifty. She'd be an old lady before she was twenty. Anyway she hadn't understood. I didn't want to participate in the lives of other individuals, I wanted to be part of a whole. When I said as much, she said, "When were you part of a whole other than in your imagination?" She must have realised how hard that sounded because she went quiet for a while before going on, "Sorry that sounded uncaring, and you know you're my dearest friend and I do care. But things are never going to get better if you won't face reality."

Gracious, she was beginning to sound like Dad.

Adrian came home soon after that and did us all a fry-up. Then we watched an Inspector Morse repeat. When I got home, Mother was on her own in the living room and called me in. She went and made us both a hot chocolate as she often used to do when I first moved in with her again. We didn't talk a lot, but I tried to get over that I understood we all needed to make adjustments to our lives, and I did understand that she deserved some peace of mind. Anyway, since she and Alec couldn't get married, there was still a chance she might change her mind, though of course I didn't say that to her.

In fact, that germ of an idea took root and developed. Suppose I could engineer a meeting between them, and Mother saw how lovely Dad was these days, perhaps the situation would resolve itself. The idea took on a life of its own. I mentioned it once to Rachel who destroyed it with a shower of icy logic, so I didn't mention it to her again. After a few gins, I worked out some magnificent scenarios that never seemed quite so foolproof in the cold light of day. Indeed, most of the time I knew I would have to proceed very cautiously.

In the meantime, I made good progress with my project and was pleased with my alcohol control. I wasn't drinking less – in fact, probably a little more – but my metabolism was coping with it much better. Once when I went out with the gang, Zoe said, "Good Lord, Nik, you've developed a head like a trucker!" which I took to be a compliment. That was the occasion of my 18th birthday, and I arrived home quite a bit the worse for wear. I'd thought Mother was out, but she wasn't and came out of the living room, took one look at me, and said, "Oh, Nikki!" in the tone I had heard her so often use with Dad.

And then Dad wrote and said he was planning to visit around the New Year, and my brain started working overtime. When he asked me about the driving lessons, I said I was starting those in the New Year, too. It looked as though 2009 was going to be a major landmark in my life.

2

In the meantime, the deadline for my project was fast approaching. For the last couple of weeks, I worked really hard on it. A few days before the date, I went through it one last time before sending it. Then I had a real need to show it to someone else. Mother had seen some of it in snatches, but not the finished item with its graphs and index. Alec was visiting, but I just barged in and said, "I must show you this."

Alec was particularly nice about it. He was a director of a marketing consultancy and used to looking over projects. He took ages looking at mine, flicking back from one part to the other as he checked my page index and cross references. Then he looked across at me, smiled, and began reading the text. I found myself watching him anxiously. After all he was a professional who employed a lot of people.

After a while, he said, "Nikki this is a very good job you have done here. Your attention to detail is excellent, but I see you also have some original ideas."

"Thanks," I said.

Alec passed the dossier over to Mother. "Have you seen this, my dear?"

"Only bits of it." Mother began going through it methodically, while I watched every twitch of her expression.

When she'd finished, we all discussed it and they had clearly understood the points I was trying to make. Alec's only reservation concerned the scientific bases for my arguments though in the end he agreed with Dad's point that it wasn't necessary for me to go into that sort of detail.

I posted the whole thing off a couple of days later, joined the gang that evening and got drunk. That was intentional. I reckoned getting drunk once a month was Okay, and I made a note of it in my diary. On this occasion I had pre-arranged to spend the night with Tracey so that I wouldn't have to face Mother's sad expression.

Now that I didn't have such a demanding study programme, I joined the gang more often. It had changed quite a bit since the early days. Of course, Matt was missing though I did have occasional news of him. It seemed that all was not so well in his relationship with Neil. Then I saw him – Matt, I mean – in the park. He was sitting, elbows on knees, head hanging down, with Dejection written all over him. He didn't react immediately when I sat on the bench next to him, then he looked slowly round and said, "Oh hello," before going back into Dejection mode.

After a while I said, "I could do with a hug," and he slowly looked round again, then straightened up and turned and enfolded me in the sort of bear hug I'd not had for a long time. I burst into tears. Matt hugged me harder before loosening one arm so he could stroke my head. "What's up Nik?"

"I had a wonderful visit with Dad in Yorkshire. Mother's fallen for a guy called Alec and won't have anything more to do with Dad. And I've missed you."

Matt held me away from him a little and grinned. "I've been dumped by Neil. I've been made redundant. And I've missed you. Problem solved."

I sniffed and fished for a handkerchief. "What happened with Neil?"

"He preferred hedging his bets. Like having several relationships going at the same time."

144

I leaned forward and gave Matt a hug. "Pity you're gay. I reckon we could have a great relationship."

He sighed. "It would only complicate a beautiful friendship. Let's go bowling tonight."

So we gradually slipped back into our old routine: bowling a couple of times a week, meeting at the leisure centre where Matt took up the gym again while I was at my yoga class, an occasional pub meal. In particular, we went to a new retro pub that Matt had heard about called the Crooked Parrot. Its focus was on re-creating the Beatles era, and I thought it was brilliant. When I told Mother about it, she looked quite misty-eyed for a moment.

At some point I showed Matt a photocopy of my project and he seemed genuinely impressed. He also said he thought I was drinking too much, so I eased off and didn't miss it. More evidence that I wasn't really addicted. Tracey rang me once and, when I said that I was busy, responded with "So it's true you're going out with that queer again," and I slammed the phone on her. Rachel and Adrian were too busy being in love to notice or comment.

When I asked Matt if he were going home for Christmas, he said, no, he couldn't face all that family celebratory stuff. So I said, "Well, why not spend it with us. There's not much family about us at the moment." When he hesitated, I said, "*Please.*" So he agreed.

Alec was there when I told Mother and she explained to him that Matt was gay.

"Oh," he said. "Well, any friend of yours is welcome, of course, Nikki." That surprised me as it made it sound as though Alec was in charge of Christmas arrangements, but I noticed Mother chipped in very quickly with, "Matt's always welcome, you know that. He's a really nice guy."

3

So that was Christmas settled. And soon after that Dad would be visiting. I talked to Matt about this and he was very discouraging about manipulating the situation, so any further planning mostly went on somewhere in the back of my head below the surface of whatever was going on at the time.

We did keep the festive season low key. For the first time ever, Mother did not suggest our usual Christmas tree with its ceremonial decorating, so I bought a smaller one anyway and initiated Matt into the art of making it into a personal creation. Alec made the usual comment about forewarning the Fire Brigade, but I couldn't blame him as almost every man had done the same thing in my living memory. Except Matt.

Mother and I did the full Christmas lunch deal, while Alec drifted about keeping us provided with coffee or sherry. Matt joined us in the late morning and he and Alec got on surprisingly well, finding they had a common interest in keeping fit. I hadn't registered that Alec went running regularly too and had even done a couple of half marathons.

Dad rang in the afternoon of Christmas Day. He called my mobile as usual, so I was able to take the call out in the kitchen. He'd bought a car and would drive down on January 5th, having booked in at a pub outside Greenley. We arranged to spend the full day of the following Thursday together and he said, yes, he would be very happy if Matt joined us for lunch. When I returned to the living room, I told them all it was Dad but not that he was coming so soon. In fact, I hadn't completely decided what I was going to do about that.

The question of how I was going to manipulate a meeting between Mother and Dad became a bit of an obsession. It had to appear natural and preferably it should be without Alec on the scene. Just after Christmas, Alec asked me whether I'd mind a lot if he and Mother joined a group of their friends for the New Year, adding that I'd probably prefer to be with a crowd of my own age anyway. He was right. Although I thought he was OK, I was getting a bit tired of playing gooseberry. They were so clearly putting on act most of the time, pretending to be really good friends rather than doting on each other, that it was getting embarrassing. My obvious first thought was to spend the New Year with Matt, but he'd decided to do a quick visit home to Yorkshire, given that he had not been there for Christmas. So I decided to join the gang.

There were a few caustic comments like "So has Matt found a new playmate?" or "So you fancy a bit of normality do you?" but they soon tired of it. Tracey had agreed I could stay with her and was particularly friendly, so after a bit I asked her, "If you wanted to bring a couple of old friends together who hadn't seen each other for a long time, how would you set about it?"

She giggled, then said, "How exciting," and then, "well, how old are they?"

"Oh, quite old," I said. "You know, around our parents' ages."

146

She thought for a moment, then said, "Well it's obvious, isn't it. You take one to an old haunt you know they had always enjoyed, and make sure the other one turns up at the right time."

I thought about it. Could it be that simple? Then I thought of the Crooked Parrot and how Mother had looked when I told her it has re-opened. After changing hands several times, it had been taken over again by the family of the former owners who were trying to recreate the original atmosphere. Matt and I thought it was great.

The rest of New Year's Eve followed a predictable pattern. We all drank too much and made a lot of noise on the street after closing time. The police were out in force and I just managed not to be picked up by slipping down a side alley where I was very sick several times. It was horrible, but at least by the end of it I was feeling marginally better. Mother clearly didn't think so and told me I looked ghastly next morning.

"You wouldn't like to make a New Year resolution, would you?" she suggested, then added quietly so that I only just heard her, "Not that it did your Dad much good." Then she softened and said, "Sorry, too many memories, let's think of something else. How about you and I do something together after the New Year? It's always a bit of an anticlimax. Matt's with his parents, Alec is away at some symposium in Brussels, and it would be fun if we could do something together."

She looked a bit doubtful when I suggested the Crooked Parrot, but then agreed and we settled on the Monday evening, the eve of Dad's departure. I still hadn't worked out the details, but at least I had set the scene.

Dad rang me as soon as he arrived and I nipped over to meet him in the coffee shop in M&S. Mother had gone to see Alec off at the airport, so there was no need for subterfuge. She was also staying on in Birmingham to meet up with a friend. The January sales were on so the town was buzzing. Dad was really looking good and on top of the world because he'd got a contract to make some of his wooden items for a chain of craft shops in the North. The candlesticks had gone down particularly well and now he was branching out into bowls and boxes. He had even produced a leaflet showing some of his designs. I couldn't wait for Mother to see them, and had to bite my tongue to stop myself from saying so, because there was a big question-mark over my devious plot.

The following day he took me for a circular drive through a number of villages in north Oxfordshire and Warwickshire, with memories of trips we had done when I was a kid. I didn't remember all of them, but some brought back vivid scenes. Among them were the views as we drove along a lane at Edgehill, looking down and way across the plains where one of the major battles of our Civil War took place. I was probably about seven at the time and all I could think of was what had happened to all the bodies of the men and the horses. At that age I was probably more worried about the horses. Another memory was when we stopped at the National Herb Centre. There was another good view from here, but I mainly remembered sniffing all the herby smells of the plants on display.

"We thought you were going to turn into a professional gardener," Dad smiled. *"We" – Mother and Dad, now about to split up. Not if I had anything to do with it.*

I said, "Matt and I recently went to a new bistro in town called the Crooked Parrot ..."

"Good Lord," Dad said. "I thought that closed down years ago."

"Well, apparently it's re-opened and is trying to re-create the original atmosphere. Of course Matt and I don't know what that was, but we thought it was pretty good. Fancy giving it a try?"

"Mm, why not? Let's see – I've promised to meet some mates tomorrow. That only leaves Monday, the day before I go."

Perfect. "That's fine. I'll meet you there, say, six in the evening?"

"It's a date," Dad said.

January 2009

1

"What on earth is wrong with you?" Mother asked.

What was wrong with me was that I was sick with worry. We were sitting at a table in the Crooked Parrot, and it was ten minutes to six. On this Monday evening in January, we were the only customers except for a young couple tucked away in an alcove.

"Probably ate too much over Christmas," I said. "Actually I feel a bit sick. I think I'll just pop over to the chemist's. Could you order me a herbal tea?"

Mother looked taken aback, but I was out of the door and across the road before she could protest. I didn't go into the chemist's but stood in its doorway and watched as a few moments later Dad went into the Crooked Parrot. I could see the table by the window where Mother was sitting. She was reading something, probably the menu. She looked up, then she stood up and even from that distance I could read the fury in her gestures.

Later Dad told me what happened. They had spotted each other at the same moment and both had exclaimed "*O-o-o-o h-h-h*" in mutual dismayed rather than pleasurable surprise. Mother had ranted a bit, and he had tried to calm her down, eventually taking a seat at her table so that she had to sit too. It was at that point I knew I had to go and face the results of my actions.

As I went through the door, I paused to let out the young couple who had been there. Mother and Dad rounded on me.

"Oh, Tuppence…" Dad said in a sad voice.

"Have you lost leave of your senses?" Mother raged. She was close to tears as she pushed past me. I turned to go after her, but Dad called me back. "Leave her,Nikki. She'll say a lot of things she doesn't really mean when she's so angry."

I went back to the table and sat down. Dad went on, "I realise you planned this with the best of intentions Nikki, but one thing you learn with time is that the only life you can change is your own."

"Even when you know other people are doing something stupid?"

"Perhaps you have to ask yourself who are you to judge?"

149

The waitress came and Dad ordered coffee and I had a blackcurrant tea, and we sat over them for an hour. It was quite weird as he explained to me quietly how much he appreciated what I had tried to do but how it was bound to backfire because I had wanted things to go the way *I* wanted them, not the way he and Mother did. When I asked him how *he* wanted them to go, he just said it would have been wonderful if Mother wanted what I wanted, but she didn't so we both had to accept that and adapt to what is, not what we wanted it to be. That was a bit involved to take in all at once, but it seemed to add up to letting other people have what they wanted while you couldn't have what you wanted. But I was too disheartened to argue.

In fact, I felt too disheartened to contemplate the future at all. I didn't want to be the child of a broken home. Well, may be not a child, but a young adult. Whatever.

"What are you going to do, Tuppence?" Dad was looking at me worriedly. "I can put off my return home if you like." *Return home. Of course, Yorkshire was home, where he had lived the whole of his life in recovery. He'd made a new start. Mother was making a new start. That's what I was going to have to do.*

"No, it's OK Dad. You go. This is something I have to sort out for myself. I'm not a kid."

He smiled. "Indeed you're not. But you must promise to keep in touch and let me know your decisions. And that you will come and stay if you want or need to."

I nodded. "Perhaps I'll go and see Rachel and Adrian."

"That sounds like a good idea. Can I drop you there."

"No, I think I'll walk a bit and sort my thoughts out."

"All right." Dad paid the bill and we went out on to the street, into a chill evening that about matched my mood. He gave me a big hug. "It'll sort out, you'll see,"

I hugged him back. "I know it will. And I promise I'll keep in touch."

I stood watching him walk back to the car. He turned once and waved, then I walked off in the opposite direction.

At the top of the road, I stopped and looked left, then right and then left again. So now what? I mentally ran through my friends and began wondering why suddenly they all seemed so boring or unavailable: Rachel already planning the rest of her life, Matt was still in Yorkshire, and Tracey .... Hold it, Tracey might not be unavailable.

I punched her number into my mobile and grinned at her response: "*Hi world, anyone interesting out there?*"

"Not interesting, just bored," I said.

"Hi Nikki. Where are you?"

I told her.

"Right, I'll pick you up in five. We'll take a look at The Zombies."

That's the good thing about Tracey. Not a moment's hesitation.

Half an hour later, we were half way through the special brew on offer at The Zombies. I'm not normally keen on the place – it's *very* loud, but certainly not boring, and there's a different special brew each evening that always packs a punch. I noticed a young man at the bar looking at us hopefully, but he didn't do anything. A couple of others, not so young, came and asked for a dance. After three more special brews and an hour later, Tracey said she'd better get home while she could still drive.

"I'll stay on, get a cab," I said.

Tracey looked briefly doubtful, pressed a note into my hand and said, "Well, mind you do."

After she'd gone, I sat near the bar looking round the crowded room, the laughing faces, feeling the throb of communal enjoyment that was as powerful as the beat of the music. I thought back over the evening to that glimpse of Mother's furious face as she pushed past me, and suddenly I didn't care about anything. I would sort myself out. Dad would help me. I'd manage – they'd just see how I would ….. It was the first time I'd ever been in a place like this alone, and the sense of empowerment was as heady as the special brew so that when an oldish man said, "Like a drink, my lovely?" I responded in a flash, "Aren't I bit young for you? Anyway, I'm already engaged."

My eye caught the amused glance of the young man at the bar. "Very neat," he said. "Are you really engaged?"

I said, "Not immediately," and he came to join me on the bench.

After studying me for a while, he said, "Perhaps I'd better look after you."

"That'd be nice." *With a bit of luck he would take me home.* I waved Tracey's note at him. "Could you get us each a special brew with this? My name's Nikki, by the way."

"Hi Nikki. Certainly can. I'm Bryn." *I'd never met a Bryn before.*

He got the drinks and we started to chat. Bryn was on benefits because he couldn't find a job. He lived with his parents, not far from Mother's flat, and knew a taxi driver who owed him and who would get us both home. By then I'd decided I would have to go home sooner or later. We swapped views on music, which weren't very similar. He didn't read much so books were a no-no. When we got on to bowling we really found common ground, even made a semi date to meet at the Superbowl.

We danced a bit. Bryn wasn't much better than me, but we stumbled along, and the feel of his arm round me was nice. Then I realised that he was much younger than I thought which was probably why he didn't seem to know what to do with me, and why he was drinking the special brews too quickly. After a couple more of these, he suddenly said, "I'm s-o-o-o tired, put his head back against the wall and went to sleep. I nudged him a few times, but the only reaction I got was "Wha'?" getting quieter and quieter until there was no reaction at all. Then I wriggled out from under his arm, which was round my shoulders, and studied him. He was asleep, really fast asleep. And I'd run out of money. And I was beginning to feel bad.

I slipped out of the Zombies. It was fairly central, and there was a short cut across the park that would take me home in about quarter of an hour, but the park looked dark and uninviting as the path curved into some trees. I found a bench near the entrance, which was well lit. The town hall clock struck midnight, reminding me that as well as feeling bad I was also very tired.

After a while, I put my feet up on the bench and stretched out, cushioning my head on my arms. How long I slept I don't know, but I was woken by something cold and wet nudging at my face. I pushed it away and sat up abruptly, which sent my head swimming. The something wet was the nose of a dog, which was on a lead. And holding the other end of the lead, his face dark with disapproval, was Tom.

2

"Nikki, what the hell do you think you're doing?" Tom's anger was fizzing.

"Fell asleep. Didn't mean to stay out so late."

"Nor drink so much? You look disgusting."

152

His contempt prodded me into answering back, "And you never were of course?" I knew it wasn't funny as soon as I said it.

"For the moment I'm not the problem." He sat down beside me. The dog whimpered a bit and settled alongside. Tom went on, "Your mother is beside herself with worry." He fished a mobile from his pocket, punched a number, after a moment said, "Hi darling. Tell Anne, Nikki's fine. We'll be home in half an hour." A pause, then, "Yes, Anne, I promise you she's fine."

"You could have rung her any time to say you were OK," Tom told me. *Yeah, I could if she hadn't walked out on me as though I were the last person she ever wanted to see again.* Answering my unasked question he went on, "She rang the flat and got worried when there was no reply; we rang your friend, Tracey."

I mumbled, "I'm sorry, sorry. It won't ever happen again."

He looked sad. "Yeah, I used to say that."

I put my face in my hands. "Didn't know you had a dog."

He rubbed the animal's head. "This is Perce. He's a rescue chap. Had a bad time. It was Sally's idea – she's got me on a health programme."

"The whole world's on a health kick," I mumbled.

"Yeah, except you. Your Mother told me about your friend Matt and his running programme. We rang him but his answering machine was on."

Was the whole town involved in my misadventure?

We drove home in silence. Facing Mother was even worse than I had imagined. It would have been easier if she had been angry like Tom, but she was just sad, desperately sad. Sally and Tom left us alone in their living room. I could only repeat what I had said to Tom. "I'm sorry, sorry. It won't ever happen again. And about Dad – he explained that I couldn't go around trying to make things fit in with what I wanted."

That at least raised a small, surprised smile. "Did he, now? One thing I will grant you – he's certainly changed."

I felt a tremor of hope. "There you are then."

"Oh, Nikki darling. Your Dad has changed – and for the better. But he's not the man I married or would want to live with. He's lost … lost his spark, his get-up-and-go…"

Apparently there was no pleasing some people. I didn't say anything for a while then asked, "And Alec, he has this get-up-and-go thing?"

153

"Yes. Yes, he has. He's full of plans for the future, even though the present is anything but happy."

"Dad would be full of plans if you gave him half a chance."

There was a moment of quiet, then Mother lost it. "***Stop it, Nikki. Stop it.*** Will you understand that I do not, repeat do not, want to go back to the past. I want to move forward to whatever there is ahead, with someone who wants to come with me. I am not, repeat not, going to fit into some cosy scenario you have worked out because you can't face reality. You are no longer a child, and there isn't a fairy on top of the Christmas tree."

She could hardly have made it clearer. Dad had put it more gently. I felt the tears pricking but willed them not to come. Mother watched me and went on more quietly. "I didn't mean that to come out so harshly, but you have created a dream that doesn't exist and I don't know how to shake you out of it."

"You've succeeded in that," I said, and suddenly didn't want to cry any more. I felt quite strong and independent. The world was at my feet and I would pick it up and shake it into shape. Once I had got rid of my hangover.

It was a horrible night. Thick sleep was interrupted by a series of dreams in which one by one everyone in my life turned their back on me and I was left in a dark fog in which indistinguishable shadows came and went. It didn't take rocket science to work out what all that was about. When I went down to breakfast, Mother, Sally and Tom had clearly been up for some time.

"We have some suggestions to make," Mother said, and this time Sally and Tom didn't go.

I was wary, but in fact the suggestions were quite sensible.

"Obviously," Mother said, "we can carry on as we are. But I think you are now of an age when you need to have more space. And perhaps I do, too. One alternative would be for you to share a flat with one of your friends."

"As long as it's not that Tracey," Tom chipped in. I wished he would mind his own business.

Sally added more sensibly, "You really need to know someone well and get on well with them to share a place." I had fleeting memories of the way Tracey left her stuff trailing all over the place, and cups from which the lipstick hadn't been washed off. Sally went on, "But there is another possibility. My sister tells me that the student who had the studio flat in the annexe has decided to take a sabbatical.

154

He may be back in six months time and said he'd love to have the flat again if it's free. How would you feel about taking it on until July?"

Wow! But …. "How much is the rent?" I asked.

"I'll cover that," Mother said.

"Or you could get a job," Tom suggested. He was becoming very irritating, but in fact I agreed with him.

"It's not exactly the best time for the job market," Mother pointed out.

I heard myself say, "I know of several part time jobs going – cleaning, shop assistants, waitressing. People don't want them because they're too short term or not well enough paid. But they'd be all right for me while I get sorted."

And so it was agreed.

January-April 2009

1

By the end of January I'd moved into the studio flat. Mother said she would help me if I wanted, but unless I asked her she'd leave me to my own devices. This time I was determined to be independent. I applied for and got three jobs and managed to make them dovetail nicely. I did waitressing three evenings a week, cleaned two mornings (for Mother and Sally, actually, but they insisted on paying the going rate), and worked at the newsagents at the week-ends. That was my least favourite as I had to get there at a dire hour in time for the deliveries and to sort out all those sections, magazines and inserts. And believe me if I got it wrong, customers were quick to complain. Anyway, all in all, I earned enough to cover the rent, buy a few ready-made meals and the odd bottle of gin. I wasn't drinking much and intended to give the gin up, but not quite yet.

I really loved planning my new home, the very first of my own: what I would take and where I would put it. The flat had its own entrance from the gardens. The door opened into a tiny hallway with a really big bed-sitter off to the right. This had a small curtained area concealing the bed and a big alcove housing the essentials of a miniscule kitchen. On the other side of the hall was a shower room and very small store room which I adapted into a tiny office for my desk and computer.

Matt came and helped, introducing a very jazzy shower curtain and giving me his old microwave. The bed-sitter had a narrow French window which opened on to a paved area on which three tubs and their contents were my responsibility. My only regret was that I hadn't a spare bed for Dad, but that probably wouldn't have been a good idea anyway.

And then there were the driving lessons which I started in the middle of January with a pleasant woman instructor who seemed to think I was progressing quite well.

On January 31st, I had an official house warming party with wine and nibbles, inviting Mother, Alec, Sally, Tom and Matt. We had to take it in turns to move, but it was great fun, and Mother began to look less anxious.

156

And so my new life began. It was quite hard at first fitting in shopping, catering, housekeeping, with my various jobs, especially as I quite often got asked to do extra hours. It meant there wasn't much time for social life initially. In fact it had shrunk somewhat anyway, as Rachel and Adrian had taken off for the Antipodes for several weeks, first roughing it in Australia, then hiring a minibus in New Zealand to rough-it there for a month. Tracey invited me to join the gang, but gave up after several refusals. And several former mates were away at uni.

Mother invited me over to her side of the building for supper a couple of nights a week, ostensibly to make sure I had at least a couple of good hot meals but also, I suspect, to check up on how I was getting on. It meant I could check up on how she was getting on, too. Alec was usually there, and his shaving things were in the bathroom so I drew my own conclusions. Otherwise Matt was my mainstay. We went bowling at least once a week and occasionally tried out one of the new coffee shops or an old favourite, though I couldn't face the Crooked Parrot for a while. I quite often wondered what I'd do if he found another partner, and then he did. But this time it was quite different.

Early in March, I passed my driving test. Matt and I decided to celebrate and were strolling down the High Street one morning soon after when he suddenly said, "Well, hi!" He stopped and went on, "Nik, this is Edward. We met at bowling the other evening when you couldn't come."

"Can't turn my back on you for five minutes," I said, grinning so that they both knew I was joking. Edward and I surveyed each other and clearly saw no evidence of threat, for he turned towards me and gave me one of those half-hugs men give each other when they're too embarrassed to make it an all-embracing one. He had tousled hair and an open-air sort of face, and a nice dimple.

"Your taste is improving," I said, then realised how that could be misinterpreted.

"S'all right. Edwards knows all about Neil. He's gone to Ibiza, by the way. Neil, I mean. Edward, we're celebrating Nikki's baptism into the world of motoring. Join us for a coffee, if that's OK with you Nik?"

And I found it was OK. So we went to the Crooked Parrot because it was the nearest, and I found the memories of that awful day had lost their edge. I didn't even mind when Matt started telling Neil about it, adding the odd detail myself.

"I did something like that," Edward said. "There was this guy and a girl who fancied each other like crazy, then fell out over something stupid, so I invited them both to my place for supper. They were so furious with me they forgot to be mad at each other."

"At least yours had a happy ending," I said.

"Yeah, though I lost two good friends in the process."

A bit later, Edward said, "I've just thought – one of my mates has just got himself a fancy Japanese car and has an old Austin he wants to sell. It's really not much to look at, but the engine's good and he'd sell at a low price to get rid of it quickly."

"No time like the present," Matt suggested, so we rang Edward's friend and arranged to meet him and his car. Edward was right. It certainly wasn't much to look at, and a weird yellow colour, but Edward knew a bit about cars and said it was a bargain. I knew Mother would advance me what I needed, so we did the deal there and then. Edward's friend called the car Beano, so I decided to do the same.

I really liked Edward. Not quite like I felt towards Matt. Matt was the brother I'd never had, and Edward was 'my brother's' friend. We did a lot of things the three of us: bowling, birding (though this clearly bored Edward to tears) and pubbing, though I was still only drinking a little. I rather enjoyed my collection of jobs because they gave variety. Waitressing was the best because I got to know some of the regular customers, and one or two even started coming on the days they knew I was on. The small restaurant was just off the High Street, run by Ahmed and Abu, a couple of Turks who kept an eye on me as though I were their daughter. And then one March day there was a customer whose face had once been very familiar indeed.

"Hi, Nikki," said Pete. "Mum said she'd seen you working in here."

I hadn't recognised him in the first seconds. He'd grown his hair to shoulder length and tied it back in a ponytail. But the grey eyes and the mouth I had once wanted to kiss were the same. I took his order for scampi and chips and a Coke and went off, my heart racing.

"Must be careful with that one," Ahmed warned as I handed him the order.

"I've known him for years and years," I exaggerated.

"So, is OK."

"How long are you in Greenley for?" I asked Pete when I took him his order.

"A while. Mum has been in hospital and, as you may remember, she's on her own now. Perhaps we could go birding? I see they've built a lot on the old marshes, but there are still plenty left. How about tomorrow morning?"

"I've got a cleaning job in the morning. But the afternoon's OK."

"Great so that's a date."

2

I rang to tell Mother as soon as I got home and she muttered, "That's good news. Perhaps you'll start a normal relationship at last. What happened to his wife?" And I realised I hadn't even asked.

I could hardly sleep for excitement. It hadn't struck me that I was lonely, and of course I loved Matt to bits in a sisterly way, but to have a date with a boy I'd really fancied those years ago, felt very special.

Next afternoon, Pete was waiting for me at the end of the path that went along the back of our old house before dipping down to the marshes. I saw there had been a lot of changes to 'our' house: an annex built on to the back, a conservatory on to the living room, and small paddling pool where Mother used to grow vegetables. Good heavens.

The first thing I did was to ask Pete about his wife. He shrugged. "She dumped me. She was beautiful but also very ambitious not just for herself but for me. And, as you know, I'm not the high-flying kind. How about you?"

"I'm not high-flying either." So I told him about my parallel universes project, and about Matt and Edward; and about Dad and my abortive efforts to bring him and Mother together again.

"So what about the waitressing and cleaning?"

So I explained about my fall from grace. He was quiet for a moment then said, "You're the last person I would ever have thought would fall into the trap of drinking too much. I mean …"

"You mean, "I interrupted, "after having to cope with my Dad?" He nodded. "Well, it was nothing like *that*, for heaven's sake. I just got in with a boozy crowd and let my hair down a bit. It didn't go on and *on*."

"Good."

"Anyway, I hardly drink at all. Except that time after the disastrous meeting between Mother and Dad. And I was *s-o-o-o* disappointed."

It was at that point Pete leaned forward and gave me a peck on the forehead. "I think," he said, "you need someone to look after you for a while." And I couldn't have agreed more.

The birding wasn't the best that afternoon, but we did see a couple of lapwing parents faking a broken wing and leading us away from wherever their nests were, just as they had that day when Pete first caught my interest. He grinned when I reminded him. "I think I fancied you a bit then," he said. And without any warning he turned and pulled me towards him, and gave me the most tender kiss I had ever had. He drew a deep breath. "And, dammit, I think I still do."

That was the happiest day I could remember for a very long time, followed by the happiest night I had ever had. After the birding, we walked back into town and had a drink at the Crooked Parrot, and I found all the dark memories of that meeting between my parents had gone. Later we picked up Pete's rather ancient green van from its parking place in town and went to the restaurant where I waitressed just for the fun of being served by Ahmed's pretty daughter, while Ahmed himself kept a watchful eye on us. It was just as well as he couldn't see inside my ahead.

Finally I took Pete back to my flat. And there, in due course, he began to undress me slowly, then he guided me on to the bed, looked down at me and said I was beautiful and began undressing himself. We lay for a long time, gently exploring each other and I had never felt so cherished. When we finally had sex, it was completely different from the other time – not very comfortable, but giving me for the first time ever that amazing sense of fulfilment that goes with becoming part of someone else. I must have gone to sleep, for when I woke up much later I was alone. Pete had pulled the bedding over me, and left a note on the bedside table. It read: *you're perfect. Call you tonight.* Then I got up and looked at myself in the mirror and knew that nothing would be quite the same again.

Pete called me that evening and came round for the night which was even better. Within a very short time, it felt as though we had been together forever. Mother said I had never looked better, and invited us both round for a meal. I guess it was what she had always wanted, that I should meet a nice boy and settle down, not making the mistake she had made. She made it obvious that she approved of Pete, and I wasn't sure she knew about him staying overnight until she suddenly accosted me with "I assume you are taking precautions." Pete was surprised I wasn't on the pill, and I felt really embarrassed about going to my doctor and asking about it, but she made it seem quite normal, and of course it made absolute sense, because the last thing I wanted was to get pregnant.

In no time we had settled down to a happy routine. Pete had saved money from his work in forest management and contributed to the housekeeping. We'd plan the menus and he often did the shopping while I was working. In the end we bought a second hand camp bed as it was pretty crowded in mine if you wanted to sleep.

A couple of days into this magic new relationship, Pete said, "Mum would like us to go round for supper. She's always liked you, so it will be fine."

Well, it was a long time since I'd seen her, but Pete was right. Everything was fine. I was surprised how old she seemed, compared with Mother, but then she had been very ill. We came to an arrangement that Peter spent most of the day with her or doing jobs for her, and then spent the evening and night with me.

All this meant I suddenly wasn't seeing much of Matt and Edward, though I didn't feel too badly about it as they had each other. Early on I rang Matt and told him about Pete, and he said he was really happy for me as long as Pete wasn't like 'that Baz guy'. In due course we all met up for a drink. It wasn't a huge success, which I suppose wasn't surprising as in a way Peter was the odd one out. So we agreed that I should meet up with them from time to time and then Peter would stay with his Mum.

Matt judged that he (Pete) was a great improvement on the Baz guy, but Edward warned that I shouldn't put complete trust in any guy until he had actually given something up for me. I wasn't quite sure what he meant, but it was certainly true that Baz hadn't given anything up, and I hadn't had a long enough relationship with anyone else to know.

Fab though life was now, I realised there is always something or someone that has to pay the price. In my case it was both. The 'someone' was Dad who vaguely remembered Pete and was pleased for me, but clearly felt left out. I said we would both come up and stay with him as soon as possible. The 'something' was my parallel universe project. It was Dad who reminded me of that.

"You've put so much work into it Nikki. What does your Peter think?" he asked over the phone.

The fact was that Pete hadn't expressed much more than bemusement, and life was OK as it was thank you, so I put it to the back of mind until I had time to think about it properly.

Three weeks after Pete had somersaulted back into my life, Rachel and Adrian came back from Australasia. As soon as Rachel rang, I blurted out all about Pete and invited them round for a drink. Of course she knew him from school days, and said she was thrilled for me. The meeting didn't go quite as smoothly as expected. Of course, my friends, tanned and healthy-looking apart from jetlag, were full of their adventures the other side of the world. Rach followed me into my tiny kitchen to help with the wine and nibbles.

"Goodness, that Pete has changed," she said.

"Well, his hair is longer," I agreed.

"And a tad more complacent?"

I pointed out that in addition to being a great help to me, he was also looking after his Mum.

"Okay, okay. Anyway as long as you're happy that's the main thing," Rach stood back and looked at me, "And I must say you look very happy."

After that, I was too wrapped in my own happiness to see much of her. The days flowed into each other, with my different jobs, household chores, trips out with Pete, and lovely nights at the end of it. It was one evening in late March that Peter dropped his bombshell.

3

He had come as usual to pick me up from my pubbing job, and he suggested a quick nightcap before we went home. There was something different about him.

"What's happened?"

Pete looked surprised. "Is it that obvious?"

"A nightcap isn't usually on the agenda."

"Mm. Well, may be I need a bit of Dutch courage." He sat fiddling with his glass.

"Well, for heaven's sake get on with it!" I was beginning to feel twitchy, and aware of the nightcap settling warmly in my midriff and spreading its warmth up to that area of my brain that doesn't like conflict.

"It's actually a good idea," Pete said, "but you may not like it at first." He went on fiddling with his glass.

"I'll never like it if you don't tell me what it is."

He took a deep breath. "It's about a new job, and it's about Mum. I've been making a few applications, had one or two interviews…"

I gaped at him. "You never said anything."

"Well, I'd tried for a couple of dozen jobs before I moved back here, and didn't think there was much hope. Then this one turned up being Assistant Manager on an estate in Cumbria. It has a lot of woods so they thought my background would fit the bill. They want me to start next month."

My heart did a quick dip. "Good Lord. That won't give you much time to find somewhere to live."

"That's what makes it so good. A cottage goes with the job." Pete paused but only briefly, "So I could take Mum with me."

Whatever I had anticipated, in my worst dreams I had not anticipated that. I swallowed hard. "What does your Mum think?"

"I wanted to talk to you before I told her." Well, that was something. But not much. I couldn't imagine her turning such an offer down. So then I came out with what was really on my mind. "And what about us?"

He put out a hand to take mine. "I know, I know. It's a terrible disappointment to break up the special thing we have. But it needn't be for long." I felt a fillip of hope. "Who knows, there might be space for the three of us. And even if not, once I've settled in I could find a small flat for Mum."

Or for me. The hope fizzled out. I said dully, "We'd better go home and talk it through."

He squeezed my hand. "No, I told Mum I'd sleep at home tonight. Then I can talk to her about it over breakfast.

That was the worst night I'd had for a long time, my mind going over and over our talk and all the imponderables that still lay behind any decision. Did I want to share a cottage with Pete and his mother? No. Even if he could find a small flat for her, how could that work out if he had a full time job? And what about my job? And seeing Dad? And….? And ….?

Finally I drifted into uneasy sleep. Pete turned up as I was clearing up breakfast things. I was cleaning for Mother in an hour's time.

"Mother's thrilled," Pete said. He looked sheepish.

"Of course, she is. So?"

"But she's really worried about you."

"So?" I was beginning to sound like Rachel again.

"Well, I'll be on a month's probation. So Mum will come with me and we'll see how it shapes. Then as soon as I get the contract – and of course Mum *knows* that will happen – I'll find a flat for her and we'll put her house here on the market. And you could join me, if you wanted to." It seemed they had had a pretty meaningful discussion over breakfast. "What do you think?"

"Do I have an option."

Pete looked more sheepish. "The thing is that it could be a perfect solution – at least for Mum and me. But I agree, not for us." He added hopefully, "Perhaps this is a sort of test to our commitment." He meant my commitment of course.

Soon after, muttering that he had some shopping to do for Mum, he headed for the door, asking as an afterthought whether I needed anything. Just then I was only too glad to see the back of him.

As soon as I got to Mother's and before I got out the carpet cleaner, I blurted out my tale of woe. She listened carefully and said, "Let's talk about it over coffee," which meant she wanted me to get the work done first. It probably wasn't the best cleaning session I'd ever done, but Mother didn't say anything when I came into the kitchen and slumped down at the table. The coffee was ready and she poured me out a mug and nudged it across the table.

"Well," she said, when she had poured one for herself and sat down, "It does seem an ideal solution for Pete and his mother."

"I suppose it is," I said, "But what about me."

Mother stirred her coffee, took a sip of it, put down her mug and said slowly, "Nikki dear, things aren't always about you."

I thought a moment. "Yes, I suppose that did sound self-centred, but I thought Pete and I had something going. Something lasting, I mean. Aren't I entitled to think I might be considered?"

"Has it been stated as something lasting, or are you assuming?" For heaven's sake whose side was she on?

"I thought I was entitled to assume when we'd been sharing everything, *every*thing, for several weeks."

"Then I must have got it wrong. I thought your modern relationships were talked through so everyone put in their bit."

True I wasn't very practised in relationships, but that seemed a fair summary – except that Pete's side of it had all been very arbitrary. I said very quietly, "Perhaps I got it wrong."

Then Mother did lean over and take one of my hands, and look sympathetic. "Life has very hard lessons, sometimes. But please, *please*, don't shut your eyes and think all the problems will go away. That's what your father did, and it almost destroyed me. And sometimes you are so like him."

May 2009

1

I took those last sentences of Mother's away with me and chewed on them for a long time. It hadn't occurred to me that I was at all like Dad. Not that there was anything wrong with him now that he had stopped drinking.

Is that what Mother had meant? But that was crazy. She had only really known of a couple of times when I went over the top. Pete came back to the flat that evening, but slept on the camp bed. He said his Mum was so excited about the move and was making plans and scattering lists all over the place of things to do, people to tell, items to buy. Lucky Mum.

Then he said, "Nik, I know it's hard for you, but it won't be for long, I promise. I couldn't let you go now I've found you again."

That made me feel so good I nearly jumped out of my bed and into his. After that things felt much better and we got back into our routine of meeting up, though less frequently, and spending most nights together. I even went and helped his Mum pack up her most precious ornaments she didn't want to leave behind, though of course she wasn't taking much at this stage as there was still a chance she might be coming back. Mother said she thought I was handling the situation very well.

In the end I spent most of Easter with Pete and his Mum as she wanted my advice on what clothes to take. I couldn't imagine Mother ever asking me for that. Anyway, Pete's Mum had always been a real townie so we went into some of the charity shops in Greenley and fitted her out with some great tee-shirts and sweaters. While we were doing it I got a couple for myself.

So the day of their departure came. Pete spent the last night with me and it was absolutely magic. He told me not to come and see them off, but I did and then regretted it because as the car disappeared round the corner there was a terrible sense of desolation. I went back into the house and had a good cry, then I locked up and went back to my flat where Mother rang me soon after and suggested I spent the rest of the week-end with them.

The first week wasn't too bad. I emailed him every day with an account of what was happening, and Peter rang or texted me. He

166

liked the estate manager he worked for, loved the job and Mum was in her element choosing plants for the tiny cottage garden. Peter emailed me a picture of the cottage with Mum by the front door. It was grey stone and a bit dark looking, but I started to imagine how I might brighten it up. I even drew a sketch of its lay-out as Pete had described.

Then one of my emails came back as undelivered as the recipient didn't have an account. I frowned at it and sent it again, but the same thing happened. Pete didn't ring for a couple of days so I texted him crossly to ask what the hell was going on. When I tried to ring him and got the unobtainable signal, I began to worry. Over supper at Mother's that evening I mentioned my concerns. She wasn't particularly sympathetic.

"For goodness sake, Nikki. You young people change your mobiles like other people change their socks. He probably found the signal or something wasn't very good and has got himself another one. And being busy in a new job he hasn't managed to tell everyone yet. You really mustn't be so dependent on people."

I refrained from saying that I wasn't 'everyone' because otherwise her comments made quite a lot of sense, and in due course she was proved right, though I had to fret a few days longer. And, while I waited, I mulled over the meaning of Mother's warning not to be so dependent on people. I decided to ask her about it.

She said, "Oh dear, I didn't mean it to become a big issue. I just meant that people are fallible and if you expect too much of them, you are bound to be disappointed. Look at Baz."

"He's hardly the best example. He cheated on me."

"I know, love. You rejected him in a way, so he dealt with it as best he could. I'm not saying he was right. Wanting your cake and eating it usually isn't. Then you wanted your father and I to get together to create that happy family unit. Even your father accepts it's too late, but you can't. I'm just worried for you."

She was worried about *me*!

I asked, "You don't think I should have any expectations from Pete? Like he has to choose between his mother and me?"

"No, I meant that you each have to make your choice according to circumstances and Pete already has a lot to deal with – new job, ailing Mum, and may be he's not quite yet mature enough to fit you into the equation as well."

167

At which point I slammed out of her flat and stalked back to mine. And found an email from Pete. It said: *Sorry for the silence. I had the bad idea of changing my email and mobile at the same time and so much is going on I didn't remember to tell you straight away. Sorry, sorry, sorry. I'm coming back to Greenley in a couple of weeks. Something's come up.*

I went straight back to Mother's to apologise and stayed for lunch. She started to say something once or twice, then changed her mind. Finally she managed, "I'm really happy for you, Sweetheart, but do remember what I said."

2

The next couple of weeks were good. There was Pete's visit dominating the future though I did wonder what he meant when he said something had come up. I made a little calendar and marked off the days. I watched a family of house martins fledge. Ahmed gave me a small rise and even the early mornings at the newsagents weren't quite so bad with the lighter mornings. On a couple of occasions I joined Matt and Edward at the Crooked Parrot, which had now become a favourite meeting place. They seemed really happy together – the sort of happy that is content to include other people. I said as much to Matt when Edward went to the loo.

He nodded and grinned. "Yes, it's great. We're thinking of moving in together."

"You really are sure this time?"

He nodded again, adding after a moment, "Which reminds me, I hope it's the same for you and Pete."

"Why shouldn't it be?"

He shrugged. "It's just that you look a bit like how I felt when I was with Neil. I wouldn't want you to go through that."

I gave him a quick hug. "No it's nothing like that." I told him about the momentary panic over Peter's change of email address and mobile number and his follow-up email, and he looked reassured.

"Do you think you'll go and join them?" he asked.

"I think so. It makes sense. And presumably I can always get odd jobs locally."

"I'll miss you," Matt said, as Edward rejoined us and asked, "Where's she off to?"

We gave him a summary of the situation. "Dammit," he said, "I'll miss you, too. But watch it. You need to be careful with these straight guys."

The days dawdled by. Almost without realising it, I started making lists of things to ask Pete when he came, and of things I would like to take with me if .... when I moved. It wasn't something I could discuss with Mother as I knew she'd say I was getting too dependent again. But I did mention it to Dad who said it would be great as I'd be nearer him. So I was feeling pretty good by the time I had crossed all the days off my home-made calendar and was waiting for Pete's arrival. I watched him park his old green van in the yard, and hurry across to my flat. He looked great. He'd cut his hair, and looked fit and outdoorsy.

I opened my door and flung myself into his embrace, which continued as he propelled me into the bedroom. A long time later, Pete said, "Wow, how could I forget how good that is?" We showered and dressed and I produced from the fridge the lamb casserole I had made that morning.

"You're a star," Peter said appreciatively after a second helping. We rounded if off with supermarket profiteroles, coffee, and then went back to bed again.

It was in the early hours of the morning that I propped myself on one elbow and said, "And how about your Mum? She is all right staying up there alone."

There was rather a long silence. At last Peter said to the ceiling, "Something's come up since I was last here."

I knew straight away that I was not going to like what I was about to hear. "Go on," I said.

"It's just this friend I had some time back suddenly turned up at the cottage. I don't know how they found out where I was ..." *So it was someone rather than something.*

"They?"

"Well, she actually. A girl I used to know."

"I see. She wasn't by any chance called Denise?" Pete turned his head away. "The girl you were going to marry?"

He sat up abruptly, clasped his hands round his knees, still did not look at me. "It wasn't like how you're making it sound."

"How am I making it sound?"

"Sly and mean. Well, it's not like that. I had no idea she was going to get in touch."

"Did you sleep with her?"

"No. Well, yes in the past. But not this time."

"So if it wasn't how I'm making it sound, how was it?"

"Like two friends meeting up. Denise has changed so much – not so brash and ambitious. Found she really missed me. I suppose she's grown up. In fact, it was Denise who made it possible for me to come to Greenley. I realised I couldn't leave Mum on her own."

Part of me could see that was understandable, but most of me was seething with disappointment and anger and resentment and jealousy all mixing in a messy cocktail, taking me over. I got out of bed, slipped on a dressing gown. "I think you'd better go."

"Why? Why? Dammit, what's got into you?"

"You really can't understand?"

"No. No, I can't. Nothing's *happened*, Nik. Denise is just helping me out of a spot."

"Well, if you can't see why I'm upset, there's no point in me trying to explain."

Pete swung his legs out of bed and sat on the edge of it beside me. "Why are you being so unreasonable, Nik? I really like you"

He tried to take hold of my hand, but I shook him off saying "And I was fool enough to think I loved you. So how do you want to leave it? Long enough to check out which of us suits you best?" I was cold with anger now. "Just take your stuff and *go*. I'm going to take a shower."

While I was in the shower room, I could hear Pete moving about, dressing, putting his stuff together. Eventually there was a tentative knock at the door which I ignored. When the knocking became louder, I shouted *"Go away, and make sure I never hear from you again!"*

I heard the front door open and close and, after a while, opened the shower room door and looked out. Not a sound. Then I went to lie on my rumpled bed and howled like an animal.

3

I don't think I slept at all that night. I know a lot of it was hurt pride, but I really had thought I loved him, and that we could make a partnership and explore the rest of our lives together.

Next morning I was snuffling over a bowl of muesli when Mother came over with the remains of a venison pie she thought we might fancy. She took one look at me, put the venison pie down on the table, and said "So what's happened?"

I tried to tell her, but it came out in gulps and sobs, so she poured herself out a coffee and sat down at the table beside me. "Do I gather that Pete hasn't quite made the grade?"

I gulped a bit more and then managed, "He's getting back with his ex-girl friend."

"Is that what he said?"

"Well, I had to d-drag it out of him. But she's suddenly m-materialised out of nowhere and is looking after his M-mum while he's away."

Mother said, "Oh dear," and sipped her coffee. After a while she went on, "It's no use my saying that it's better to find it out now than later?"

"N-no. I really l-loved him. I d-don't know what I'm going to do."

Mother put her mug of coffee down. "What I suggest you do is come and stay with us for a few days. I can take some stuff out of the box room and make a bed up there. It looks over the gardens. We can put the old tv in there."

As if I'd be feeling like watching telly. But she was doing her very best to make me feel wanted and unalone, so I got up and gave her a hug and said, "You're a star, Mother." Then I remembered that's what Pete had called me the previous evening, and burst into tears again.

Later that morning, we went back to her flat and organised the box room. Alex was out playing golf so thankfully I didn't have to do any explaining to him straight away. By the time he came home I was under more control, and anyway he was very nice and sympathetic.

The following days dragged by. Pete sent me some emails which I deleted without reading. Everything seemed pointless, but I went through the motions of my various jobs on automatic. I got told off at the newsagents for making a muddle of the various Sunday supplements. Even Ahmed complained that he had lost his little ray of sunshine. In the end it was Tom who gave me the first nudge in the right direction. I had not seen him for a while, but now he happened to be home when I was cleaning for Sally. While I was doing the en suite for their bedroom, he came to lean on the door jamb and said, "I hear you've dumped your boyfriend."

"Mm."

171

"I gather he's cheating you?"

"Mm."

"Cheating on people is a sign of immaturity. I imagine you're feeling a bit sorry for yourself."

I straightened up from cleaning the bath. "Is this leading anywhere, Tom?"

"Just showing a friendly interest. And I remember how an emotional jag affected me and sent me flying to the bottle."

"Yes, but I'm not an alcoholic."

"No, of course not. Want a coffee?

"Thanks, but I've got an interview for another possible part time job."

"Good for you." Tom was about to go then turned back. "Just wondering - now you've got some work experience whether you might like to think of something a bit more permanent."

"Such as?"

"For example, hotel work. Greenley isn't exactly the hub of the universe, but there are several quite pleasant country establishments within a reasonable radius. I gather you've got a car now, so that would help."

I gave a final polish round the rim of the bath. "That's not a bad idea, Tom. I'll check out the possibilities."

"Try Hillside Manor, just off the main road going north."

"Thanks, I'll do that."

"The Assistant Manager is James Meredith. I'll give him a buzz."

The next day I took Beano for a thorough clean and valet. It cost me most of my week-end earnings at the newsagent, but was worth it. He didn't exactly look any *grander*, but he certainly looked cared for.

Hillside Manor was ten miles from Greenley, a couple of miles down a side road and sitting on the side of a hill as its name implied. I felt a bit self conscious parking Beano among the row of large shiny cars in front of the hotel, but she was certainly cleaner than several of them. A Jack Russell in a neighbouring car yapped furiously, so I pulled my tongue out at it. Then I stood back and looked at the imposing façade of Hillside Manor. It looked like – and probably had been – a stately home at some point in its history. Later I learned it was 17th century with 19th century additions.

As I was heading for the main entrance a man approached and said, "That was my dog you were pulling your tongue out at."

Over my shoulder I said, "Sorry. Don't like yappy dogs."

The receptionist said that James Meredith was at a meeting (you wouldn't believe how much time people spend at meetings) but would be out shortly – and would I like to take a seat and someone would bring me a coffee? So I sat in the foyer in an armchair from which I could look out on to stately gardens while I was brought a tray with a pot of coffee and dainty cup from which to drink it. It was very restful and I was still enjoying the coffee and the view when I was aware of someone sitting on a neighbouring chair and looked round to see the owner of the yappy dog.

"I know Dennis can be irritating…"

"Dennis?"

"Dennis, as in Dennis the Menace. That's the name of my dog. And I'm James Meredith."

I'd flipped through enough copies of Beano to know of its association with Dennis, and giggled. "My car is called Beano."

James Meredith grinned back. "Perhaps that's why Dennis was getting so cross." The grin made him look younger and really quite good looking. "Do you want some more coffee?"

"No thanks. And I think I'd better come clean straight away and explain that my experience of hotel work is limited to a bit of waitressing, cleaning and shop work. All part time."

"Well that's refreshingly honest – and in your favour, it happens. We won't have to train you out of too many bad habits." He drew some papers out of this pocket and consulted them. "The next training course starts in two weeks. Can you manage that?"

I hadn't thought in terms of training courses, and asked, "How much is it?"

"Good heavens, nothing. You get board and lodging free, but have to sing for your supper. In other words while you're in training you're supervised by existing staff to do the jobs you will end up by doing when you've completed."

"Where is it?"

"In Wiltshire, not far from Marlborough. Our group headquarters are at Forest Lodge, a few miles south of the Ridgeway. So, shall we see you there?"

June-September 2009

1

Mother wasn't very keen on me living away for a month, but Alec pointed out it would get me some proper qualifications and do me the world of good. So I enrolled and enjoyed the course so much that I barely thought of Pete after a while. For a start, much of the time I was too tired. The training was non stop and in between any tuition there was endless bed making and room cleaning. You wouldn't believe how many things you need to know about preparing a room between the departure of one guest and the arrival of the next. Or how disgusting some people are.

Some of the other trainees were fun, too, and came from all over the country. In fact there were a couple of rural dialects I could hardly understand and we had a few hysterical sessions over misunderstandings. Our rooms were along a corridor at the top of the building, presumably once the servants' quarters, but at least we each had a room to ourselves, poky as it might be.

One of the other trainees came from Northern Ireland and I took a bit of a fancy to him. He was one of those whose dialect I found difficult to understand, largely because he exaggerated it just to confuse us. He was called Liam and reminded me a lot of Matt, though he made it clear very early on that he was not gay. During the course, we were strongly discouraged from forming relationships, and we were not allowed in the bar. So, at the end of the first week, when our free time coincided, Liam and I went off in his car to explore local hostelries. It was quite a small car and not very comfortable when we decided to have sex in the back of it.

"So you aren't spoken for?" Liam said, while we were tidying ourselves up. Well, I wasn't, was I? But it was amazing to discover how soon Pete ceased to matter. After that we found ways of popping into each other's rooms. Usually I went to Liam's as he had an endless supply of Irish whiskey which I discovered was spelt with an 'e' and tasted quite different from Scotch.

By the end of the course, Liam and I had become an item. We both passed, though I didn't do so well in the kitchen which certainly would not have surprised Mother, while Liam got glowing reports

174

from Chef. Apparently my talents lay with communication and people, so it looked as though I was destined for front of house.

Fortunately Mother took to Liam, and made no comment when he moved in to my flat while we put ourselves on the job market. In the meantime we both took part-time jobs. Ahmed was very pleased to see me back but I don't think approved of Liam. He kept asking where that nice young man Peter was, so I said he was working in a different part of the country which, after all, was true. I was getting quite good at being selective with my truths.

One evening Liam came home late and found me with my feet up watching a film on TV and half way through a bottle of red. He plonked down beside me and said, "You're drinking too much Nik," and of course he didn't know about the bottle I'd already had. We started rowing quite a lot about my drinking, so it was probably as well that towards the end of July Liam got offered a job in the kitchens of a fine establishment in Wales. He said that would be just great for when he wanted to catch the ferry back to Belfast.

Reception jobs seemed a bit harder to come by at the time, so I had to wait longer. But that was OK. I carried on working for Ahmed and also took a week-end slot with a department store. By then Rach and Adrian had an August date for their engagement, and it was fun helping to plan that. I also saw more of Matt and Edward. They were now settled in a smart flat near the park. Matt was working full time as a garage mechanic, and Edward, who was on the administrative ladder in some council department, liked to call him his 'bit of rough'. But I didn't start going out with the old drinking gang again. I preferred to have my own supply and just enjoy it relaxing with a TV programme, or going back over my notes on parallel universes. Neither Pete nor Liam had showed much interest and, since Matt had partnered up with Edward, he had other preoccupations. They were, after all, in their mid to late twenties so getting on a bit. I suppose I was also drinking quite a lot, but there was no one to notice, and I'd usually slept it off by morning.

One evening Mother turned up with her 'we-ought-to-have-a-talk' face.

"Are you all right, Sweetheart?"

"Fine, fine. Why wouldn't I be?"

She slipped into the kitchen and put the kettle on. It looked as though it was Cosy Chat time.

"You don't seem to be having much of a fun time. Alec and I are quite worried about you." *Alec and I.* Perhaps I should start worrying about them. "And you don't seem very fortunate in your choice of boyfriends."

So that was it! "Don't worry, Mother – and tell Alec not to. Unlike Rach I've absolutely no desire to settle down for ages yet. OK, I made a bad choice with Baz, but I suppose I was a bit young. And Pete – well, I badly misjudged him. But Liam was never more than a lot of fun, and he was starting to get very bossy...."

"Well, that wouldn't suit," Mother interrupted with a smile. "Anyway, as long as you're happy."

"Yeah, thanks. Have to say I'm a bit restless. I'll be really glad when I get a proper job sorted out."

And sorted out it was the very next week. The letter came from the natty James Meredith. It read, *Dear Miss Wood, I apologise that it has taken longer than I had hoped to write to you, but I think I can now offer you a position for which you are admirably suited. It is as receptionist at the Forest Lodge, involving some secretarial duties. When hosting conferences in some of our other establishments, we may also call on your waitressing or other skills. Perhaps you would kindly call my secretary, Julia Adams, to make an appointment when we can discuss details.*

2

I rang and made an appointment to go over the following Tuesday. Julia Adams ("please call me Julia") was very chic and I felt a bit under-dressed at first though I was wearing my latest designer suit, straight out of Oxfam. Over coffee, she said, "Mr Meredith spoke very highly of your progress at the course," and that was surprising as I had hardly seen him during my time there. But Julia assured me he was very good at spotting talent.

She gave me a very thorough tour of the premises, though I was already quite familiar with them from my time on the training course. It was the sort of place you could imagine being used as the setting for a TV series for an early 20th century drama, but so cleverly adapted that every room had all the modern facilities anyone could possibly want. I thought some of them were a bit 'o.t.t.', like the bath taps that did not exist, but you waved your hand in front of an outlet, and water suddenly came out. There were cosy sitting corners on each floor with old furniture and tables strewn with magazines. The dining room was very elegant, but there were little cafés and a buttery dotted about for more intimate meetings, not to mention three different bars.

At my first interview, I had assumed that I would come in every day according to my shift hours, and Julia agreed this was fine, but said that during busy times, like conferences, when staff often worked overtime, it made sense to stay overnight. She asked if that would be a problem, and I said not at all. In fact, the idea of being able to alternate between my own flat and my own place of work gave an extremely pleasing sense of independence. She left me to wander round the grounds while she made some phone calls and arranged lunch, when we would be joined by James Meredith. The grounds were extensive and there wasn't time to explore more than a fraction of them, but I did a circuit of a small lake, and followed a path into woodland before returning through more formal gardens.

When I got back to reception, James Meredith was waiting and so was Julia. I noticed she called him James, but thought I'd better not until invited. Still it looked as though inter-management relations were friendly.

"Julia says you'll slot in very nicely with our team," James Meredith said over plates piled high from the most lavish cold buffet I'd ever seen. "And that's good news, as we have several big conferences in various venues this summer and will need all the best quality staff we can get."

"I still have a lot to learn," I said, and it was by no means with false modesty.

"Of course you have. That is why it would be excellent if you could start as soon as possible and get some experience before the rush. Would you be able to start, say, next Monday?"

Wow! I hadn't expected it to be that quick. But when he mentioned the salary, that was higher than expected too, so I didn't hesitate for long.

When I got back to the flat and nipped over to tell Mother she suggested I stay for supper to celebrate. "You must have made a good impression, Sweetheart. I'm proud of you."

It was a lovely evening and Alec said he was proud of me, too. Then at the end of it, he said more seriously, "I don't want to dampen your success, but I think it's only fair that you know that my wife Marion has now been diagnosed with liver cancer with no possibility of surgery. They give her probably ten to fifteen weeks. Your mother is my greatest support." He got up and kissed her on the forehead. "And I'm so glad she has you to support her."

I think that was the most serious speech Alec had ever directed at me and for a moment I felt quite wobbly. With so many people being proud of me, I thought it was worth a little extra celebration when I got back to my flat. There was a half of a bottle of gin at the back of my wardrobe, so I poured a good measure into a glass and topped it up with tonic. Then I settled down to call Dad, who greeted me with "Wherever do you get to these days? For goodness sake get yourself an answering machine."

I promised I would and gave him my news. He kept interrupting with little exclamations of 'Good Gracious,' and 'Well, I never', and finally said, "That's my girl. Wait till I tell the gang here – we'll probably descend on you mob-handed." I very much hoped not, but he soon added "Not serious. Though I certainly plan to give the place a once-over before long."

In the end it was quite long because the subsequent weeks were so busy I never seemed to have a moment to myself. And though I did get myself an answer-phone and Dad left lots of messages, I had to keep ringing to say, "No, not next Tuesday-Thursday-Friday – there's another big group coming then." I even had to cancel going to Rach's engagement do. In fact I wouldn't have thought it possible to work so hard, then get up the next day and do it all over again, and again. Julia became a good friend. It was clear that James Meredith relied on her entirely for organising his schedules and, indirectly, the running of the hotel. From time to time we'd have a night cap in my room and do a post-mortem of the day. She had a boyfriend called Robert who looked soft and cuddly but not very bright. Other people's choice of partners is sometimes very odd.

Even Mother commented that I was looking ragged out, but actually I was loving it. It was partly because I now felt a useful part of a team, and partly because I knew I was good at it, and getting better. This was confirmed by Julia who told me that James had described me as a great 'find'. Well, that was a surprise. He'd always been rather distant with me and sometimes I caught him watching me with a distinctly critical look. On the other hand, he was also good at handing out pats on the back if he thought you had done a good job.

All the same, I was conscious that I was beginning to rely on a stiff nightcap to help me unwind before I went to bed, and its morning equivalent to get me going next day. Still, this unusually busy patch would not go on forever and then I would get back to normal.

And then something extraordinary happened. It was the fourth day of a big regional conference for some major charity when everything started going wrong. At least I started doing everything wrong. Even Julia, who was harassed herself, began to lose patience when I got the numbers wrong for how many were having which menu, having already double booked three couples, and provided double-bed accommodation for aficionados of twin beds. James Meredith must have overheard something for he caught my arm as I was flying from A to B and said, "For goodness sake pull yourself together Nikki."

The final straw was when I overheard him apologising to one of the organisers because 'one or two of our staff are not quite as trained as they should be.'

I eventually stumbled up to my small room on the top floor, poured myself a large gin and burst into tears. It seemed so unfair when I had worked so hard and was so anxious to get everything right.

A short while later, there was a quiet knock at my door. I opened it, clutching my glass and gaped through damp swollen eyes at James Meredith.

3

He slipped in, pushed the door shut behind him, removed the glass from my hand and enveloped me in his arms. And then he guided me to the bed. I think I was too drunk to protest and anyway the whole thing was so weird I couldn't begin to analyse it. Not least I was enjoying it. For a long time he just held me, murmuring that the last thing he wanted was to upset me, but everyone had become rather overstressed in recent days. Then he made love to me in a way that had more tenderness than passion in it and it was like nothing I'd experienced before. It felt so good, I let it happen. I sensed him slip out of bed but must have fallen asleep, for the next thing I was groping my way back into consciousness, gradually recalling what had happened, then sitting bolt upright and wondering how the hell I was going to face James Meredith.

When I got down to the office it was to find not James but Julia, frantically sorting through mail, checking through menus and dealing with the non-stop ringing of the phone. She looked as haggard as I probably did.

She paused breathlessly to say, "Hi Nikki. James has been called away – something to do with his daughter. Thank God it's a quiet day." She stopped, looked up. "You look about as dreadful as I feel. You're overdue for some days off. James'll be away for several. I'll square it with him as soon as I've caught up with this lot." She waved an arm over the papers scattered over the desk.

After a strong black coffee I drove home. A lot of things needed sorting out in my head, but I wasn't in state to do it just yet. Except examine Julia's words: 'something to do with his daughter.' Despite the coffee, the first thing I did on getting home was to sleep for several hours. When I awoke I found Mother had been in and put a note on my bedside table. She had written *Hadn't the heart to disturb you. Come across for supper and we can swap news.* The idea that I wouldn't have to cook supper was very appealing, so I rang and accepted, even though I had no intention of swapping all news.

I made myself a cup of coffee and sat in the living room, staring out at the garden and reliving last night. Though I had thought James quite dishy, I hadn't thought of him in *that* way, and it was hard to grasp how it had all happened so quickly. Presumably we'd all had rather too much to drink. Did I want it to happen again? Yes, I did, because I had felt really cherished. But he was married, and I didn't do married men. Did I?

It was at that point that the phone rang. It was Dad. He said, "Got you at last. So how are you coping?"

I'm exhausted and I've just slept with my boss didn't seem the right answer, so I simply said, "We've had a crazy few weeks, but I think we're coming out of it, so we should be able to meet up soon. At the moment I'm about to join Mother and Alec who apparently have news."

"Oh." From Dad's tone with that one syllable, I realised that perhaps I shouldn't have mentioned that, but he changed the subject and went on to tell me how well his sales were doing..

In the event, it turned out that Mother and Alec did have major news to impart. Alec had moved Marion to a local hospice as she clearly did not have much longer to live.. I felt sorry for him. In the way he was reacting, he managed to combine anxiety, guilt and a deep sadness. Mother said very little but touched him or gave him little hugs at every opportunity.

In the light of this, their interest in my news was minimal, though they were pleased and encouraging at the success I reported, and commiserated with my mistakes 'which were hardly surprising given the pressure you were under'. I said it was OK, because my boss had been very understanding.

"Well, don't start falling in love with him," Alec said, his mind clearly somewhere else.

As I let myself into the flat, the phone was ringing. "Oh thank God," said James Meredith's voice. "I've been so worried, my dear. Did you get my note?"

"No."

"I thought I left one in your mail box…. Perhaps I didn't. It was such a frantic time this morning…." *Could it only have been that morning?* "I thought I left a message to say that I had to rush off because my daughter Sammy had come back unexpectedly from Uni with a lump on her breast. My wife took her to the hospital today and they are doing a biopsy tomorrow. I've been trying to call you all day – I was so worried about how you might be after last night."

I managed "I was probably asleep and have just got back from supper with Mother and her partner. I'm fine. Perhaps a … a bit surprised."

I sensed his smile. "Not half as surprised as I am, my dear. I just don't do this sort of thing. Though things have been a bit difficult lately."

After a small silence I said, "I do hope the biopsy shows there's nothing too wrong with Sammy. Anyway, she must be quite young so that'll be in her favour."

"Mm. About your age."

The silence hung between us. "Nikki, it would help enormously if we could meet up, say, for lunch. Just that. As friends. Obviously it can't be more."

"Shouldn't you be with Sammy?"

"Good heavens, her mother hardly leaves her for a minute. The poor girl won't want both of us. How about tomorrow? I know a great little place not too far from here. You're taking a few days off, aren't you?"

"All right, if you think it's OK."

"I'll pick you up at noon. Take care, my dear."

September 2009 – January 2010

1

And so began my first real affair, though I doubt if most of my peers would have called it that. For a start, it was more intellectual than physical. And if that sounds unreal, well that's just how it was. James even used the word 'unreal' and said he had never felt that way before. I didn't have many comparisons to go by, but this was no way like anything I had felt for Baz or Liam or even Pete. We did have sex occasionally (though not as often as I would have liked), but that was usually if James had had quite a bit to drink. I'd had quite a bit to drink rather often.

What I liked was when we were somewhere quiet where we could talk and talk, and I'd watch his changing expressions as he made some argument. It was James who got me back thinking about parallel universes, so that I unearthed all my old notes. He was also quite critical.

"My dear, it is no use putting forward a proposition while skimming over some point that you don't quite understand. You must go back over it until you do understand."

So I underlined all the woolly bits in my notes and went back on line or to the library to check points such as the relevance of parallel universes to 19th century literature and medieval legends. Then I could at least present James with properly researched argument. Sometimes during one of our discussions he would break off midsentence and give me a smile that made me want to leap straight into bed with him, and say, "I love this searching mind of yours." More often than not, our evenings ended with him looking at his watch, "Good God, is it so late already! I must get home."

I did ask him about 'home' quite early on. There was a photograph of his wife, Jenny, on his desk, looking very elegant and pretty in a mature way. "Oh Jenny," he said. "She's over the top of her head in good works. That's not a criticism, mind you. When I was head-hunted for a career in this group and saw what the prospects were, I worked all the hours of day and night. Jenny needed her own stimuli, and she's absolutely ace at organising committees, getting money out of businesses and making sure things get done. So we've sort of drifted, I suppose. But of course I'd go to the ends of the earth for her."

So that was that. It was difficult to understand how he could feel like that about Jenny, yet spend so much time with me. It was probably one of those things that people said "you'll understand when you're older." How much older do you have to get? On the other hand, given the fact Jenny had chosen to fulfill her life in her own way, I didn't feel guilty about the time I spent with her husband.

It was all very unsettling and frustrating except for one magic week-end. It was my week-end off and James rang me late on the Friday evening to say he had to meet someone on business in North Wales, and would I like to come. He had booked us into a hotel and disappeared for some hours to meet this 'someone', but the rest of the time I had him to myself. The only awful moment was when one of the receptionists asked me to pass a message on to 'my father'. Fortunately she turned away before my face flared scarlet.

James did not speak much about his children. His son was away at boarding school. Sammy had squeezed through with a B.Sc. Econ. degree and was now doing work practice somewhere in London and sharing a flat with friends. Fortunately her benign lump had been removed and she'd made a quick recovery. Reading between the lines, I guessed Sammy was a bit of a disappointment to James as her main interests were partying and pop concerts.

In early November, Alec's wife Marion died. I supported him and Mother as much as I could, through the preparations for the funeral, the event, and sorting through her things afterwards. I also promised to spend Christmas with them – in fact, was glad to as being on my own certainly wouldn't be much fun. At work, the autumn was fairly quiet but it was clear as December approached that the pre-Christmas period would be frenzied. Before that, Dad and I finally managed to get together. Firstly I had to promise not to manipulate any more meetings with Mother, but I had learned my lesson the last time. And I warned Mother so that she could keep out of the way. Despite his protests, I let him have my bed and I slept on a camp bed in the box room crammed between the desk and the book case.

I took a few days off and we arranged to have lunch at Forest Lodge on his last day. It was so good to see Dad and he looked really well, though he couldn't apparently say the same about me. We talked and talked. I told him quite a lot about James though, of course, not everything. He looked a bit worried and said to be careful, though it was good that James had got me thinking again, as Dad had felt I had been backsliding in that direction.

Then he had a brilliant idea. "Why don't you start a blog? On parallel universes? It's obviously a question that a lot of people are interested in. You might include a forum. It might even lead to one of those '*How to ?*' books. That friend of yours – what's his name – Adrian? He knows about computers and could help you, couldn't he?"

Adrian certainly could. I stored that in the back of mind for investigation in the New Year. I'd had a word with James prior to our lunch at Forest Lodge, so he came over in the middle of our first course, looking suitably obsequious, to ask if everything was satisfactory for sir and madam, and smiling to show he was not to be taken seriously.

"May I offer you a bottle of Chateau Bourignac on the house?"

Dad said, "Not for me thank you. But I'm sure my daughter would enjoy a glass."

James joined us for coffee.

"You must be very proud of your daughter, Mr. Wood," he said.

"No one prouder," Dad rejoined. "Unless it's her mother. Anyway I understand Nikki s doing well here."

"I've never had a trainee transform so quickly into a key member of our team."

"That's very good to hear. You think she has a career in hotel management?"

"No doubt about it."

I had my own back by telling James about Dad's new career. James said he'd have a look at the website when it was up and running, and may be order some items for the hotel shop.

On the way home I ventured, "So what did you think of my boss?"

"A tad smooth. But he obviously has a very high opinion of you. Be careful though."

"Oh, don't worry. James just thinks I have a beautiful mind." I joked.

"Mmm," Dad said non-commitally.

James was more enthusiastic about Dad. "What an enterprising man. I wouldn't have minded a brother like him."

That was a shock. Then I realised that, yes, they would be the same generation and could be brothers, even if with quite an age gap.

2

The Christmas season slowly enveloped us. I guess all of us at the hotel felt we'd had a surfeit of Christmas before it arrived. Day after day glittered with decorations, jingled with Christmas carols, crackled with parcel-opening, juddered with laughter and jollity. We were all worn out by the end, and James' family had had a sudden influx of relatives from Australia, so I saw little of him, though he often managed to call me at home.

I made up for it by 'taking over' our family Christmas. Needless to say Mother's preparations for it were very subdued. In the end I said I'd take charge. In view of Marion's recent death, we'd keep it very low key, of course, but I thought we could just have a small Christmas tree, which I would decorate, and invite round a few friends. We decided on two small groups, Sally and Tom, and the Lewises, who owned the house where we rented our flats, for one; and then Matt and Edward, Rachel and Adrian for the other.

I even offered to have the parties in my flat. Alec took me completely by surprise when I suggested it by coming over to give me a big hug. "You're a gem, young Nikki. It could be a touch tight in your flat. We'll have the parties here, it will bring a bit of life into your mother's Christmas, and stop me from being quite so self-absorbed."

And so it was. All our guests knew the situation and acted appropriately. And I began to see how really difficult it was for Alec. After all, Marion had given him a terrible time, but he had loved and married her, so his feelings must have been very muddled up. It helped to understand what Mother had gone through with Dad, too. Though, of course, Dad wasn't dead, thank God. He kept in touch regularly, reporting soaring sales on Ebay.

I was working on Boxing Day, but had Christmas Eve and Christmas Day off, so we arranged to have Sally, Tom and the Lewises on Christmas Eve, and Matt, Rachel and partners on Christmas Day. Matt came over one evening to help me decorate the tree, because he knew how I liked it, and that was a nice evening. In fact, everything went better than I dared hope.

And then, from one moment to the next, everything went horribly wrong. One late morning in the first week in January, I looked up from checking the following week's bookings on the computer and found myself facing a young woman with an enquiring expression. She was very pretty in an in-your-face sort of way - that much I noticed before she repeated the comment I had obviously not heard.

"I have an appointment," she said, "with Mr. Meredith. Mr. James Meredith."

I felt curiosity mixed with a twinge of resentment. In a flash I registered the up-to-the-minute hair style: what I thought of as the one-sided look, with the hair curving at length over one cheek while pulled well back from the other. She was wearing an extremely short splashy red dress over black leggings.

I picked up the internal phone. "May I say who is calling?"

She was checking her nails whose red matched the dress. "Sammy Meredith," she said. "His daughter."

A heavy object seemed to hurtle from my throat to the depths of my stomach, but I managed a steady voice as James answered the phone and I said, "Your daughter is here to see you Mr. Meredith." He was out in a few moments, hugging this elfin creature and saying to her, "Sammy, I want you to meet my Number One Assistant, Nicole."

"Hi Nicole," Sammy held out a limp hand.

"Hi Sammy," I returned.

"I'd hate to work for Dad," she went on. "He's so *strict.*"

"He likes a job done properly," I agreed. "But at least he appreciates it."

Sammy pouted. "I s'pose. I probably don't try really hard enough. It's a lot to live up to with Dad married to the hotel, and Mum married to Committees."

James intervened briskly with, "Stop talking rubbish. And come on Sam, I've booked the table."

"And I'm sure you have a whole line of meetings this afternoon," Sammy said cheekily, slipping a hand through his arm.

I watched them head for the main dining room with a knot like stone in my gut. They passed through the shafts of sun slanting through from the entrance hall and into the shadow where the corridor divided. And just for a nanosecond, with the colour washed out of the scene, the view of James as he looked down at Sammy reminded me of the sight of Dad as he came home from one of his sales tours, back in those long-ago days of normality. The distress was like a tidal wave: Sammy and Dad, James and I. .... Age-wise there was hardly anything in it. Then I imagined Sammy chancing upon James and I in a restaurant, out and about somewhere.

"What's up Nikki?" Julia was at my elbow. "You look as though you have seen a ghost."

"Just something reminded me of someone," I muttered vaguely.

As soon as I could, I went to the loo and was violently sick. Then I sat on the loo with my head in hands, asking myself whether this really was my life ambition, potentially to become the instrument for breaking up a perfectly normal family?

Soon after I returned to Reception, Sammy and James returned from lunch.

Sammy pronounced it as 'yummy', and added, "Dad said he couldn't manage half as well without you. I wonder if anyone will ever say that about me."

James batted her gently on the side of head, "Go home and tell your mother that, if she can tear herself away from whichever committee meeting it is this evening, I'd be glad as the Masons are coming over for a drink." Then he noticed me. "Nicole, are you all right?"

"Mm, I do feel a bit rough."

"Well, go home and get yourself an early night."

It was the worst night I'd had for a long time. The Lewis's house was old, and there were plenty of cracks in the ceiling. I had lain in bed often enough staring at them, but never before had they created so many possibilities of interpretation, especially faces with down-turned mouths. There were a lot of initials too. Any number of 'N's, but no 'J's unless I cheated and counted in a bit of a cobweb hanging down.

I felt so absolutely terrible about …. about everything that I didn't know what to do. I crawled out of bed and had a couple of gins, crawled back again, dozed off, woke up again. And still didn't know what to do. So I had another couple of gins and stared at the ceiling working out … really trying to work out why everything suddenly seemed so totally dire. But of course it wasn't rocket science. For the first time I had looked at my relationship with James from the outside and seen it for what it was: a father-daughter relationship that had crossed the boundaries of acceptable behaviour.

Actually that's not true. I didn't see it like that straight away. What I thought was that if James' marriage was properly OK he wouldn't spend so much time with me. Even Sammy agreed that her mother was married to committee meetings. If Jenny spent more time at home, Sammy would be less self centred and James' attention wouldn't wander.

So it was all Jenny's fault? I had another gin or two while I worked it out, and must have drifted off. But when I woke up again with a thumping headache, I still didn't know what to do. Then I wondered if anyone in the world had ever felt as *alone* as I felt just then. Everyone else had someone. Mother had Alec, Rach had Adrian, Matt had Edward, Dad... Well Dad didn't have anyone as far as I knew, but he had managed his life OK, found out who he was, where he wanted to go. Or at least that was the impression he gave.

Who was it who had said that I always seemed to need someone to depend on. The gin had fogged my mind up a bit and I couldn't remember, so instead I tried to work out what that actually meant. Yes, it was true that there had always been a Someone in my life who was important at that particular time, and then if they became distracted – like Rach with Adrian, or Matt with that awful Neil – my life seemed to fall apart. Though it had been all right earlier on, like when I was aiming for exams. Perhaps the exams replaced the people. And that was when gin had become my friend. As it still was. Had I become too dependent on it?

There wasn't a lot left in the bottle and just to prove to myself that I was *not* dependent, I took it in to the loo and tipped it into the pan. As I flushed it down, I felt a shiver of dismay, replaced in the next moment by a twinge of relief as I remember the two bottles of white wine left in the fridge. Just at that moment the thought of opening one was not appealing. In fact, I felt rather sick, soon followed by the act of vomiting. Of course, my mind was still an emotional tip following the events of the day.

After that, I was so tired there was nothing left but to go to sleep.

I woke up to the ringing of my mobile. "Good morning, my dear," said James' voice. "Are you feeling better?" *No I wasn't.* "I've been thinking." *That sounded ominous.* "It seems we've been caught out by our own success this year, with so many Christmas bookings. I didn't realise until yesterday – well, actually Sammy commented on it – how hard I've been working you and Julia in particular." *Why the hell couldn't Sammy mind her own business?* "I've had a word with head office, and they're sending us a team of extra staff. So I want you and Julia to take time off – I hadn't fully realised how exhausted you both are."

This was ridiculous. "But we're your key staff," I protested, not even pausing to hear how arrogant that sounded. "Just give us another day and we'll be fine."

James almost snapped. "No, Nik. It's not only about you and Julia. I've only just learned that Jenny collapsed at some conference last week-end – one of her colleagues rang me. I think it was sheer exhaustion, but I'm going to have to give more time to the family. I've booked Jenny and I on a Caribbean cruise – we'll be away a month." There was a small pause. "Hey, my dear. The world won't completely stop if we get off it for a while. Then we'll really make up for it to celebrate the new decade. Don't you agree?"

"Of course," I said, though I didn't.

January - April 2010

1

A month! He might as well have said a lifetime.

It was the first time I'd ever started on alcohol at that time of the morning, but these were special circumstances. The first couple of glasses of wine steadied the wobble in my midriff. By the end of the first bottle I was beginning to get things in perspective: a month wasn't that long. I fished my calculator out of my desk drawer: less than 0.002% of my life so far.

It turned out that wine doesn't make a good opener for breakfast, so I skipped the cereal and brewed myself some coffee. Then I used the calculator to see what percentage a month would be of my whole life if, say, I lived to seventy or eighty, however hard that was to imagine – well, the Grampies had both made it that far. And that made me think how long it was since I had thought of the Grampies and I started to cry. Perhaps a second bottle of wine would help? But just then all I wanted to do was go to sleep again. So I did.

Once again I awoke to the ringing of my mobile. This time it was Julia. "You OK, Nik. You sound weird."

"Fine, but I've just woken up." I could hear myself slurring.

Julia giggled. "So you're taking James' advice literally! Oh dear, it feels so strange suddenly to have eons and eons of time with nothing to fill it. A month!" So I hadn't dreamt it. "What are you going to do?"

"Dunno, haven't worked it out yet." I stifled a yawn.

"We could go on a trip. You could do a really long trip in a month." Yeah, like a Caribbean cruise. "Where would you go if had a completely free choice, Nik?"

"Dunno." I pulled myself together to give the question proper thought. "I think I'd just go," I said, "without any plan, choosing this or that way at every crossroads and see where it might lead."

And quite suddenly I knew that that was precisely what I wanted to do.

To Julia I added, "I've got stuff to do this morning. I'll call this afternoon and perhaps we can meet up."

In fact the only 'stuff' I had to do that morning was make myself look as normal as possible before facing Mother. I took a shower, spent a lot of time on my face getting rid of dark circles and blotches. Then I called Mother and invited myself over to lunch.

She greeted me with "You look as though you could do with making up some sleep."

"Mmm." I had no difficult in stifling a yawn. "Yeah, it's been kinda busy. But James Meredith has been great. He's given both Julia and me some time off. Like, a month."

"Really, well that is generous." Mother was putting the finishing touches to a home-made quiche. "So what are going to do with it?"

"That's what I came to talk to you about. I've saved up quite a bit, and I thought I'd just take off in Beano and, like, follow my nose. Or his bonnet. I've always fancied doing that."

She looked a bit doubtful. "On your own?"

"I was thinking about asking Julia to come with me."

"Yes, well she seems a sensible young woman. I do wonder how James Meredith will manage with you both gone."

"It's a quiet time coming up. I believe they are bringing in a temporary team. Anyway James won't be there. He's taking his wife on a Caribbean cruise."

Mother nodded in approval. "Good for him. They could probably do with seeing a bit more of each other. Why don't you set the table while I make the salad?"

Over lunch, Mother let me gabble away about my plans, or rather non-plans. She even made one or two suggestions about places to go that she and Dad had enjoyed, including with me when I was far too small to remember. Then she said, "A month you say? So you'll be back by mid-April?"

"What's happening in mid-April?"

"Alec and I were thinking of getting married."

"Of course, I'll be back." Suddenly my head was full of questions that weren't to do with me. Who would give her away? What would Dad think? Would I be bridesmaid? Did you even have bridesmaids at a second wedding?

Mother switched back to my plans and I scribbled down her suggestions, then said I thought the best idea was to check out the library for maps and books. And anyway Julia might have ideas, too. If she wanted to come. When I rang her that afternoon, it turned out that she did.

We arranged to meet at the Crooked Parrot that evening and I went along armed with maps and gazetteers. "Wow!" Julia exclaimed as I dumped them on the seat beside me. "Were you really serious when you said you would just drive off and decide at each cross road which way to go?" She giggled.

"Well, broadly speaking. But I think I'd want an overall general plan." I waved a hand at the pile of maps. "For instance there are some places I'd really like to see, so I'd want to make sure they got included. Like, places associated with my childhood. And, of course, any places that you're interested in."

Julia giggled again. "It's such an amazing idea. My Robert didn't really take it seriously when I told him." Her Robert? Oh, that moony chap that sometimes called to collect her. Pleasant, but probably not very imaginative. Julia went on, "Do I need to tell you now? I mean about the places I'm interested in?"

"No way. We're not leaving today. Or tomorrow. But planning is half the fun." And it was great to realise I wasn't just saying that but meant it. No, I hadn't miraculously forgotten James and his priorities, but they were no longer centre stage. "Anyway, you think about it, and we'll meet up in a couple of days. Come round to my place on Thursday. Six o'clockish."

In the interval, I continued my own researches, including in the library. My instincts were to go north, not just because Dad was in that direction, though I intended to include him in our month of meandering. My list kept getting longer: several places in Shropshire, some Potteries spots in Staffordshire, birding reserves on the Lancashire coast, and pretty well the whole of the Pennines that we could criss-cross at will.

On Wednesday morning I had a shock call from Julia saying she had heard from James, virtually as they were leaving for the airport, asking if she and I would go in the next day just to give some guidance to the new team that was arriving. It seemed weird to me that James hadn't planned all this out earlier, but then he had been acting strangely of late. And why had he rung Julia rather than me? Then I worked out that would have been awkward for him if he had just been leaving for the airport and the rest of the family were about. Anyway Julia and I went in. The new team turned out to be rather a superior lot so it was quite satisfying to show them they didn't know as much as they thought they did. They even asked us if we'd give some back up over the week-end, so we did. After all, a couple of days here or there didn't matter.

They were long days, so we stayed over in the hotel, but met up to discuss our plans when we could. I hadn't realised before how much Julia giggled and began to hope that it wouldn't become irritating. I also rang Dad to say that he was included on our itinerary.

"That's great," he said, but didn't sound as though he thought it was as great as I expected.

"How's business?" I asked, thinking maybe that had something to do with it.

"Couldn't be better." I could sense him making an effort to take an interest in my plans, and filled him in as much as I could. He made one or two suggestions, including some that Mother had made, but I still felt his interest was half-hearted.

"What's up, Dad?"

And then I heard him smile and he said, "It's not something I'd want to keep from you, Tuppence." A pause. "I think I've met someone."

Great. Dad had met someone. I asked: "Anyone I know?"

"No, she was away when you visited. She runs a crafts shop and sells some of my stuff." The lift in his voice was audible. "When you come, you'll be able to meet her. She's called Tess." Why did I want to cry though I was really pleased for him?

When I told Julia, she said, "Isn't that great, just as your Mum is getting married?" And giggled. Yes, there was a risk that giggle could become irritating.

2

Julia and I left on our adventure the following Wednesday. Our plans were nowhere near complete, but then we didn't want to be too tied down by detail anyway. I spent a couple of evenings with Mother and Alec and they made some sensible suggestions and requested that I call them at least every other day at a fixed time. One of the sensible suggestions was that we should at least book accommodation for our first couple of nights. Alec, who seemed to know a lot about moving round the country, checked the internet for a group of inns called Best Budget and we booked in to one near a place called Much Wenlock. Alec also told me something very interesting about Much Wenlock.

So we set off on the M40 then M42 and finally the M6. It was one of those nondescript February days when it's neither misty nor clear and you keep thinking the sun is about to break through but it doesn't. Julia was rather subdued and finally admitted that her Robert wasn't keen on her going off into the blue like that. She'd promised to ring him every day. Then she giggled which seemed a good sign that she was getting back to normal.

I'd checked the junction for the turn-off for Much Wenlock. Julia woke up from a doze just as I was checking the signposts.

"Look out for Much Wenlock," I told her.

She giggled. "What a funny name."

"Something very important happened in Much Wenlock in 1850," I told her.

About half an hour later, we found our Best Budget and checked in. It wasn't what you would call classy: long corridors with rooms off them, and basic furniture. But we had our own shower room and what could you expect for the price we were paying?

Julia plonked herself on one of the twin beds, stretched luxuriously and said, "So are you going to tell me what great event happened in Much Wenlock in 18-something?"

"1850. Yes, well it was the very first of the modern Olympic Games, and it still happens here every year."

Julia didn't giggle. She burst out laughing. "Surely you can come up with something more convincing than that?"

I'd come armed with print-outs off the Internet. She subsided into silence while she read them, then said "Wow!" and "Wow!" again.

"You can actually walk an Olympic Trail," I said, though I guessed she wasn't in to walking. While she was reading, I fished a bottle of wine from my bag, and waved it at her. "Like a glass?"

Julia giggled. "No, thanks, but you go ahead." I did.

We had a bottle of wine in the little Italian restaurant in the next block, but Julia only had a couple of glasses. She said, with a hint of admiration, "You can certainly put it away," as I finished it off.

I slept well and Julia still was fast asleep when I got up and showered. My hope was to walk the Olympic trail, but she wasn't too keen so we wandered round shops in Much Wenlock and Ludlow before returning quite early to Best Budget. Wandering round shops wasn't really my top priority and I was beginning to learn that sharing the same workplace with someone wasn't the same as going on holiday with them. Still it was early days. We hadn't booked any further accommodation and a quick check on a library computer showed there were no Best Budgets on our likely route for quite a while, but as Julia said, at this time of year it couldn't be difficult to find a room almost anywhere.

She drank a bit more wine that evening and was livelier. I stayed in the bar and had a nightcap while she went up to our room and did her daily call to Robert. When I rejoined her, she was rather tearful. She said, "He's missing me terribly. I hope you don't mind, but I said he could join us for the week-end."

I did mind very much. In fact I was appalled. Julia realised she'd probably got it wrong because she said that I could choose what we did next day and she'd fall in with it whatever it was. So I took her for a several-mile slog on a marked trail near Ludlow, then felt guilty because she got blisters on one heel. We left it rather late to look for a room and ended up in a b & b on the outskirts of Ludlow with a grumpy landlady. Still, she did a very good breakfast, slightly spoilt by the realisation that it was now Saturday and we'd be meeting Robert off the train at Ludlow station at midday.

We spent the morning in the library looking for accommodation and found a budget motel not too far up the M6. I said it was OK if Julia and Robert shared a room, and I'd have a single. In fact it was rather a relief to be on my own, and I got through my other bottle of wine, no problem. I also remembered that I hadn't rung Mother as promised and made up for it with a long call. She made me laugh by telling me of the first time she went on holiday with a student friend and ended up hating her. So generation after generation we continue to make the same mistakes.

Actually, Robert was OK. Delighted to be reunited with his Julia, he was glad to fit in with any plans. And, after all, I imagine my interests in birding and parallel universes were as boring to him as his passion for the minutiae of cars and computers were to me. So it was a bonus when I found that Much Wenlock's status as the home of the modern Olympics really excited him. There wasn't time to do the trail, but we did get to visit the museum. This housed the archives of the farseeing Dr. William Penny Brookes whose annual Olympian Society's Games inspired de Coubertain, the acknowledged founder of the modern Olympic Games in 1896.

So, after a great morning together, it was all the more of a shock when, over bowls of pub soup, Robert began sheepishly, "You're going to hate me Nikki …."

"Oh I dunno," I broke in cheerfully. "We've had a fine time so far."

That must have put him off his stride, because he stumbled about getting words mixed up before he finally blurted out, "It's just that I miss her so much, I want her to come back with me."

I gaped at him, then at Julia who was staring fixedly at her feet.

"You mean you want her to go back with you," I more or less repeated.

"I said you'd hate me."

Just at that moment I felt more exasperation than hate. "And what does Julia want?"

We both looked at Julia who continued to stare at her feet.

"Julia!" I said sharply.

She looked up reluctantly. "I think," she said, "I think I want to go back." With a bit more spirit she went on, "I'm not like you, Nikki, all independent and able to cope." *Hell, is that the impression I gave?* She went on, "I need people, someone to give me sort of guidance." *Good heavens, was this the young woman who had the staff scurrying in all directions getting things sorted for the guests?* I must have said it aloud because Julia said a bit snappily, "That's my work. That's what I have to do."

There didn't seem much more to say. Robert had already paid for their room and even for mine for another night, and he'd ordered a taxi to take them to the station. He'd thought of everything. It was quite surprising, but I could see he was just the sort of person Julia needed. It seemed too mean-spirited not to see them off, so I told Robert to cancel the taxi and took them to the station myself. When the train had disappeared from sight, I went into the bar and had a large gin, and asked myself whether I really minded this turn of events. Either I or the gin answered that, on the whole, no. I was about to order myself another gin when I thought that was probably not very wise, so I nipped in to the nearest mini market and bought a bottle of wine.

On my return to the motel, I found something very odd had happened. The receptionist greeted me with, "Good evening, Miss. Adams. Your friends asked me to give you this when you returned." She handed me a something in a fancy wrapping which was obviously a bottle of wine. I was about to explain that I wasn't Miss Adams when I saw an envelope attached to the bottle. The message inside was in Julia's sprawling hand, and read *sorry, sorry we've changed your identity but I'm keen it shouldn't get around that I was sharing with Robert.* I was first cross and then amused and then wondered what on earth she would think if she knew about me and James.

3

I returned to my single room well supplied for an evening of oblivion. After a glass or two, I paused briefly to wonder why I wanted oblivion, but the sensation I was enjoying was far too pleasant to question so I stopped wondering and poured another glass. At some point I went past the point of no return, fell asleep, woke to be sick, fell asleep again and finally awoke to a splitting headache. The one problem with oblivion was that it did not last.

The next week or so passed in something of a blur. I decided to go back to the first motel. During the day I explored the countryside, doing occasional walks, visiting old churches and a couple of castles. In the evenings, I returned to the Italian restaurant, disposed of the previous day's empties and replenished my stocks. Sometimes if there was a good special offer, I'd get half a dozen and keep them in the boot of the car.

Towards the end of that week while I was having my evening meal at the Italian, a guy came over and asked if he could join me for coffee. It was an obvious pick-up but I was well through my bottle of wine by then, and didn't mind. He was called Mark Latham, and was a sales rep for a new fashion firm: niche fashion, Mark hastened to add, explaining this was sold in particular to boutiques in touristy places. It also meant they were pricey. I quite took to Mark, who was older than, say, Pete but way younger than James Briefly I wondered about James, but after all he was in the bosom of his family, so I didn't object when Mark suggested I came to look at some of his stuff at the hotel where he was staying. This was in Ludlow and a good deal smarter than my Budget Motel as well as the sort of place where they don't seem to notice extra people coming and going.

Mark had some amazing luggage, like very high and thick suitcases, that he undid and, hey presto, inside were a whole lot of things on hangers. There was some really cool stuff. He let me try some tops on, and then a leisure suit. I'd bought my usual bottle of wine with me, but he said he'd already had enough to drink, thank you, and perhaps I had too. All the same, he was very good about it when I found I was too sloshed for sex and fell asleep on his bed. Next morning, when he found I hadn't any fixed plans, he suggested that I moved into his hotel. By the time we met up the following evening, I found he'd moved to a double room and told reception his wife had joined him.

"Have you got one?" I asked. "I mean, a wife."

"Not quite. My girl friend Lena wants us to get married, but I'm not sure I'm good at commitment. How about you – any husband?" I refrained from saying 'not my own' because it wasn't really very funny.

We slipped into an easygoing relationship, making few demands on each other. I was glad to have a drinking companion even though he didn't drink much, and Mark seemed to like my company too. He decided it wasn't worth going home at the week-end as Lena was away and he might as well stay put and explore some new markets over in Worcestershire. So we carried on, changing hotels a couple of times, while Mark widened his marketing area and I widened my experience of my homeland.

And then I forgot to ring Mother.

She left several increasingly cross messages on my mobile and finally caught up with me one morning as I was going down to breakfast. "What's going on, Nicole?" *Ouch, when she called me Nicole that was bad news.* "Alec and I have been worried stiff."

"Sorry, sorry, Mother." Best to be honest. "There's no real excuse. I've been travelling a lot and I suppose I just forgot. I'm really sorry, and I will ring regularly from now on."

Mother said, "Well, mind you do. I had a call from Julia, saying she'd come back as Robert was missing her. She seemed a bit worried about you. Thought you were drinking rather a lot."

Damn Julia. I managed a laugh. "Compared with Julia, almost anyone would be drinking a lot. No, I'm OK, Mother. Really. Just sorry I've been amiss in my calls." Amiss? Remiss? It didn't help that my head was thumping with hangover.

A couple of days later, Mark said much the same thing. "Don't you think you're drinking rather a lot?"

"Does it bother you?"

"Well, no. But you kind of move on to another planet about half way through most evenings. Still, it's not my business." No it wasn't.

He didn't mention it again, but the following Friday he decided to go home and check up on Lena. He took my mobile number and said he'd ring some time, but didn't seem all that sorry to be saying goodbye.

I wasn't all that sorry to see him go, though I missed his jokey companionship. The trouble is that other people's timetables tended to interfere with drinking. That sudden realisation made me stop and think. Had drinking become that important? Of course not. I could stop any time, if I really wanted to. In fact, I'd stop that very day just to prove it. For the immediate future there were more urgent preoccupations, like where I was going to spend the next night. The hotel had computers available for the use of guests so I logged in and found that Best Budget had two or three motels scattered about the area and one of them said they would be delighted to quote a special price for a week.

While I was packing up, Dad rang. "I thought you were coming to see me."

"I am, I am. Things got a bit complicated. Julia decided to go home early, and then I got side-tracked...."

"So I hear," Dad's tone sounded dry. *How the hell had he heard?*

"I'll be over at the end of next week."

"Mm. And what about your mother's wedding?"

Dear God, where had time gone and how had I got into this mess? Not to mention that I'd be due back at my job. I said, "It's OK, Dad. I'll sort it."

I rang off and loaded the car. Well, at least I'd got a place to stay for the following week, and enough to pay for it. But behind that comforting thought I was worried. How could I so completely have lost track of time that I hadn't realised that I was almost due to see Dad, and ran every risk of not getting home for Mother's wedding? Well, I'd told Dad I'd sort it, and I would.

The Best Budget motel in the Cumbrian foothills was some degrees classier than those I had experienced so far. The view from the window of my room to the low hills topped by higher and rockier crags helped to start with. The walls carried a series of pleasing water colour prints, and there was a heavenly shower gel of a kind I had not come across before. By the time I'd luxuriated in a long hot shower and made myself a pot of strong tea, I was feeling not only good, but optimistic and, above all, content with my own company. My hand reached automatically for my bag and the bottle that should so reliably have been there. And then I remembered. In order to make my day of abstinence easier, I had decided to leave my supplies in the car. There was, I told myself, nothing to stop me from going to collect a bottle. But it was important – really important – that I showed myself how capable I was of managing without it.

It was a terrible night. At two o'clock in the morning I used the facilities to make myself a cup of tea and that helped a bit. Then I sat on the bed hugging my knees and wondering how it had come to this. For some reason I remembered Tom telling me about the time he was in Rehab. Some of his fellow patients had the most awful withdrawal symptoms, hearing and seeing things.

Yeah, but I wasn't that bad. It was just my system had become used to a certain level of whatever, and was now demanding it. If I went down to the car and got a bottle, I'd be fine. But Tom's voice was still there telling me how bad it could be, and though obviously I wasn't at that stage, I'd always thought that control was the answer. So I sat the night out, with the help of a surge of caffeine as I reduced the stock of tea- and coffee-bags in my room, and watched darkness lighten to deep then light grey and finally welcome daylight.

My achievement really lifted my spirits. If I could do it once, I could do it again whenever I felt it necessary. I used up the last coffee bag and sat by the window sipping it looking out at the hills. There were still problems to overcome: like visiting Dad, getting back for Mother's wedding, making some money. And deciding what to do about my job, and James. I went on looking at the view, trying to conjure up a picture of those days not so long ago when he had dominated my thoughts: those long evenings of discussion and his expression as he watched me. Not just conjure up a picture but the feelings that went with it. But I couldn't. It was like an episode that had been great at the time, but had ended: a step on the ladder to my new independence.

So what was I going to do with this new independence? I fished out some Best Budget notepaper from the drawer of my bedside table and started a list: i) Visit Dad, ii) Mother's wedding, iii) Earn some money.

After studying it a few moments, I picked up the phone by my bed and dialled Dad's number. His voice lifted as soon as he heard my voice. "Of course you can come any time you want. We'll be delighted to see you."

We? Of course, I was soon going to meet the new woman in Dad's life.

April 2010

1

So what did I know about her? She was called Tess and ran a crafts shop that sold some of Dad's carvings. Not a lot to go on. "So is Tess still selling your things in her shop?" I asked now.

"She certainly is. In fact, she's expanded and now has three shops. Small ones, of course. But she's even had a feature in the local rag, and that brought me in a few orders." I could hear his voice smiling with enthusiasm. "I'm sure you'll get on – she's so looking forward to meeting you."

"And where did you two actually meet?"

"Oh didn't I tell you? She's a member of that self-help group I belong to. There's one that meets just a few miles from here."

So it looked as though I were in for a few dry days.

We arranged that I should arrive at the cottage on Friday evening. When I'd rung off, I looked at my list and carefully crossed out 'i) Visit Dad'. Mother's Wedding seemed a bit more than I could handle just then, so I turned my attention to 'iii) Earn some money'. With my background, my best bet would be some kind of hotel work, but this was just about the worst time of the year for casual work. Well, no harm in checking. That morning I asked the receptionist if I could have a word with the manager.

She checked the diary. "Mr. Craddock is away this morning looking at one of our new sites. I'll put you down for three o'clock this afternoon."

And so I heard from Roger Craddock that afternoon that Best Budget were expanding not only in numbers, but also in style. He seemed impressed when I told him of my training background. "But unfortunately not yet. At the moment, if anything, you're over-qualified, but the new place due to open in a few weeks could do with just your sort of training."

"If you're keen to stay up in this part of the country I could ask around," he said. "In fact, we could do with you the week after next when we've got a visiting horde of travel agents from Europe checking up on what our group has to offer."

I explained about my visit to Dad and my Mother's wedding. Roger raised an eyebrow. "You seem to have an interesting if complex family," he commented, but he agreed if I could get back by the day before the group was due to arrive, it would be OK as long as we had all the arrangements in place in advance. So I spent the next couple of days in the office matching rooms to individuals. Most of them were French-speaking which was fortunate as mine was quite acceptable. I really enjoyed being back in that atmosphere of planning for a major group, especially preparing those extra touches that were not perhaps part of Best Budget's usual style. Roger was pleased and grateful for my input and said I could keep my room without charge in the meantime and even gave me £100 to take my Dad out for a meal. That would be some meal, I thought, and certainly enough to treat Tess as well.

I wasn't sure what to expect from Tess – probably somebody rural and motherly. I'd, like, thought it probable that she had moved in to the cottage with Dad, but she hadn't, though she was already there when I arrived, helping him to prepare an evening meal. And she was a real surprise: quite tall and willowy and young-looking in a way that some older women manage to achieve. After I had given Dad a greeting hug, she came out of his kitchen, wearing an apron and wiping her hands on a towel, and said, "I'm so very pleased to meet you Nikki."

She'd prepared a tray of tea and we sat round the coal fire in the living room while I told them about my new job. I thought Dad would be pleased, but his first reaction was "But how are you going to fit that in with your mother's wedding?"

Tess said, "Give her a chance, Jim. It's very enterprising of Nikki to sort out a way of staying independent if she's not going back to her old job."

Clearly she was more intuitive than Dad who simply asked "But why aren't you going back to your old job, Nikki?"

"I think it's time I widened my experience," I said. "Best Budget feels more like part of the real world than Forest Lodges. And I'll get to meet these foreign agents." In fact, that came into my head as I was speaking as I hadn't given it a lot of thought, except that I wanted to hang on to my new-found freedom in which relationships didn't seem to get in the way.

Tess added, "And with a broader background of hotel management she should be able to get a job anywhere."

It seemed that Tess and I were going to get on famously. All the same I was conscious of being watched – not in a staring way, but

202

in an awareness of everything I said and did. The awareness stayed with me through Tess' excellent *boeuf bourguignon* and apple crumble, washed down by a glass of local spring water. Wine was offered but I declined. Afterwards we sat by the fire discussing Dad's growing success with his woodwork, and my future.

Dad said, "You strike me as being much more restless than before Nikki. Are you sure you're doing the right thing, chucking in a good job for something that sounds a little tentative to say the least."

"Come on Jim. When is it OK to be restless if not at Nikki's age?" Tess intervened.

"I suppose. As long as she's not starting on a series of geographicals."

Tess looked exasperated. "Don't start seeing a geographical in every situation."

I asked "What on earth are you both talking about?"

"Nothing," Tess said. "It's a term used around here when people start acting a bit unconventionally."

"Well, Dad should know all about that."

Tess grinned. "*Touché*, my dear"

The next morning we went to see her shop in nearby Settle and have lunch in the compact flat above it. I was really impressed by the range of local crafts she had on sale, and the way she had displayed them. Dad bought me a carving of an old forester which took my fancy.

There was a good local museum and that evening I took them out to a meal on Roger's generous bonus. As no one was drinking alcohol we accepted the chef's recommendation, which was also the most expensive dish – and very good it was too. Less enjoyable was the 'talking to' I received from both of them, though Tess' contribution was mostly agreeing with Dad. His took various ways of telling me that I was letting myself go in terms of health and my appearance and that I'd better smarten up before I went to the now imminent wedding.

To this end, we did the round of Settle's shops which had quite a lot of the sort of boutiques that Mark Latham would have been glad to supply. In one of them I found a great outfit with a long skirt and fitted jacket , nipped in at the waist, which looked good on me as mine had recently become quite small. Tess said it reminded her of the 'A'-line style her mother used to wear when Tess was a child, and that there hadn't been a more flattering fashion since. Father remembered a girl friend who had worn it. I liked the way he and Tess were together, like long-term friends.

Over breakfast on the day that I was to drive south, I asked Dad what he really thought about Mother re-marrying. Without hesitation, he said "Of course I minded when I first heard about Alec. But realistically I made a mess of her life as well as mine. We've both changed and if we had met for the first time recently, I doubt we'd have become an item as you would say. But I'm glad we did back then, or we wouldn't have you."

I grinned. "Not sure I'm that much of an asset."

"You will be, given a few more years." He grinned back to show he was teasing.

I arrived back in Greenley a couple of days before the wedding. The Lewises had a small flat that was empty and let me use that. Mother and Alec were so well organised that there wasn't much for me to do. They were getting married in the local Registry Office and Tom was best man, so he came round once or twice to discuss arrangements. I took the opportunity to see Matt and Edward who seemed as comfortable together as Mother and Alec did. I thought Tom was a bit cool with me but that was OK. We'd both moved on since those days when he'd just come out of Rehab.

Mother looked beautiful on her wedding day, in a simple lilac suit and deep contrasting high-necked blouse. And happy. They left for a honeymoon on a Caribbean cruise next day. Mother gave me a mega hug and said, "All I want is for you to be as happy as I am one day."

2

I don't think I had ever felt so lonely as I drove north again next day. Half way, I left the motorway and stopped at a pub for a sandwich and a large gin. It felt really good as it slid down and warmed my midriff and sent a sense of lightness up to my brain. Here at least was a friend who wouldn't go away. I was tempted to have another, but that would have been silly given the long drive ahead.

Roger gave me a great reception and as soon as I'd dumped my stuff in my room, we met for a working meal. He soon got me up to speed over the number of agents arriving and any of their special needs. I made one or two suggestions about putting a couple of miniatures and fruit juices in the fridge for each room, and said I'd get some friesias in bud from the posh florist in the next village so that we could put a small vase containing a spray of them on each dressing table. We had a bottle of wine over the meal and by the end of it I knew everything was going to be all right, and that it was all right Mother and Dad having found new partners because I'd also found the life style I wanted to live. For good measure I had a large gin as a night cap and slept like a baby.

I'm not quite sure what happened after that. We worked round the clock preparing for our guests, greeting them, serving them, informing them, feeding and watering them, cleaning for them, solving their large and small problems. Most of them spoke quite good English and all of them were amazed by the surroundings, our attention to detail, and the fact that they had hit a bright spot, meteorologically, so that the sun shone upon them. "Where are all zese umbrellas and bolleur 'ats you 'ave ?" I was quaintly asked on one occasion.

With one or two of them I ended up in bed. I'm not clear which of them, but they spoke French and thanked me for an interesting night, of which I could remember virtually nothing. Following one of these nights Roger called me to his office and informed me I was not behaving appropriately. I can't remember what my response was but it seemed to satisfy him. At least I thought it had until the group and their bus disappeared down towards the main road when he called me into his office again.

"Nicole," he said, "I do want to express my thanks for all the work you have put in to make a success of the visit for our foreign agents. They were all impressed by what we had to offer, and I am sure we are going to get some bookings from them in due course…"

He paused. I noticed that he was looking down at his desk rather than across at me, so I broke in with a cheery, "It's been a pleasure. I'm really pleased it went so well."

He nodded, then did look across at me. "But there are a few things that trouble me. There's no doubt that you're a natural for this job, but some of your methods do seem a little…. a little, say, unusual. For example, you do seem to have a fondness for drink."

This time it was me who nodded, and tried to look as rueful as I felt. "Yes, Roger, I'm sorry. When I'm working full stretch, I have to say the odd drink seems to keep me going, and I probably don't realise just how much I'm getting through. I really am going to take it in hand."

Roger looked pleased. "I do hope you will, because I'd hate to lose you. And it has been noticed by one or two of the staff." Yes, I had been aware of the odd snigger. He went on, "We'll say no more about it, then. I hope you can stay on for the next month anyway. The coming week should be quiet, so we'll all be able to relax a bit. But there's a Best Budget sales conference coming up the following week and I'm keen to put on a good show for that. We'll have the directors from Leeds here."

Then things went badly wrong. I did really well the following week, helping to plan the conference, sort out the accommodation, making sure there was a set of documents ready in the room of each participant. And I didn't touch alcohol for over a week. Not until after everyone had arrived, the conference was under way and we were being told what a great job we had made of the arrangements. It was that evening, quite late, that I decided to celebrate with a nightcap in the bar, and there I met Jumbo. The name was a joke, because he was really rather thin, but he apparently had a voracious appetite both for food and booze. We shared the latter over the next few days, moving from the bar to his room, where we continued to indulge, quite chastely but apparently more and more noisily.

Roger told me to pack my bags as soon as I surfaced the day after the conference finished, and while my hangover was so great that I did not realise the full impact for some time.

April-May 2010

1

There is a clear memory of Jumbo appearing as I was loading my car.

"I gather we've both been expelled," he said cheerfully. "Can you give me a lift to Kendal?"

While I was in the process of giving him a lift, we decided we might as well stick together for a while. Thankfully, from my point of view, he was divorced so had no one to whom he had to hurry home. It also turned out that Jumbo, whose real name was Jack Slater, was a very good salesman and had won a handsome bonus. When I commented that therefore Bargain Budget were very stupid to get rid of him, he explained that he had blackened his copybook quite a number of times already and anyway it was time to move on.

He added, "I'm probably doing a geographical." I knew I'd heard that expression before but couldn't remember where, so let it go. Anyway, he put a portion of his handsome bonus at our disposal to find us a room for a few nights, and we both agreed that it made sense to go down market to make it last longer.

We found a pub in the back streets of one of the Lake District towns – I can't even remember which one now. Our room was just about clean and had a queen-size bed that had seen better days, but it was fine for drinking in, which is what we mostly did. Jumbo seemed more interested in oblivion than sex, and I doubt if either of us were capable of much of the latter. We alternated drinking with oblivion. From time to time one of us went out to get a take-away. No one seemed interested in cleaning our room, so we piled our discarded take-aways outside the door and they duly disappeared.

"What d'you wanna do with your life, Nik?" I remember Jumbo asking.

"I'm into palarell univershes," I said.

"What happens there?"

"That'sh what I'm trying to find out. I think s'what happensh or would've happened if you make another deshishon. S'ppose my dad hadn't been a drunk, I'd be in a palarell universh."

"Can I be there, too?"

"I don't shee why not. Not sure you can be in someone else's palarell universh."

"No harm in trying," he muttered before crashing out.

Something of the conversation must have stayed in his mind because whenever we both woke up he said, "I'd like my palarell universe to be in India. ..... They sheem to get the hang of things there."

I was intrigued. A distant memory stirred. "Have you read the Baga-something?"

Jumbo was sitting up in bed hugging his knees and he hugged them for a while in silence before saying, "You may mean Bhagavad Gita?"

It sounded about right so I said, "Yup," trying to remember where I'd heard about it. I'd like to have carried on this conversation but Jumbo decided it was time for a take-away and by the time he got back I was probably asleep again.

I've no idea how long this went on for. Jumbo must have paid in advance for however long it was, as no one bothered us. Then one morning or afternoon or evening I woke up and he'd gone. It took a while to work this out as I assumed he'd gone for a take-away, but when he didn't come back, I started looking around, and found his note propped up on the shelf above the wash basin.

It's been great, he wrote, *but I must move on. Not a geographical. Need to do something. Feel terrible. You need to do something too. Hope we meet up.*

But he didn't tell me what I needed to do.

There was no alcohol left and I felt too ill to go and get some. So I curled up in the middle of the rumpled queen-size bed and sweated and shook it out. At one point the walls of the room seemed to be closing in on me, and I thought I screamed. But perhaps I didn't as nobody came. Then when I tried to straighten up the bed, I found an envelope under the pillow and some money inside, enough for several more nights.

I read Jumbo's note again. *You need to do something too.* Whatever that meant, I didn't think it meant shivering and sweating in this grotty room. I staggered over to the window. It was day time, late afternoon by the look of the sky and deepening colours behind the hill. The walls of the room had stopped closing in and, though I felt dire, I'd stopped shaking. I looked out of the window again, and saw Beano parked in the yard, just where I'd left him. The sight of him gave me a sudden lurch of nostalgia and I started to cry, and then I couldn't stop, sobbing and retching and howling until I ached all over and there was nothing left but to curl up again on that wretched bed.

2

When I woke up again, it was daylight but the next day. I felt dreadfully weak and sick, but something like the faintest flicker of hope reached through along with the thought that if Beano and I could get away from this place and find somewhere to hole up for a while, things might – just might – get better. I had a shower, opened my bag for the first time in days and fished out clean underwear and tee-shirt. Then I checked the room for stray items, stuffed them into the bag and went down to load the car. Finally I returned to reception where a girl with hennaed hair and a strong foreign accent confirmed that my man had paid up to date.

I was free to go. But where?

Fortunately I was good at reading maps – one of the better legacies of my relationship with Baz. I sat in Beano, the big road-map book spread open across the dashboard. I found a red biro in Beano's bowels and marked the place where I was. Then I surveyed the double-page spread as a whole and let my attention be drawn by the closest contours and the wriggling lines that marked minor roads leading into them. And somewhere above Ambleside, nudging into the lower slopes of the Langdale massif, I saw a track. Switching to a larger scale I map, I found it again and noticed that beside it were the small indications of habitations. Of course, they might be crumbling barns; or they might be derelict cottages.

"You won't know unless you go and find out," I said aloud. Anyway, I had a good feeling about this.

It was one of those days that Cumbria specialises in: the clouds low concealing some of the tops, and resting on others. It wasn't raining, but you knew it might at any moment. I'd written down a list of road directions as Baz had shown me all that time ago. The first part was easy, along numbered roads, then it became more complicated and I started feeling tired. So I stopped at a pub and had a sandwich and a black coffee. When the guy behind the bar asked me where I was going, and I told him, he said "Not a lot up there."

"I'm looking for somewhere quiet," I said.

"Then you've likely found it." He was polishing glasses. "I've heard tell there's a cottage for sale on that track."

Really? Well, I wasn't in a position to buy but perhaps they'd rent it out for a while.

The barman went on, "But I reckon it's a mite lonely for a lass like you. There's a pub – the Shepherd's Rest – nearby. You could ask there." He scribbled on a pad with directions on the best way to get there and sent me with a warning to be sure to top up with fuel as there weren't too many petrol stations ahead.

Despite the weather, it was a memorable drive. As I wound slowly up from one valley and over a pass to drop down into the next, the mist rolled away on either side of me below invisible tops, and out of the greyness I heard the mournful bleat of sheep, and occasionally met the equally mournful gaze of one looking back at me before scampering ahead down the road in front, ignoring my admonishments to *'for effing sake get off into the safety of the heather.'* Occasionally I passed a farm, more often a derelict barn or cottage. I hoped the one the barman had mentioned would be more habitable than these seemed to be.

It was then it struck me that for hours I had not thought how dire I was feeling or how badly I needed a drink to put things right. Perhaps I'd celebrate when I got to the Shepherd's Rest. Certainly I could do with something – I felt really hungry. And that was an unusual sensation, too. When I first saw it, I thought it was shut, but it turned out that the landlord wasn't expecting much custom on a cloudy weekday out of season, and as soon as I pushed open the door he went round putting all the lights on. He was called Herbie, short for Herbert, and looked older than my Dad.

Without much delay, he told me I was a sight for sore eyes without sounding in the slightest as though he was making a pass. Then he said I looked as though I needed fattening up and he could recommend his good lady's all-day breakfast. While we waited for it to come, I told him I'd heard there was a cottage for sale nearby – not that I wanted to buy it, but perhaps rent it for a while. After a few moments of puzzlement, he said, "You must mean Ben's Bothy – a couple of hundred yards up the track. It's not a cottage, but a sort of walkers' hut. Some fancy school in the south bought it. They were going to bring up groups of youngsters on courses. Orienteering or something like that. But it didn't work out, so the owners have put it on the market. My guess is the enquiries will come in when the weather gets better, so they might well take a short-term tenant. It's well fitted out – rooms with bunks, a shower room, kitchen. I took a look – it's OK. Twelve or more bunks so you could have a different bed every night. And my good lady could fix you up with a meal when you wanted. She's a grand cook."

'My good lady' materialised at that moment with my breakfast and she was indeed a grand cook. I hadn't felt so hungry for a long time and, as I ate, I thought over what was becoming an increasingly attractive idea. While I started on my second pot of coffee, Herbie rang the owners of Ben's Bothy who agreed the place would be better not left empty and appointed Herbie to negotiate. Before long, I was standing in the Bothy's kitchen, the temporary proprietor of all I surveyed.

3

There followed the happiest few weeks I could remember. Herbie and his wife Mary kept an eye on me and agreed I had made the place look really homey, with a table cloth, lamp shade and cushions from a local charity shop, and a couple of pots of African violets. Several times a week I had lunch at the Shepherd's Rest, otherwise relying on a supply of ready-made meals from a local supermarket. I slept and slept and in between walked and walked. In the evenings I explored a shelf of books left by previous occupants and found a number of recent award winners that had escaped my distracted attention. I even wrote to James to say I thought it better if I didn't return to Forest Lodge. He didn't reply. And then my thoughts began to return to earlier paths of exploration. Amongst a muddle of papers I found some barely legible notes I had scrawled while I was with Jumbo.

And finally for the first time my mind catapulted back to Greenley and then Yorkshire and the fact I had not been in touch with anyone, not anyone, for a very long time. And that it was an equally long time since either Mother or Dad had sent a reminding text message. A stone seemed to plummet from my throat to my bowels. I got there just in time and sat on the loo seat, gulping deep breaths as I disgorged what felt like a week's accumulation. Then I sat there for a long time more, waiting for calm to return. Then I heard a voice.

"Nicole .... *Nicole* .... Are you there?" It was Mary. She had always refused to shorten my name.

I croaked, "Coming Mary. I'm in the loo."

She went on happily, "I've just done a really *cordon blue* thingy ...a cassoulet. You really should come round for supper."

I yanked up my trousers, pulled the chain, tried to look normal. Mary took one look at me and flung her arms round me, clucking, "Dear child, what on earth has happened?" And I burst into tears and blubbed out a shedful of pent-up misery, the words falling over each other so that all she could do was rock me back and forth and say, "It'll be all right. You'll see, whatever it is, it'll be all right."

When I'd finally begun to calm down, she took the key from the hook by the door, led me out, locked up the bothy and held my hand, like a child, as we went down to the Shepherd's Rest. As soon as I saw Herbie, I burst into tears again. "Give her a tot of brandy," Mary said, and I stopped bawling long enough to wail *"No brandy."*

I don't know how long I sat snivelling but when I was back in some control again, Mary had gone back to the kitchen, and Herbie was behind the bar drying glasses. Happily there were no customers.

"You need to tell us Nicole," Herbie said, "if we're going to help you."

Mary came through with a bowl of chicken broth and a hunk of home-made bread. "It was a bit muddled what you told me, but there was something about your father. And drink," she prompted.

So slowly, as I ate my broth and bread, I unfolded the story. OK, so it was an edited version, because they were such nice people and I didn't want them to think badly of me. I told them about Dad and his problem and how it had affected me; and then later I had started drinking and thought it was OK as long as I kept it under control, but somehow I hadn't, and now I was really, really trying.

To my surprise, Mary's homely face broke into a wide smile. "But that's grand," she said. "No wonder you didn't want that brandy."

Herbie came out from behind the bar and put a beefy hand on my shoulder. "You're a grand lass. But now you've come so far, why are you so upset?"

So then I was even more economical with the truth and explained that my own sobriety was still in its early stages; that prior to that, without going into too much detail, I'd had been through quite a wild time. And that in the process I had completely forgotten to keep in touch with either Mother or Dad.

Mary tut-tutted in sympathy. "Is that all, my dear?" she said. "When you've been a Mum you'll understand a bit better, but I reckon your parents will be thrilled like anything to know that you have recognised your problem and done something about it.

Later, I sat at the window of my bothy, looking out at the hills, the Langdale tops still layered with snow. In my ear the phone burr-burred its contact with distant Greenley. And then the burring stopped and Mother's voice, uncharacteristically flat-sounding, said, "Anne Chapman." I hadn't rung her since she'd become Anne Chapman. My throat tightened. I wanted her there beside me, reassuring me that everything would be all right.

"Mum," I croaked. "Mother."

A pause. "I'm sorry? This is Anne Chapman here."

"Mother, it's me, Nikki. I'm so sorry…."

A longer pause, then "*What?*" The flat-sounding voice was transformed. I could never have imagined such cold anger could be injected into one word. "You're sorry?! You disappear from the face of the earth, hole up with strangers, and you call to say you're sorry!" The cold anger had deepened to vitriol.

"I – I haven't b-been well," I faltered.

"Oh yes, indeed. I've heard how unwell you've been and the men you've been unwell with. But I'm afraid I'm really not concerned. You of all people know what I've been through, and it's not happening again. Nor am I putting Alec through it. He's been through enough. We've both been through enough."

I struggled to get a word in. "But I've stopped, Mother. I'm O.K. I haven't had a drop for three, nearly four weeks."

She burst out laughing and it was the harshest sound. "Three, four weeks? Ring me again when it's three, four years. Not before, d'you hear?"

There was a scuffling sound, an exclamation, then Alec's steady voice. "Nikki? I'm sorry, your mother isn't quite herself. I think the years of worry have finally caught up with her. She's really not very well."

I tried to keep my own voice steady. "And I suppose I haven't helped."

"No, well …"

"Look after her, Alec," I said, and put the phone down before the big sob gathering in my throat broke out.

I sat sobbing for a long time even though I had already decided my next move. I'd ring Dad. He'd understand. Only I wanted to be in control first. It took quite a long time. I had a cup of coffee, went for a walk, had more coffee. While I was walking I thought about what Mother had said. I thought of those terrible years of Dad's drinking, and how we had shared the awfulness together, though I could see it must have been much worse for her. And then suddenly the problem had come back, only this time with me.

It would be different with Dad. He knew what it took. As soon as I got back from my walk, I made another coffee, got my mobile, and punched in his number. It was Tess who answered.

As jauntily as I could, I said "Hi Tess. Nikki here. Sorry I haven't been in touch for a while. Is Dad about?"

"I'll see." No *'good to hear from you'* or *'how are you?'*

Nothing happened for a while. Dad must have been in the garden. Then his voice, loud and harsh. "And what the hell do you think you've been up to?"

I allowed a moment's pause. "Hello, Dad. Yes, sorry it's been a while...."

He interrupted, "*A while!* Your mother has been frantic with worry. So have I. It didn't help to hear you'd been holing up with some unsavoury company."

Hear from whom? When? Where? I said, "Well, you could have done something about it."

"Only you could do something about it. Like I had to."

"I'm not like you," I shouted.

I'm not sure who cut the line first. I took a gulp of coffee and found I was out of breath as though I had been running. Then I heard voices and looked up. A small group of walkers were passing my window, chattering and laughing; they stopped right in front of me, arguing about the route. I couldn't hear what they were saying, but they were animated, in touch with each other, and for the first time I had a feeling of what it might be like to be in a parallel universe. One of the girls leaned forward to peer through my window, saw me, looked embarrassed, waved. They moved on, their voices faded and I felt like the last person in whatever universe I inhabited.

One thing would help, but I hadn't got any, and the Shepherd's Rest was the last place I could get some. Herbie and Mary had been so kind. They were probably the only people left who had a good opinion of me. Without thinking too much about it, I began collecting up my things and loading Beano. I left the cover and the cushions for the next occupants, gave the African violets a good watering and hoped Mary would take them under her wing.

Then I manoeuvred Beano down the track and drove on without looking back.

June 2010 – November 2011

1

The order of events for the next fifteen months are completely scrambled in my mind, even though I have been over them again and again. But I can remember the earlier months, and a few periods of clarity along the way.

After leaving the Shepherd's Rest, I made my way back, dale-hopping, to the place where Jack and I had holed up those weeks ago. I found the route directions I had scrawled down on a piece of paper on the floor at the back of Beano and though I went wrong several times, I eventually managed to get back on course. It was better weather than the last time, so the tops were visible and there were good views, but still the same silly sheep fleeing ahead of me as I crossed a pass. Anyway I wasn't much in the mood for admiring views. I thought how nice it would have been if Jumbo had still been with me. At that point I stopped the car and began to snivel. The escaping sheep stopped and turned to look at me with inquisitive expressions, and were so comical that I started to laugh, and the laughter and tears got mixed up until I was stricken by a major attack of hiccups.

Then I came upon the pub where I had stopped for a sandwich those weeks ago. The man behind the bar recognised me. As I ordered my first gin for all that time, he asked "So did you find that cottage in the Langdales?"

I took a sip of the gin and nodded. The glow of it seemed to take possession of the whole of me and reassure me that everything was going to be all right. While the barman ordered me a sandwich, I told him that I'd had a magic time there, and he smiled and said, "But now it's time to get back into the real world?"

"Something like that."

I had never been more tempted to order another gin, but from somewhere a nano-grain of commonsense reminded me that if I wanted Beano and myself to stay in one piece, a coffee would probably be better. The coffee was good and I managed to push the sandwich down, then I went on my way and found the pub where

Jumbo and I had stayed. The same woman with the hennaed hair was at reception.

"Wanna room?" she said.

"Yes, but I was wondering if you had any jobs as well."

"Go'n ask Manuel," she said and disappeared.

A while later she came back with a man, sort of swarthy, not bad looking. "You wanna work?" he asked.

"I'd like to stay here a while, but I don't have a lot of money. But I can work."

"You clean rooms?"

"Yeah, I'm a good cleaner."

"OK, we try for one week and see how good cleaner you are."

This time the room had a narrow bed, an even narrower cupboard, a chair and a washbasin in one corner. The loo was down the corridor. My room looked out on the car park so at least I could see Beano.

That week I worked really hard. In fact, I doubt whether Manuel or many of his guests noticed how spotless their rooms had become. But at the end of it, my new boss called me in and said, "Yes, you good cleaner. I give you room and food and you get salary and keep baksheesh." The salary was very small and I wasn't counting on much baksheesh, but I'd noticed the gin in the bar was easy to access and I'd got pretty good over the years at watering bottles down. After that first week, my standards became a bit less spotless but I doubt if many people noticed.

I settled down to a routine that became OK. The mornings were the worst. The two hours or so before it was time to get up, when the fear in my midriff began spreading up into my head and I just wanted not to wake up at all. Eventually I found a quite small nip of gin helped that fear to go away, but had to be careful because it was easy for one small nip to become several and then I went back to sleep and Manuel came thundering on my door.

Days turned into weeks and then months and I noticed that summer had blazed into autumn and finally winter while I wasn't looking. At Christmas, Manuel gave me a bonus and told me to get some new clothes. I had noticed they were beginning to fall off me, but no way was I spending good money on clothes, so I had a good dig round the charity shops before checking out the supermarkets for the cheapest gin. That evening I had a shower, a biggish gin, and put on my new-old clothes.

"You are pretty girl," Manuel said, with a smile that was more a leer. It was a while earlier I had decided I would spend the night with anyone – not for the sex, but for the feeling of someone else being close. But Manuel didn't make any move in that direction. So I spent the night hugging my pillow.

My routine was quite unchanging. Getting up took time for me to pull myself together. Breakfast was a lot of coffee, then later in the morning I'd mix myself a packet of invalid food because I didn't want to get really ill. I did the rooms, had a spell on reception, served at lunch if we had guests, then around tea time I crashed out for some hours. During the day I had nips of gin from a small bottle in my pocket. After my sleep, I served in the bar which is when the more serious drinking started. If there were customers, they often bought me a few drinks. When I went to bed, I had several gins quickly until I crashed out. With this routine, there was no time to think, and by the time there was, I was in my room preparing for the night's oblivion.

It was during the post-Christmas and New Year doldrums that things suddenly changed. I was just clearing the only two breakfast tables when Manuel said, "Mr. Slater in Room 7 is asking for you."

A memory stirred. *Jumbo?*

When I let myself in to Room 7 there was nothing to be seen but a big mound of bedclothes which seemed to be shaking uncontrollably. The shaking paused and then resumed. Finally half a face appeared above the bedclothes, and then a whole face. I would never have recognised him. Skinny Jumbo who had earned his name as a joke could now claim it for real.

After he'd focussed on me for a while his pudgy face broke into a grin, and that I did recognise. He heaved himself further above the bedclothes and I saw his enlarged face was matched by an overweight body. "Been looking for you," he said. "Forever."

I sat on the edge of the bed. "What happened, Jack?"

He screwed his face up. "Went into clinic. Difficult. Too difficult… " He broke off, began to say something else, was violently sick. I mopped him up as best I could, stripped the bedclothes off. He was in an awful mess and there was blood too. Then I went to find Manuel and we called for an ambulance.

2

The incident shocked me into a few days of sobriety. The paramedics asked a lot of questions I couldn't answer, as I knew nothing about

Jack except that he had been a good salesman for a brewing company. They said they would pass the information on.

"Very sick man," was Manuel's comment.

The following day was my day off so I drove to the hospital. I must say Jack looked better in a pair of clean hospital pyjamas. A doctor came to talk to me and I explained again that I was just a friend and knew very little about him. He told me that tests of Jack's liver showed that it had been seriously affected by his drinking and if he didn't stop he would be in serious trouble. Did I have any influence on my friend. I doubted it, but said I'd try.

"After the last time, he said he couldn't cope with the withdrawals," I added.

"We can do something about those." Doc mentioned a drug with an easily forgettable name which he said would make the process much easier.

"Yeah, he told me that," Jack said when I tackled him later. "Not sure I trust any of those medics. Not sure I trust anyone. Except you perhaps." He looked at me through sad eyes. "Would you stop, if I stop?"

I really wanted him to get better and I didn't think it through. "OK," I said.

A light seemed to go on behind his eyes. "It's a lot to ask. Perhaps I could get hold of some of that drug for you."

"It's OK, Jack. I'll manage."

And I really, really thought I could.

And I did for quite a while. My new routine helped. I went to see Jack on my afternoon off and Manuel let me take a couple of evenings off most weeks as things were quiet. And I learned more about him in those few hours than in the weeks we had spent together.

From an early age he found he was good at selling stuff. Only seven, he was caught selling unwanted Christmas presents at primary school. Though he had no academic ambitions, his parents insisted he went to university where he took economics, got mixed up with student high life and drink, flunked his exams, left home and got himself a job as salesman. And did well. He'd had several jobs before I met him at the Bargain Budget sales conference. His parents had kind of given up on him even before his father died of cancer and, two years later, his mother remarried.

218

"To an awful man," pronounced Jack. "I'm not even sure where they live now." He drained his mug of tea and held it out to me. "Could you get me a refill?"

"I'm not your slave," I said, but I went anyway. We were in the day room and the tea trolley was parked by the nurses' station. Jack was due to go into rehab at the end of the week, and wasn't sure if he'd be allowed visitors.

Over the refills, I gave him a rundown of my own growing up years.

"Yeah, well, they do say it's hereditary."

"What is?"

"Alcoholism."

"I'm not an alcoholic," I said crossly. "I just drink too much sometimes."

"Yeah, well," Jack said. "Only you can decide that."

Before I left I checked with the ward doctor whether I'd be able to visit rehab. His take on it was that they'd want Jack to settle down for the first week, and then I probably could.

I stayed a bit cross about Jack's comment for quite a long time, which had the effect of keeping me right off alcohol just to 'show him'. In fact, it wasn't that difficult now it was out of my system. I was even getting hungry and eating well. At this rate I'd have to start buying more clothes. One morning I studied myself more closely in the mirror: skin tauter, eyes more alert, back straighter. Yeah, there was something to be said for keeping things under control. Well, I'd always thought that.

When I next saw Jack, I noticed how much better he was looking: still overweight, but less flabby; bright-eyed; articulate if a touch holier-than-thou.

"So what do you actually *do* here?" I asked.

"A lot of talking, both one-to-one and group therapy." He noticed my grimace. "No, it's OK – to find suddenly there's a whole lot of people in the same boat."

"You mean people who've drunk as much or more?"

"No, I don't mean that. It's not a competition. Anyway, tell me what you've been up to."

"Oh, the usual. We're not so busy at the moment, so there's a bit of decorating and repairing going on. If the weather's good, I go for walks."

Jack smiled. "I must say it suits you."

219

"How about your liver? And how long are they keeping you here?"

"It's under discussion. The usual course is six weeks, but they think I might need longer."

'Usual course'? Did you have to pass an exam at the end?

The Rehab centre was housed in an old country house at the end of a long drive. It reminded me a bit of the place where Dad had gone in the days when he still lived at home. The staff seemed nice, mostly dressed in ordinary clothes, but it still smelled of institution to me. Jack seemed to get on well with them all, and with the other inmates. In fact, there was almost a clubby atmosphere when they got together. I even began to feel I was interrupting when they called him away. It was rather as if my only soul-mate was turning away. But I went on visiting him regularly, and keeping off the gin, and was aware of my own increasing feel-good.

Then one week-end in March I arrived to find him packing.

"They're sending me to another place," he said, sounding more excited than I had ever heard him. "It's more of an open prison than this, and you get all sorts of stuff like training programmes."

I forced some enthusiasm into my voice as I said, "That's really good. But I'll miss you. Where is this place?"

He came over and gave me a hug. "I'll miss you too. It's in Somerset." *Too far for my days off.* "But of course we'll keep in touch."

I helped him to pack while he babbled on about a training course he was considering on woodwork – 'something I've always wanted to do' – and the happy coincidence that two of his new mates were also being transferred. It made me think briefly of Dad.

By the time I left him, my sense of isolation was beginning to take over. But that wasn't the only thing that sent me plunging into a very dark place. When I arrived back at the pub, I found an extremely unpleasant letter awaiting me. It was from Rachel, and it read: *I probably shouldn't write this letter, but I will because I thought you were my best friend and someone has to tell you what a mean, self-centred, unreliable person you have become. When you didn't answer our wedding invitation ....* **What** *wedding invitation? .... I assumed you would just turn up full of bounce and be the centre of attention as you like to be. Fortunately, because everyone was so marvellous and it was such a magically happy day, I didn't miss you too much at the time.*

After a while I started to worry and went to see your Mum, then wished I hadn't because she was obviously worried sick too. In fact, she seemed really ill. She said she'd heard that you were drinking a lot and seeing different men. Then I went to see Matt and he was worried too because he'd heard the same, but like he's your good friend, too, and said maybe you had to get something out of your system because you had this weird complex about yourself. I thought he was talking psychobabble, then I remembered various incidents when I realised actually Matt was right. Like you need to possess people and if you can't you turn into some manic drama queen.

Well, I've had enough. I'm pregnant now. It's a boy and he's due in October – perhaps you'll both share a birthday. I've always thought you would be the godmother of my first child, but an unreliable alkie is absolutely no use to me or to him. With deep sadness, Rachel.

I was totally devastated. Without pausing to think, I tore the letter into several pieces, then rushed down to the office to get sticky tape to put it together again, weeping as I did so and the various sentences came together before my eyes. Then I sat holding the sheet of paper and thought and thought and thought of that wedding invitation. I had absolutely no recollection of it, but then I had no recollection of a lot of things.

Re-reading the letter, certain phrases jumped out at me: *centre of attention as you like to be, need to possess people, turn into some manic drama queen...* Was that really what she and Matt and probably others thought of me? And then that strange comment: *she (mother) said she'd heard you were drinking a lot and seeing different men.* Yes, Mother had said as much on the phone. But heard from whom, and when and how?

Was I being watched?

I got up, stood at the window, looked out at the car park and saw Beano. We had to get away. Go somewhere. Anywhere. Jack was OK. He didn't need me. Nobody in the wide world needed me as far as I could see.

November 2011 – autumn 2012

1

After that everything is very hazy, except for the first few days. I told Manuel I'd had bad news and must return home. He was so nice, insisted on giving me quite a tidy bonus for helping to get the place straightened out, and fed me a good lunch that I didn't really want. It was nice for a few moments to realise that I had actually done something positive and helpful.

The bonus meant that at least I could stay for a few nights somewhere reasonable, and I found a comfortable bed and breakfast place a few miles off the M6. The landlady was really homely, and so kind that in the end I told her I was having a bad time, broken up with my boyfriend and needed to be somewhere peaceful for a while. It was awful how easily the half truths were invented and believed.

And then I saw myself in the mirror. Of course I saw myself in the mirror quite often: every morning when I got up, several times a day when I combed my hair or tried to tidy myself up. But this was the first time I saw myself as in noticed and registered what I really saw. It was a pallid face, long straight hair bereft of any styling, wide mouth, short nose with a hint of an upturn at the end. Brown eyes quite wide apart. Brown dead eyes.

I studied them Were those the eyes that had looked with love at Mother and Dad; with affection at Matt, Rachel, a dozen others; with desire at Baz, Pete and perhaps one or two more; and in recent months with raw need at nameless men whose comfort I needed, most recently Jumbo?

As I stared at myself, the dead eyes filled with tears. So who was there to offer comfort now, or even care? Except perhaps for that mysterious informant who had been reporting on me to Mother and Dad. Not that they could care that much to let me continue in that state. I felt terrible. It was as though my whole head had been stuffed with darkness. So much for sobriety I thought.

But I felt safe where I was. My landlady insisted that I stayed in the b. and b. over Christmas. She had a very extended family, most of which tipped up over the festive season so my presence was barely noticeable until a nephew from Australia caught me nicking gin. I didn't wait to be asked to leave.

After that things just got steadily worse though I can't say in exactly what way as the more I drank, the deeper the haze that became my life. How I actually got the stuff isn't clear. I think I nicked most of it – in half bottles which are easier to conceal than full ones. I slept anywhere, instinct leading me to sheltered places that might be warm – usually bus stations, roadside shelters, garden sheds – surprising how people leave their sheds open. In one bus station I struck gold in the shape of a wallet that someone had left on the seat. In fact this happened a few times. There was never a lot in it, but enough for several packets of Complan, tins of baked beans, ravioli or spaghetti hoops and a tin opener, which kept me going for days. Occasionally someone would stop by and ask me if I was all right and once or twice they took me into a nearby café for a sandwich or bowl of soup. From time to time I got a job washing up somewhere and got some money that way. On another occasion I found a rucksack someone had abandoned. It was in a bad state, but I patched it up and it was fine for carrying my meagre possessions.

I had no idea of the passage of time except that the weather changed, the days got longer, and I knew if I could only hit the right level of alcohol in my system everything would be OK. It was just so difficult to find it. I think I remember trying to call Dad several times, but hit the 'off' button as soon as I got the ringing tone. Sometimes I thought back to Rach's letter and Mother's comment implying that someone had been checking up on me, then I'd get quite paranoid about being followed for a while. This got really bad in the summer when everywhere was crowded and it was easy to imagine you kept seeing the same people.

It was around midsummer that I decided the best thing would be to get up into the hills and hole up in one of the many bothies or huts run by different climbing or walking clubs. This felt like a brilliant idea and I spent a lot of time planning it. I even convinced myself that I might overwinter in one of them – there was usually a supply of wood for heating, and I could probably steal or scrounge enough to keep body and soul together. I knew I wasn't fit enough to do a strenuous walk, so I went to one of the tourist information offices where a very helpful woman gave me a booklet on treks graded according to difficulty. She even let me have a copy very cheaply as the cover was torn. As I wasn't feeling too well, I found a shelter near one of the national park's camp sites. During the day when there were a lot of people about, I used the camp's shower facilities and sat in the café with a cup of something studying my booklet and checking the routes against a huge detailed map of the area which covered one wall.

While I was doing that, a male voice asked "So where are you planning to go?"

He was middle-aged, fit-looking. I said, "Oh just something modest – I'm a bit out of condition." I pointed to the route I was considering. "I'm thinking about that one – it doesn't look too difficult."

"Oh that one's really easy. And there are a couple of good huts along the way if you want a rest." It was just what I wanted to hear.

I spent the next couple of days making preparations. Funds weren't great though they'd had an unexpected boost by finding another wallet (really, people were careless). By doing some careful research round the supermarkets, I found an unknown brand of gin going cheap and had enough for half a dozen half bottles – well, I'd just have to eke it out. The rest went on Complan, tinned food and special-offer chocolate. Then I went into a health-food shop and nicked a strip of homeopathic sleeping aids. Four of those gave me the best night's sleep for a very long time.

It seemed sensible to start on a full stomach so I had poached egg on toast and black coffee at the camp café and set off. Even then, in spite of the good night, I found it really hard going. After all, I hadn't walked more than a few hundred yards since … well, probably since those walks from Ben's Bothy. So I had a few swigs of gin to help and actually reached the bothy by late afternoon. It was a shock to find it occupied by a group of four brewing tea. They tried to be friendly but soon gave up when I pretended to go to sleep. And, to my great relief, they decided there was still plenty of daylight left to get to the next bothy and upped sticks around six o'clock.

Later I worked out I must been there quite a long time. People came and went, but they were always in pairs or groups and didn't bother me when they found me unsociable. If I was lucky, they left quite a bit of food behind – tins or the remains of a loaf, and even some cans of beer. On one occasion I made a huge effort and went down to the valley to stock up with gin. I'll never know how I managed it. For a while I tried rationing it out, but that didn't last long. And suddenly I was half way down the last half bottle and I knew I didn't have the strength to get more.

By the time I'd finished it and gone to sleep and woken up in the dark and found I'd been sick all over myself, I wasn't capable of sensible thought. Certainly I wasn't capable of taking in the fact that while I slept someone had come into the bothy. I heard them breathing first and my heart started thumping.

"Who's there?"

There was the sound of shuffling and then a click and flare of light from a torch.

"So," a male voice said, "Have you had enough yet. Nikki?"

2

The strangeness of finding someone in this remote place who knew my name overcame any sense of fear. In fact, I wasn't aware of any feelings except the sensation that this was the worst moment in my life and I didn't care if it ended *now*.

The light wobbled as the whoever-it-was moved over to the table by the window. A lighter flared, two candles on the table spluttered into life. The brightness made big white patches in front of my eyes, and then settled to flickering softer light with shifting shadows that played on that corner of the bothy and on the man's face. It looked familiar, but I couldn't put a name to it. It said, "Don't be scared, Nikki. I've come to help."

How could anyone help? How could anyone possibly know what I was feeling?

Then I knew who it was.

"Tom," I said.

"That's right."   Ah yes. Tom had had a problem and been in rehab. But, even then, he could never have felt as I did. No one could.

"I have some idea of how you're feeling," Tom contradicted. "Though you probably can't imagine that." *Good heavens, a mind reader, too.* I giggled, and then I don't remember what happened because my head burst into a crazy mish-mash of images and sounds, and I felt completely out of control. Finally I was aware of arms holding me tightly and reassuring sounds that everything would be all right if I would only hang on in there. He went on talking to me, and some of it I took in. Something about he had kept a regular eye on me and had seen how low I was sinking, but knew that if he came to the rescue too soon, I'd soon feel better and start all over again. So he would leave the odd old wallet lying around for me to find with a bit of money to keep me going.

It was a while – a very long while – before I could begin to piece things together.   For the moment there was the major logistical

225

problem of getting back to the road, and even more urgently how to stop being sick.

Tom apparently had a solution. He had some anti-nausea medication prescribed by his own doctor. And, magically, he had half a bottle of gin. It was a half empty half bottle, but nevertheless it was gin.

"You're wonderful, Tom," I said.

"You won't think so for long," he said. And he was right. He poured out a minuscule amount and refused to let me have any more for what felt like hours.

Later I learned we were there two more days, me alternately retching, sleeping, trying to force down invalid food that Tom prepared. A few people came and went, but the weather was bad and there were not many walkers. When I stopped retching, we went for short walks. On one of these suddenly I noticed a shape soaring on the thermals in the sky. I stopped and stared at it, thinking how fantastic it must be to be able to do that. Then I announced firmly it was a buzzard. When I resumed walking I saw Tom was smiling.

"What?" I asked.

"I think we're over the hump," he said. 'We'? It seemed a long time since I'd been part of 'we'. That was nice.

It was probably that evening he began to tell me the sequence of events that had brought him here. He didn't spare my feelings. Mother, he told me, had been getting increasingly worried by my phone calls or lack of them. The severe depression into which she had fallen following years of coping with Dad and then worrying about me, had made her very ill. Eventually he and Sally had decided to have a few days in the Lakes and had booked in at a bed-and-breakfast in Kendal. Tom had eventually tracked me down at the time of my first stay, with Jack. Manuel had filled in some of the gaps following Jack's rehab. Enquiries had given him some additional insight into my life style.

Mother had begged them to keep tabs on me. Then a few weeks after taking over Ben's Bothy, I had made those calls to Mother and then Dad. By then Mother was seriously affected by depression. Both she and Tom had been in contact with Dad which accounted for his reaction to my phone call, but he had managed to trace it. Tom explained that while I was still denying that I had a problem, there was little anyone could do. But from my call they had managed to glean roughly where I was, and Tom eventually landed at the Shepherd's

226

Rest where Herbie and Mary gave a glowing account of my stay matched by utter puzzlement at my departure. It was instinct that had brought him back to Manuel who had pointed him in the direction of Jack's rehab. centre and eventually to Jack himself.

"How is he?" I asked.

"Doing well. Worried about you." Tom got up and put the kettle on. "I've told your mother you're OK, but I think it's time she heard your voice."

I'm not sure whose voice was the wobblier. After her initial shock, then joy, the need for reassurance, she asked "So what happens now, darling?"

"What happens now?" I asked Tom.

"I'm driving you over to your Dad's tomorrow or the next day. Then hopefully you can begin the rest of your life."

"I heard that," Mother said. "Sounds good. As long as it includes all of us."

The walk down the next day was horrendous. I'd thought I was much better and, comparatively, I suppose I was. But I was so weak through lack of proper nourishment and normal living that I didn't think it would be possible to be more tired and still alive. Tom gave me a lot of support but the emotional struggle had taken it out of him too. When finally I saw Beano in the car park, I would have burst into tears had I had more energy.

We stayed overnight in a small pub and I was happy to let Tom drive Beano to Yorkshire, leaving his own car wherever he had parked it. Through my tiredness, which seemed to cling to me like a shruggie, I wondered how I was going to cope with seeing Dad again, and later Mother, and then the whole complex mystery of Life.

Finally, as the afternoon was turning into a golden evening, Tom drew Beano to a halt outside a church hall.

"What happens here?" I asked.

He put a hand on my shoulder. "You'll find your Dad in there," he said. "The next few steps you take could be the most important in your life."

I watched every one of them as I walked up the gravel path. There was a scattering of early autumn leaves and a deep red one drifted down and brushed one of my shoes. At the door I looked back. "Go on!" mouthed Tom.

The door was heavy and opened on to a small entrance hall. Beyond was another door and from behind it came voices. Several voices. One of them Dad's.

I pushed it open. There was a square room, quite big, with a table at one end and several rows of chairs in a semi-circle facing it. Heads turned as I opened the door.

Behind the table was Dad. He stopped talking when he saw me, his face crumpled and he opened his arms, and I hurried across the room into them.

"Oh Tuppence," he said into my hair. And everyone started clapping.

Postscript 2013 –

That happened a few months ago. Since then I've been in rehab and come out it. I've taken a room in the village and during the week work for Tess. I've found I'm quite good at window displays and organising promotions. Parallel universes are on the back burner for the moment, but I guess I have a better idea about them now than most. From time to time I join Dad at his self-help group meeting. Sometimes, if he's in the area, Tom joins us.

While I was in rehab, Rachel came to see me with her baby boy, called William after her father. We've made our peace with each other and I shall try and be a good godmother for William. After rehab I stayed with Mother and Alec, and renewed contact with Matt and Edward.

Around Christmas, Jack who has started his own craft workshop, came to see me and I hardly recognised him – fit, almost slim, certainly no longer identifiable as Jumbo. He told me he's looking for a partner and wants to talk to me about it. He also kissed me, and it's the first time I remember him doing that, which is weird. It was worth remembering, too.

In fact, all round, the partnership sounds rather an attractive idea.

If this sounds like a 'happy ever after' story, I'm not taking it for granted. Already I've seen people come in to recovery and go out. I know I've only just started on this journey of hanging on to the courage to change, one step at a time, one day at a time. In the end, today is all that any of us has.

About the Author: Sylvie Nickels spent much of her working life as a travel writer, returning to her first love fiction in later years. One of her particular interests has been the effect of war on the children and grandchildren of participants and this has provided the theme for several earlier novels (details: http://tinyurl.com/SNickels-books)
Courage to Change is her first book for Young Adults.

In the 1970s, Sylvie moved to north Oxfordshire with her explorer-lecturer-photographer husband George Spenceley, who died early in 2013. She is planning to complete his memoirs and talks of these on her blog at www.sylvienickels.wordpress .com

CPSIA information can be obtained
at www.ICGtesting.com
Printed in the USA
BVHW081307070719
552773BV00001B/85/P